Have you read them all?

Treat yourself again to the first Miss Seeton novels—

Picture Miss Seeton
A night at the opera strikes a chord of danger when
Miss Seeton witnesses a murder . . . and paints a portrait
of the killer.

Miss Seeton Draws the Line
Miss Seeton is enlisted by Scotland Yard when her paintings
of a little girl turn the young subject into a model for murder.

Witch Miss Seeton
Double, double, toil and trouble sweep through the village
when Miss Seeton goes undercover . . . to investigate a local
witches' coven!

Turn to the end of this book for a full list of the series,
plus—on the last page—**exclusive access to
the Miss Seeton short story** that started it all.

People may sometimes have wondered about the early career of Emily Dorothea, and how she became the quiet Miss Seeton who, many years after the war, retired from teaching art to live in the village of Plummergen.

This book tells you at least part of her story.

The world can't get enough of Miss Seeton

"A **most beguiling** protagonist!"
New York Times

"Miss Seeton gets into wild drama with fine touches of farce . . . This is a **lovely mixture of the funny and the exciting**."
San Francisco Chronicle

"**You can't stop reading.**"
The Sun

"**Depth of description and lively characters** bring this English village to life."
Publishers Weekly

"Fun to be had with a **full cast of endearingly zany villagers** . . . and the ever gently intuitive Miss Seeton."
Kirkus Reviews

"Miss Seeton is the **most delightfully satisfactory character since Miss Marple.**"
Ogden Nash

"**She's a joy!**"
Cleveland Plain Dealer

Miss Seeton's
Finest Hour

A MISS SEETON MYSTERY

Hamilton Crane
Series creator Heron Carvic

This edition published in 2017 by Farrago, an imprint of
Prelude Books Ltd
13 Carrington Road, Richmond, TW10 5AA, United Kingdom

www.farragobooks.com

First published by Berkley in 1999

ISBN: 978-1-911440-85-7

This book is dedicated to those 520 of

The Few

who gave their lives for freedom
in the summer of 1940

The Beginning

What General Weygand called the Battle of France is over. I expect that the Battle of Britain is about to begin. Upon this battle depends the survival of Christian civilisation. Upon it depends our own British life, and the long continuity of our institutions and our Empire. The whole fury and might of the enemy must very soon be turned on us. Hitler knows that he will have to break us in this Island or lose the war. If we can stand up to him, all Europe may be free and the life of the world may move forward into broad, sunlit uplands. But if we fail, then the whole world—including the United States, including all that we have known and cared for—will sink into the abyss of a new Dark Age, made more sinister, and perhaps more protracted, by the lights of perverted science.

Let us therefore brace ourselves to our duties, and so bear ourselves that, if the British Empire and its Commonwealth last for a thousand years, men will still say, "This was their finest hour."

—Winston Leonard Spencer Churchill, PRIME MINISTER OF THE UNITED KINGDOM OF GREAT BRITAIN AND NORTHERN IRELAND, in a broadcast to the nation, 18th June 1940

Chapter 1

The tubby policeman—to call him overweight would have hurt his feelings—pedalled his regulation black bicycle slowly along the road. The hot summer sun gleamed on the chrome of his handlebars, the steel of his helmet, and the buttons of his uniform jacket. If the inspector hadn't made such a point of telling him it was Official Business, he might have risked undoing the topmost button, but orders were orders. Police Constable Badgery knew that he had the reputation of the Hampstead force to maintain.

Against one plump—that is to say, well-padded—hip the bulky canvas bag slung on its strap diagonally across PC Badgery's shoulders bumped in time with his weary pedalling. Sunbeams glimmered on his well-polished boots as they rose and fell, rose and fell—left, right, left, right. His breathing was laboured, his forehead damp. Flaming June had given way to scorching July, and speaking for himself, he couldn't wait for winter . . .

He arrived, thankfully, at his destination, dismounted, and as he held the bike upright with one hand, with the other he fumbled in his trouser pocket for a large white handkerchief. He tipped back his helmet, mopped his streaming brow, and sighed. He could feel a wide, deep dent where the webbing had rubbed. He promised himself that he'd have a word with his wife about that, standard issue or not. A spot of padding, perhaps. A little snip here and there to make it an easier fit . . .

PC Badgery contemplated the bare brick pillars on either side of the gateway for a few moments before he sighed once more, adjusted his helmet, and started to push his bike up the short paved path to the front door. His Blakey-tipped boots made dancing sparks as iron met stone with a heavy, clumping, rhythmic tread.

He reached the house, propped his bike against the wall, and marched up the short flight of steps to the bell, which he rang in his most official manner. Waiting for someone to answer, he straightened his helmet, tugged at his jacket, coughed, brushed his boots on the mat—and grew suddenly hot as puffs of gritty dust drifted out of the plaited coir to dull the red waxed shine of the earthenware tiles that covered the porch floor.

Coughing now for quite a different reason, the unhappy constable was about to back away when the curtains twitched at the side window. Through the brown, paper, antisplinter tape that patterned the glass, a pair of blue eyes peeped out at him. The curtain fell, and after a moment or two there came a rattle at the door as the handle began to turn.

The door swung open, and PC Badgery found himself touching his helmet in salute to a small, elderly woman—a woman no more than five feet tall, and to the younger, plumper man enviably slim—who stood looking up at him with a smile of enquiry in her eyes.

Police Constable Badgery cleared his throat. "Er—Miss Emily Dorothea Seeton?" he said in his most official tones.

The grey-haired little lady shook her head in courteous reproof. "Come now, Mr. Badgery," she said in a soft voice. "I will agree that I am not much given to gadding about the streets, but you must know very well who I am."

"Er—yes, Mrs. Seeton," said PC Badgery, hotter than ever and wishing his collar didn't feel so tight.

"Yes, indeed," returned Mrs. Seeton, the enquiring smile now a twinkle in her blue eyes. "But if your true intention was to speak with my daughter, I'm afraid she isn't here at the moment. She is helping at the canteen—King's Cross, you know, for the troops—and I don't expect her home for at least an hour." She saw his face fall. "You could come inside to wait for her if you like," she invited. "If your business with her is important." She saw him hesitate.

"You could," she suggested, "hold my wool for me if you felt obliged to make yourself useful." Now the twinkle was almost mischievous. "My daughter," explained Alice Amabel Seeton, "is very good about helping me wind the skeins into balls, but one's arms grow so tired after a while, and when she is so busy in so many other ways, I am always reluctant to ask her. She would be most pleasantly surprised were she to come home this evening and find today's batch already completed."

"Er," said PC Badgery, shuffling his feet on the mat and then, as more dust appeared, growing hot again. "Well . . ."

Mrs. Seeton took pity on him. "Of course, your bicycle must be something of a problem," she said kindly. "I can well understand your not wishing it left outside when there are such very strict warnings about leaving motor vehicles unattended. And one would think a bicycle even more of a temptation, as it makes no noise, and could easily be ridden away without your noticing."

"Don't," begged PC Badgery, blanching at the very idea of being charged with Aiding and Abetting the Enemy—which had to mean prison, at the least.

At the least. There were rumours—not that he believed them, but he couldn't help hearing people talk—of one or two folk who'd been actually hanged—some said shot—in the Tower, for treason. Well, if letting some passing spy or fifth columnist pinch a police-issue bicycle counted as treason . . . well, if it did or if it didn't, it was a risk he wasn't prepared to run, seeing as how the only way of immobilising a bike was to take the blessed thing to pieces, and the day was too hot for that sort of carry-on.

Mrs. Seeton seemed to read his mind. "And it is," she continued, "far too hot for you to carry your bicycle up my front steps into the hall, where an eye could be kept on it. On second thoughts, Mr. Badgery . . . I trust that you will not think me rude if I withdraw my invitation?"

"Not at all," he assured her, and ventured to grin. "Er, thanks, Mrs. Seeton. You're right, I didn't ought to leave my bike where it can't be watched—and it's only a message, after all. I'll come back later on—when it's cooler," he added. "If that's all right with you."

"For my part I see no difficulty, but I cannot promise that you will find Emily at home even then," Miss Seeton's mother warned him. "Should another troop train arrive at King's Cross, they will need every helping hand they can muster. My daughter is a good, conscientious girl and does her best to telephone when there is a delay—but of course there is a war on . . ."

"If there wasn't," said PC Badgery, "I could've left my old bike outside your house and never worried."

4

"You could have propped it against the front fence." Mrs. Seeton said, the wistful note in her voice an echo of Police Constable Badgery's earlier sigh as he contemplated the bare brick pillars. No longer did spearhead iron railings guard the perimeter of the neat front garden; no longer did a curlicued model of the blacksmith's art hang on ornate hinges in the gateway. There was a war on.

In May of that year the government had asked for—had demanded, by Order in Council—the country's scrap metal to be turned into guns, shells, bullets, tanks, ships . . . and Britons up and down the land had responded with a magnificent swiftness that was cheerfully cavalier as to what might be meant by *scrap*. Cherished decorative ironwork was ripped from walls, balconies, and even domestic appliances to be handed over without a murmur. Over the past two months people had grown accustomed to the ubiquitous sound of hammers and hacksaws, and to the sight of holes in masonry and concrete—holes they regarded with patriotic pride tinged with only a slight pang of regret for past glories. Alice Seeton recalled her aunt, her mother's only sister, telling how, as a child, she had watched the city's gates and railings being painted black in mourning for Albert, Prince Consort. Aunt Dorothea had always hoped that one day they might all be returned to their original bright colours. She could never have dreamed that a time would come when they would all be taken away by order of the government and melted down . . .

"And my best saucepans, only yesterday," murmured Alice. Lord Beaverbrook's public appeal for aluminium to "turn your pots and pans into Spitfires and Hurricanes, Blenheims and Wellingtons" had struck a resonant chord with the

Seetons. The minister of aircraft production's promise to make good use of Britain's "kettles, vacuum cleaners, hat pegs, coat hangers, shoe trees, bathroom fittings, and household ornaments, cigarette boxes, or any other articles made wholly or in part of aluminium," had resulted in an energetic few hours of sorting for Alice and Emily before they could feel their consciences clear, their duty done. A telephone call to the local headquarters of the Women's Voluntary Service, a visit from one of the green-clad ladies, and her departure with a clanking cardboard box in her arms had left both Mrs. Seeton and her daughter happy to have done what little they could in defence of the country they loved so well.

"My missus, too," said PC Badgery. "All in a good cause, I won't deny, and we parted with a tidy lot and glad to do it—except there was no persuading her to give 'em her jam pan, even with sugar at eight ounces a week and like to be rationed shorter still before it's long again." He gave his tummy a quick, rueful pat and chuckled. "She goes on and on at me to cut down the spoons in my tea, too. She will have it that sweet stuff in the shops is bound to go on ration sooner or later . . . but she makes a tasty marmalade, she does." He smacked his lips and then sighed. "When she can get the oranges," he finished sadly.

"When, indeed," echoed Mrs. Seeton. "And I am sure Mrs. Badgery will agree that having to buy them by weight still seems a little . . . peculiar."

Mrs. Badgery's loving spouse grimaced. "The whole blooming world's gone peculiar." Forgetful of government exhortations to spread neither alarm nor despondency, he thumped at the canvas bag slung diagonally across his hip. "I mean, gas masks—on a day like this! Time was we would've been out enjoying the sunshine, not wondering if that devil of a Hitler, begging your pardon, was getting ready to poison the very air we breathe. I don't mind telling you, I keep my eyes skinned when I pass by a pillar-box just in case that warning paint looks like to change from yellow—and I've a whistle right here in my pocket, and a rattle in my saddlebag, all ready to let everyone know to take cover."

Alice Seeton winced, but did not answer. In the circumstances it was difficult to know what to say.

PC Badgery blushed. "I'm sorry, Mrs. Seeton," he said quickly, his embarrassed boots raising further clouds of dust in the little porch. "Spoke without thinking. I, er, I'll be off now and pop back later, shall I?"

"I cannot promise at what hour my daughter will return," Mrs. Seeton reminded him. "She is usually home in good time to hear the six o'clock news, but . . ."

"But there's a war on," supplied PC Badgery, his blush fading as he saw his way clear to depart. "Well, I'll leave it for a while and hope for the best, shall I?"

"We must all hope for the best," Mrs. Seeton chided him gently. "As my nanny used to say: 'Hope for the best, expect the worst—and take what comes.'"

"Ah," said PC Badgery with a wise and thoughtful nod and a ponderous sigh. "If only we knew what was coming, it would make life a lot easier, Mrs. Seeton. I mean—it might well be the worst, but if we could know beforehand at least we'd be sure we were ready for it."

"We would have braced ourselves to our duties," said Mrs. Seeton with a faint smile.

"It'd be our finest hour," agreed PC Badgery, neatly capping the phrase first uttered by Winston Churchill less than a month before and already famous throughout the world. "It *will* be," the policeman amended firmly. "Oh, we'll show that Hitler what's what, Mrs. Seeton, just you mark my words. The Frenchies and the rest may have gone down—but it's not so easy to walk over the British as he'd like to think. We may well be left on our lonesome own to stand against the blighter—but we aren't licked yet!"

Chapter 2

"Captain Grange?" The grey-suited man behind the desk in the anonymous office in the Tower of London addressed the telephone in crisp, clear accents. "Chandler here. I've just had a message from Hampstead—"

"Then scramble this bloody call!" came the quick interruption in a voice more accustomed to giving orders above the roar of a mid-ocean tempest. "Great heavens, man, don't you realise there's a war on?"

"Sorry, sir." After a few moments Chandler resumed the conversation. "It's hardly conclusive," he told the still-simmering Captain Grange. "According to our information, the girl is helping out at the forces canteen and won't be home again for some hours, at least."

"Canteen? What blasted canteen?"

"King's Cross station, according to her mother."

"According to her mother?" Once again Captain Grange's bellow had the startled Chandler holding the phone away from his unhappy eardrum. "Good God, Chandler, some mothers will say anything in defence of their offspring. You should know better than to trust a feeble alibi like that. Has anyone made a . . . an independent sighting?"

"N-not yet," came the admission after an uncomfortable pause. "Our Hampstead chap—Steptoe—the one who started all this—was told off to go and look for her, but we're still waiting to hear from him."

Captain Grange's lengthy silence made Chandler feel even more uncomfortable. He felt little better when the other man finally spoke.

"She could be miles away by now, Chandler. She could have prepared her damned signals for an entire squadron of parachutists and gone into hiding where we wouldn't stand a hope of catching up with her before . . . it was too late to matter, one way or the other."

"Unlikely, sir," protested Chandler. "From all we've heard, she's devoted to her mother, who isn't in the best of health, and—well, to be honest, does anyone really believe all the stories about fifth columnists laying flight paths for enemy aircraft with stones and sheets of white paper?"

"Enough people believe it to have 'em phoning the police when the damned woman keeps being spotted prowling about on Hampstead Heath—an open space, let me remind you, where parachutists could drop in their hundreds and hide in the scrub without being noticed—"

"Which is why," broke in Chandler, "the Heath has more barrage balloons and pillboxes and ack-ack guns per square yard than anyone could shake a stick at. The blighters wouldn't stand a chance if they landed—which I doubt very much if they'll try—"

"Prowling about on the Heath," resumed Captain Grange as Chandler drew breath, "with her sketchbook under her arm and her pockets full of pencils! That's the sort of thing that makes people nervous, Chandler, when it's fifty to one we'll be invaded before the end of the month . . ." There was an uneasy pause. "Or worse," the captain grimly acknowledged. "That devilish Hun has rolled up Norway, Denmark, Holland, Belgium, and France, not to mention Czechoslovakia and Poland and Austria—and, great God Almighty, the Channel Islands as well. British soil, remember!"

Chandler, who remembered all too well, said nothing.

"The Germans," Captain Grange went on after another uneasy pause, "are a damned methodical bunch—and method coupled with madness makes 'em as dangerous as they come. A megalomaniac like Hitler won't take too kindly to the idea of a bit of the world within easy reach preferring not to join his nice, tidy European empire. He'll invade, Chandler, and it's up to you and me and the rest of our crowd to see that this island of ours isn't—isn't handed to him on a plate by innocent-seeming schoolmarms who go sketching on Hampstead Heath!"

"We could have her in for questioning," suggested Chandler, after yet another pause.

"If she's guilty she'll have her story ready. If she's genuine," said Captain Grange, scepticism in every syllable, "then she still needs a warning shot across her bows—for upsetting everybody."

"The same as the haystack artist?" enquired Chandler, and Captain Grange emitted a furious snort.

"That damned artist," he said through obviously clenched teeth, "was sketching what could have been a vital military installation. The L.D.V. have spent the past two months preparing roadblocks and building camouflaged redoubts and ammunition dumps—camouflaged, Chandler, remember!" Then, for the first time, certainty wavered. The captain coughed. "The fact that on this particular occasion," he hurried on, "the lady happened to sketch a—a genuine haystack is—is neither here nor there in the general scheme of things. At a time like this you—we—can't be too careful."

While Chandler was inclined to agree with the captain in principle, it was his private opinion that the Local Defence Volunteers had objected to the lady artist's sketch more on account of the pub in the background than the haystack in the foreground. Haystacks were by nature anonymous, transitory structures: public houses endured and could be identified. Yet it still seemed a case of overreaction on the part of the amateur soldiers. Were Hitler's troops ever to find their way to the pub in question—an oak-beamed pub in an ancient village as far from the sea as geography allowed—they would be unlikely to ask its name, or the name of the village. It was the sort of village to which nobody went unless they already knew of its existence; to which nobody went unless they had good cause. Debt collectors, bailiffs, shotgun-toting fathers of despoiled virgin daughters—yes. Nazi storm troopers . . . no.

Or at least he hoped it was highly improbable . . .

"What was that, Chandler?"

"Nothing, sir." Chandler pulled himself together. "Or rather—yes, you're right, we can't be too careful. I know about 'innocent until proved guilty,' but I have to agree with you—Miss Seeton seems . . . too innocent to be true."

"My point exactly," said Captain Grange in triumph. "If you're a fifth columnist or any other sort of damned traitor, you cover your tracks—try to fit in with the people around you—lull them into accepting you as one of them. You take care you don't do anything to excite their suspicions that you're getting ready to sell 'em down the river. But good God, man, by all accounts, this Seeton girl's never lulled anyone in her life. Wouldn't have had so many of 'em phoning in about her—her queer cavortings, if she had. Never fitted in, they say . . ."

"Artistic temperament?" offered Devil's Advocate Chandler as the captain paused for breath.

Captain Grange made clear his opinion of temperaments, artistic or otherwise, in one crisp nautical phrase. Chandler deemed it wise to say nothing.

"It's a cunning double bluff," said Captain Grange at last. "The female of the species, remember, Chandler. With her family background the girl *ought* to be above suspicion—and that could be what they're relying on."

"Surely you don't think her mother—"

"The Huns, you fool, not the family—but wait." Chandler duly waited. "Your man Steptoe," said the captain after a moment or two. "Checked the mother out with her doctor, didn't he?"

"He did his best," Chandler told him. "Blood out of a stone, though. The doctor's hot stuff on professional etiquette and the Hippocratic Oath. All he was prepared to tell us—once Steptoe had waved the Official Secrets Act under his nose—was that Mrs. Seeton is genuinely delicate, which says everything and nothing at the same time. It's a pity half the neighbours have evacuated to the country—not so much gossip around as there might have been—but from what we can gather, it's one reason the girl never left home: her mother's never been the same since the flu epidemic of 1919. Wore herself out nursing her husband and the younger child, according to rumour—not that the doc would confirm it, of course."

"There you are, then," said Captain Grange, once more triumphant. "The woman knows she may not have long to go—heart, perhaps—so she's prepared to take the risk of turning her daughter into a damned pacifist—or worse—so that she'll be . . . well looked after when the Nazis get here. Not that they will," he added sharply.

But the pious phrase *I hope* was all too audible to Chandler's inward ear, unspoken though it was . . .

"Double bluff, as I said," concluded Captain Grange with a thunderous clearing of his throat. "We can't be seen to persecute delicate old ladies without concrete proof, but the daughter's young enough to take care of herself. If we *are* making a mistake—well, better a mistake now than leave a traitor on the loose for the future—a future that's damned uncertain, Chandler."

"You hardly need to tell me that, sir."

"No." Captain Grange cleared his throat again. "If," he said heavily, "the girl really is the—the innocent patriot she'd like us to believe, then she'll be happy with an apology for the misunderstanding and a pat on the back for helping the war effort by keeping quiet about it all. But get her in for questioning, Chandler—and make it soon!"

It was not, in truth, a long walk home from Finchley Road underground station, but the weary Emily Seeton found herself counting every step and marvelling at how slowly the lampposts seemed to pass. She had been on her feet for hours, and the chance to sit down had been denied her even on the tube. It had been the start of the rush hour when she finally left Euston, and only her slightness of frame and youthful agility had allowed her to squeeze into the crowded train to stand, too short to reach the strap, so close to the door that each time it opened she had to step out on the platform to allow those farther along inside the carriage who wished to get out to do so.

When Alice Seeton heard the door click shut, she hurried down the hall to greet her daughter. "Emily, dear, you look exhausted," she said. "I've had the kettle filled and ready to boil for the past half hour, so by the time you've taken off your hat and freshened up, the tea will be ready."

Emily smiled at her mother. "I'm sorry I wasn't able to telephone—I hope you weren't worried—but they asked for King's Cross volunteers to help at the Euston canteen, and of course one could hardly refuse."

Alice, smiling back, gently shook her head. "Remember what your dear father used to say was the motto of his men? 'Never volunteer: you have no idea what might happen next.' "

Emily quickly stifled the thought that in these times nobody, volunteer or otherwise, had any idea what might happen next. For her mother to mention her father—who after twenty years remained a cherished, seldom-spoken memory in his grieving widow's heart—must be a sign that she was worrying more than she wanted her daughter to know. Her daughter would humour her in her loving deception.

"What happened next," said Emily with a rueful chuckle, "is that I washed quite as many cups at Euston as I'd been filling with tea at King's Cross. If not more," she added with another, fainter, chuckle.

"Tea," responded Alice with gentle firmness. "We'll take it through to the drawing room, and we can listen to the

15

wireless while we eat." She glanced at Emily and hesitated. "Did you . . . hear the News earlier, by any chance?" she asked, trying to sound casual.

"At four-fifteen," replied her daughter, "I was travelling the Northern Line between King's Cross and Euston—but everyone on the afternoon shift has been talking about what happened at one o'clock." She patted her mother gently on the shoulder. "If, that is, you are asking whether I know about . . . the names."

Alice, suddenly unable to speak, winked away tears as she nodded. Emily patted her mother's shoulder again.

"Tea," she reminded her, "in the drawing room. I'll be down in five minutes—no, four," she amended as she looked at the grandfather clock beside the hall stand. "In time," she said bravely, "for the six o'clock news."

In the drawing room mother and daughter were silent as they arranged the cups and plates, the teapot, the milk jug, and—though it was empty—the sugar bowl. Neither of the Seeton ladies cared much at the best of times for sweetened tea, and had in any case resolved to do without for the duration: but the empty china bowl was a gesture of defiance against the dictator who wanted to disturb far more in the world than England's teatime ritual.

Still in silence, Mrs. Seeton reached out to turn the Bakelite knob. The wireless, warming, hummed slowly into life. The chimes of Big Ben rang out and died away.

"Good evening," said the announcer. "Here is the six o'clock news, and this is Frank Phillips reading it."

The two women listened without speaking to the rest of the recital. When it was over, Emily, after a glance at her mother's face, switched the wireless off.

"It is only a precaution," she said. "So that we will recognise at once should they . . . succeed in breaking into the same wavelength as the BBC to—to tell us even more of their wicked lies."

"Should they invade, you mean," said Alice, and Emily did not—could not, truthfully—deny it. "There are armed guards," her mother continued, "outside Broadcasting House, so I have heard." She suppressed the quiver in her voice. "Which is of course no more than another, very wise, precaution," she went on in tones intended to be bracing. She drew a deep breath. "And," she ended firmly, "no more than one would expect of Sir John Reith, who has a good deal of common sense."

"Indeed he has," agreed Emily, and raised her teacup as if drinking a toast to the Scottish founding father of the BBC. "Although I am sure it will come very hard with the Nazis if they ever attempt to parachute decoy newscasters—or anyone else—into this country, no matter where they might land."

There was a lengthy pause.

"I have been looking through your dear father's things," said Alice at last as Emily sipped her tea. "I thought—that is, I wondered . . . his army revolver, you know. It is still in the wrappings as he . . . left it. We ought perhaps to think of—of cleaning it in readiness . . ."

Emily stared at her gentle mother. When, earlier in the week, the word had been passed round the Hampstead ladies that helpers would soon be needed to remove twenty years' worth of storage grease from the Great War rifles expected any day now from America as arms for the newly formed Local Defence Volunteers, Alice Seeton had shivered at the

17

very idea of handling a lethal weapon. Emily, with her neat artist's ways, would have been far handier than her mother and had every intention of offering her services . . .

And now it seemed her services might be required rather sooner than soon—and rather closer to home.

But before she could reply, the front doorbell rang.

Chapter 3

"There!" said Mrs. Seeton, rising to her feet. "How silly of me to forget, but when you were late home . . . That is, Mr. Badgery was asking for you this afternoon, and I told him to come back in the evening."

"Constable Badgery?" Emily, now also on her feet, was at first puzzled, then resigned. "No doubt one or two of the children have been misbehaving again. Oh, dear. I had hoped, with so many extra classes . . ."

"Mischievous children will never be short of mischief," said Alice with a faint smile as Emily, waving her mother back to her chair, prepared to hurry out into the hall before the bell should have to be rung a second time, which would hint at discourtesy on the part of the hostess to an expected guest.

When, however, she opened the door, Emily Seeton stood and blinked at the man in the porch—a man she had most certainly not expected. While his face, on reflection, had something familiar about it, the man who had just finished brushing his feet on the mat in no way resembled the plump, uniformed PC Badgery. This grey-suited stranger—no, not a stranger: she had seen him in the High Street from time to time—was tall and thin, with an air of distinction from which his trim moustache detracted not a whit.

"Miss Seeton?" the man with the moustache greeted her, and raised his hat politely.

"I am she," said Miss Seeton, equally polite.

"My name is Steptoe," said the man, replacing his hat with one hand as with the other he held out a folded card, about three inches by four, overprinted and stamped in what seemed a highly official way.

Automatically Miss Seeton took the card and opened it. From inside, the rectangular black-and-white image of the grey-suited Steptoe regarded her with the blank, frozen gaze customary in such documents—although for a moment, until she blinked, she thought she could, behind the blankness, see the anguished eye of a man of action who had been forced to endure the static demands of the camera lens.

Miss Seeton blinked. The sharp, soldierly features at once dissolved into those of the man who, in his grey suit, was bureaucracy personified.

She turned to the front of the folded card. She'd been right: Mr. Steptoe was a civil servant. *Ministry of Information*, she read. *Subsection P(F/S)*.

"Publicity," supplied Steptoe as he saw her quick frown, "and fact sheets, you know."

"No," echoed Miss Seeton, the pucker still between her brows. "I'm sorry, but I fear that I do not. I had thought you—that is, Mr. Badgery—wanted to talk to me about the children."

It was Steptoe's turn to frown. "Children?" He shook his head. "Badgery? Oh—the beat bobby, you mean."

Miss Seeton nodded, pleased that her acceptance of Mr. Steptoe as a neighbour had been correct.

"No," said Mr. Steptoe, "my department has nothing to do with the police, or with any children—but we do indeed want to talk to you."

Miss Seeton, blushing, recollected her manners. "Won't you come in?" she invited, handing back the folded card and stepping aside as Mr. Steptoe smiled, pocketed his identification, and removed his hat.

"Thank you, Miss Seeton." Mr. Steptoe brushed his shoes once more, though they hardly needed it, and crossed the threshold in one long stride. Miss Seeton paused politely for him to hang his hat on the mahogany stand—he did no more than flinch at the remarkable summer straw that was its neighbour—and then led the way into the drawing room.

"Mother, this is Mr. Steptoe . . . from the Ministry of Information." Emily tried to sound calm, as a gentlewoman should, but her voice held a note of uncertainty. "Mr. Steptoe, this is my mother."

"I'm sorry to intrude on you at teatime, Mrs. Seeton." Steptoe's regret sounded genuine. "There's almost nothing worse than stewed tea, is there?" His eyes met those of Alice, who, like Emily, had expected someone else and found it hard to conceal her surprise. Mr. Steptoe smiled. "And with the ration only two ounces a week," he went on, "I know you can't afford to pour it away and start again. Please, don't let me interrupt you—what I have to ask your daughter won't take long."

Once more Miss Seeton recollected her manners. "If you would care to sit down . . ." she murmured, as her mother returned Steptoe's smile with a wary twinkle and prepared to play the hostess by offering the stranger a cup of tea.

"Not for me, thank you." Mr. Steptoe divined her intention before she could speak, and bowed a graceful refusal as he took his seat and turned, with another smile, to Alice's daughter. "Miss Seeton," he began. "I understand that you are something of an artist."

Miss Seeton blushed. "A teacher of art," she corrected him politely with a sigh. "Those who can," she explained as he seemed about to protest at her modesty, "do—as Mr. Shaw has so pithily expressed it. Those who cannot . . ." She sighed. "Teach," she concluded sadly.

"My daughter is an excellent teacher," Mrs. Seeton chimed in as Mr. Steptoe appeared likely to let this mournful utterance pass without further comment.

"I have every reason to believe that she is," said Mr. Steptoe, and Alice subsided with a blush that was as proud as her daughter's was embarrassed.

"Your school, they tell me, was evacuated," Mr. Steptoe pressed on. Miss Seeton recovered herself to confirm the events of September 1939 as they related directly to the pupils and staff of the private establishment where she had been the art department's deputy head.

"Your chief has remained with the pupils and most of the other teachers in the country. You stayed for a while and then came home," said Mr. Steptoe.

Emily glanced fondly at her mother. "Yes, I did," she agreed. "Once the children were properly settled—one or two were a little unhappy in their billets at first, and changes had to be made—but as we were sharing the premises of another school, which already had an excellent teacher of art, it seemed to me that I could be of rather more *practical* use to the war effort here at home. Not every parent took advantage of the evacuation scheme, you know."

"I certainly do," said Steptoe with emphasis.

"And many of those who did," Miss Seeton went on, "began bringing the children back to London once the immediate threat of . . . gassing and bombs appeared to be groundless." She glanced at her mother again. "And even now, when the situation is so grave . . ." She coughed. "You see, with so few teachers to—to keep them under control, and with most of their parents busy with war work of various kinds, it made sense for me to offer my services as a—a part-time tutor, so to speak, though I know little of much except art, beyond my general reading—for of course one tries not to become too *narrow*—but it has been difficult to organise curriculum lessons while so many are away from home, studying at a different rate. Yet one has to keep them out of mischief during the day—or rather"—and once more she blushed—"one has to try. Which is why I had supposed you to be Constable Badgery, bringing another friendly warning about what my young charges might have been doing while I was occupied elsewhere."

Mr. Steptoe chuckled richly. "Nothing so sinister, Miss Seeton. They tell me"—he was careful not to identify the source of his information—"you've been sketching around the place on and off?"

"In my free time, yes," said Miss Seeton with a guilty blush. "Such as it is—and perhaps it *has* been something of a self-indulgence, but I had supposed—with all my work at the forces canteen, and the various excursions with the children, and the lessons . . ."

23

"I'm sure you've been doing a splendid job," said Steptoe quickly. "Everyone deserves a spot of relaxation, if they can get it, when they're under pressure, and wartime—well, let's agree it's not exactly a picnic. But talking of picnics—you've been up on the Heath, I gather."

Miss Seeton's eyes glowed. "Yes, indeed, although not, of course, for a picnic. Such a wonderful view right across London—like a huge outdoor aquarium with the great flying fish of the barrage balloons, changing colour at different times of day with the sun and the passing clouds—and the excavations, where the different colours are—are real, not caused by the varying qualities of light. Red and brown, orange and ochre—just as one has seen the Grand Canyon in cinema features, only smaller, of course." She came suddenly, sadly, to herself. "And artificial, not natural. And of entirely different purpose."

"I'm glad you've said that, Miss Seeton." Mr. Steptoe sat up straight and fixed her with a cool, efficient gaze. "You've been sketching the excavations, and you know all too well what they were—are—for. Well, I'd like to look at your sketches, with a view to using them in Ministry of Information leaflets about air-raid precautions."

"Oh," said Alice faintly.

Her daughter said nothing.

"Perhaps I could borrow your sketching block, Miss Seeton," said Mr. Steptoe. "Or blocks, plural, if you've visited the Heath as often as I infer that you have. I take it you date your sketches?"

Miss Seeton, with a wary nod, indicated that she did.

Mr. Steptoe smiled. "That's excellent," he told her. "We might like to try something along the lines of before and after, you see—it all depends on what we've got. On what you've drawn. I'll give you a receipt, of course."

He was so calm and self-assured as he drew a gold pen and a notebook from his inside pocket that Miss Seeton found herself hurrying upstairs to her room almost before she had fully grasped what she had, by her silence, evidently agreed to contribute to Britain's war effort. Her cartoons and sketches of sandbags being filled—of plunging depths and soaring heights of richly coloured soil, Cheddar Gorge in miniature, the rabbit-nibbled turf of Hampstead Heath scored and slashed and lacerated by a thousand desperate delvings from rich, restful green into a more grim and gory hue . . .

Miss Seeton reached her bedroom door, went inside, and found that she was shivering. The Ministry of Information. Publicity and fact sheets. Before and after—peace and war—bombs and gas, death and destruction—

Miss Seeton frowned and then took a deep breath. "'We must,'" she reminded herself, " 'brace ourselves to our duties.' " She found her spine stiffening even as she spoke the words. " 'And so bear ourselves that, if . . .' "

But, inspired though she was by Churchill's oratory, she could not finish the sentence. Who dared now to say, in all honesty, if the British Empire and its Commonwealth would last for a thousand hours, never mind a thousand years?

Miss Seeton shook her head. "It is up to all of us to ensure that it does," she told herself firmly. "Or to try our best, at the very least," she added as she crossed the room to stare into the looking glass at her pale, resolute face. Rather too pale. She must not upset her mother by letting her guess how worried she might be. She patted a little colour into her cheeks, and then pulled out the bottom drawer of the tallboy in search of the few sketchbooks she had left.

"But I cannot help wondering," she murmured as, having shut the bedroom door, she hesitated on the landing, "if Mr. Steptoe has been entirely frank about his reason for wanting these? Yet he is, in a way, a neighbour—I cannot believe there is anything wrong . . .

"I am afraid these three are all I could find," said Miss Seeton as she returned to the drawing room, where her mother and Mr. Steptoe were conversing amicably together, the stewing tea abandoned. "One of them is not yet full, and I should be pleased to have it back in due course—but I had quite forgotten," said the owner of the sketchbooks as she handed them over, "about the children, you see."

"The children again," said Mr. Steptoe, achieving a smile as he accepted the books with a hand Miss Seeton might (had she been less preoccupied) have noticed shook a little.

But Miss Seeton did not notice. She was too busy trying to explain to the government's representative her apparent lack of cooperation. "It is," she began, "my habit to sketch on only one side of the paper—which in times like these may seem extravagant—unpatriotic, indeed, when the money saved could be put into one of the national schemes, which is what I try to do by making economies in other areas. But as long as I still have some of the blocks I bought before the war, I confess that I prefer it—although once they are full I shall buy only enough for teaching purposes, and none at all for private use—if, that is, any shops will stock artists' materials by then. Which is why I have made such detailed notes

26

on those of my later sketches I hope to turn in—in happier times into coloured works, because once my paints and crayons were exhausted, I hardly cared to buy any more. And it is not," Miss Seeton struggled to make clear, "as if the paper is put out for salvage right away, although naturally we save all our bones and tins and so forth as we have been asked to do—but when young people are short of pocket money, as so many are, I feel it does no harm if they are encouraged to use the empty backs for their self-expression, which is so very important . . ."

"It's what we're fighting this war for," agreed Steptoe as she paused for breath. "The right to be ourselves, not some Fascist lunatic's mindless puppets."

Miss Seeton nodded. "Freedom is worth a sacrifice," she said quietly. "And so I tell the children, hoping to set an example even in the smallest things. One of my used blocks may be shared between half a dozen youngsters on the strict understanding that, should they be unhappy with what they have drawn, they are to put it out for salvage rather than tear it up or burn it without thinking. Which they tell me they do," she concluded, ambiguously but with pride.

"I'm delighted to hear it," said Mr. Steptoe as she subsided. He had done no more than receive the sketchbooks as she offered them, and put them thankfully to one side while she talked. Now he opened his notebook, uncapped his pen, and wrote out in an elegant copperplate the promised receipt for *three quarto sketchbooks, property of Miss E. D. Seeton, 13th July 1940*. This he signed with a flourish, blotted the ink with a piece of blotting paper produced from the back of his notebook, and passed to Miss Seeton . . .

Who observed only after his departure—and did not care to mention to her mother—that Mr. Steptoe of the Ministry of Information, Subsection P(F/S), had left no telephone number or address at which he could be reached.

Chapter 4

Mr. Steptoe, recognised by Miss Seeton as a neighbour passed occasionally in the street, in truth lived no more than a mile from Alice and Emily. On his long legs it took the MI5 man under ten minutes to reach home: where, the minute he was inside, he tore off the string and brown paper with which the sketchbooks' owner had insisted on making a neat parcel—a gentleman does not normally carry a parcel, but in time of war such a solecism was surely permissible—and began leafing through the first of his three prizes.

Halfway through he closed the book with a slam and passed a hand over his steaming brow. He opened the second book at random, turned half a dozen pages, and felt himself grow cold. He breathed deeply, and hurried to the telephone.

The operator had no idea that the number to which she put him through had its own private link to another number—a number so secret it was never written down. After a quick exchange of password and countersign, followed by what seemed an eternity of connecting clicks, Steptoe was pouring out his tale to Chandler in the Tower of London.

"I was right about her," was the gist of his frantic babble once his superior had managed to soothe him to a more normal rate of delivery. "That woman wants more than watching, I tell you—she needs talking to. Fast!"

"Then bring the books here now," he was told. "Faster than fast. Any chance of finding a taxi?"

A hollow laugh was all the answer he received. "Faster than fast," reiterated Chandler, and banged the telephone into its cradle. His hand hovered by the scrambler button, but he decided against talking to anyone else in the group until he had seen and judged the evidence for himself. It was not that he couldn't trust Steptoe—it had, after all, been Steptoe who first alerted them to the possible dangers posed by Miss Emily Dorothea Seeton—but as Steptoe's line superior he would like to make up his own mind. An hour's delay, even when the Huns were expected any minute, couldn't make that much difference—could it? The girl had had time enough to tell the enemy what she knew. There was nothing he and his kind could now do about the past. It was the future that was their concern . . .

Making sure that Britain had one.

"Great heavens," said Chandler weakly, as Steptoe opened one of the sketchbooks and stabbed with an urgent finger at the date on the bottom of the page.

"And what about this?" demanded his subordinate, turning to another paper marking slip and once more emphasising the date noted carefully by Miss Seeton in an out-of-the-way corner of the drawing. He heard his superior draw in his breath with a hiss, and nodded. "And this?"

Before he could find the next page, Chandler had snatched the sketchbook from his hands. "You've marked them all, I take it?" he demanded.

"Just the worst of them. I was in a hurry," came Steptoe's reply as he dropped into an armchair and left Chandler to get on with it. "And believe me, it wasn't easy on the tube, with everyone giving me funny looks and obviously watching out for spies. I'm amazed nobody warned a guard and set the Transport Police on my trail."

"Spies," muttered Chandler as he turned a page. "How I dislike the use of—good grief!"

Steptoe nodded in satisfaction. "Thought you'd appreciate that one," he said.

"Are they all . . . as bad as this?" Chandler asked after an unhappy pause.

"Yes," he was told. "All those I've marked, that is."

"And when you think what else must have been going on in other departments that we know nothing about . . ."

"Yes," said Steptoe grimly. "I told you so."

Chandler wasted no more time. He seized the telephone, pressed the scrambler button, and when informed (in a tone of some reproach) that Captain Grange had gone home for the night, cursed the informant roundly and gave instructions that the captain should report to the Tower for nine sharp the next morning. Yes, he knew very well it was a Sunday. Hadn't Grange's crowd (the military man sneered) realised yet there was a war going on?

The Royal Navy always works five minutes ahead of everyone else. Ask a sailor to rendezvous at seven, and he will be there at six fifty-five.

Captain Grange was at the Tower of London by half-past eight on Sunday morning, and even then he was not the first to arrive. Chandler's urgent message of the previous evening had rung warning bells in all who had received it. Miss Emily Dorothea Seeton might or might not be a traitor, a fifth columnist, in league with the enemy; they had to make up their minds about her, and they had no time to spare for giving her any benefit of the doubt.

"This drawing here, for God's sake." Captain Grange could hardly bring himself to look a second time at the sketch dated, in Miss Seeton's clear hand, *22nd May 1940*. "I ask you—how did the bloody woman know about it all days before anything happened? While it was still being planned? She *must* have a contact at the Admiralty, and that can only mean . . ."

" 'It' being Operation Dynamo," said Chandler for the benefit of his less quick-witted colleagues, as the horrified sailor subsided with a groan and closed his eyes.

"It certainly looks like some sort of electrical thingummy," said Cox of Subsection R, a group of innovative boffins whose job was to produce those items essential to effective espionage that other people said were, if not impossible, then luxuries. Fountain pens that could also squirt tear gas, miniature compasses and gyroscopes that fitted in uniform buttons, fuses and timers and switches that looked like anything but what they really were—these were the province of Cox and his colleagues.

"Yes," he went on, judiciously squinting at the sketch he held at arm's length. "It looks like a dynamo, all right—a female's idea of a dynamo, that is," he added sourly. Cox (it was whispered) had been disappointed of a wealthy young widow early in his courting days, and seemed unlikely to amend his misogynist habits for the duration.

"Operation Dynamo," snarled Captain Grange, opening his eyes and glaring at the assembled group of military and airforce intelligence men as if he held them personally to blame. "Just tell me, if you can—how in the devil's name did that girl *know*?"

The sudden collapse in mid-May of neutral Holland and Belgium, overwhelmed by the Nazi invader, coupled with the surprise German breakthrough of France's supposedly impregnable Maginot Line, had led to the perilous entrapment by enemy troops of the entire British Expeditionary Force. So sudden, indeed, had been that collapse of the Low Countries that many spoke of treachery within, of spies and fifth columnists aiding the parachute troops who fell from the skies in a terrifying, invincible, deadly rain. Small wonder that the British now watched the heavens more anxiously than ever they had done before . . .

The BEF, dispatched across the Channel in answer to the desperate pleas of Britain's smaller neighbours on the European mainland, had been forced to retreat before the brutally efficient, ever-closing pincers of the conquering Nazi armour until the beachhead of Dunkirk was reached. The BEF had been pushed back to the sea; there was nowhere else for them to go; they were encircled—and the circle was pulled tighter hour by hour.

In his chalk tunnel fortress beneath the castle that was the glory of the white cliffs of Dover—Hitler was said to boast that his first meal on British soil would be eaten in Dover Castle—Vice-Admiral Bertram Ramsay and his staff had worked around the clock to prepare the evacuation plan that was, in its incredible success, to thrill the whole free world. With less than a week's notice, so sudden had been that Low Countries collapse, Ramsay arranged for ships of both the Royal and Merchant Navies—corvettes, destroyers, mine-sweepers, trawlers, cargo vessels, ferries—to carry the beleaguered troops from Dunkirk harbour. It was hoped that, with luck, some forty-five thousand men of the BEF might be rescued before the port was at last overrun.

Little Dunkirk, upon which the whole fury and might of the Nazi enemy was then turned, held out courageously for longer—far, far longer—than the anticipated forty-eight hours. The navies of Great Britain steamed to and fro, to and fro across the minefields of the Channel, being bombed and shelled and strafed by German artillery on land and by Nazi aircraft that swooped in roaring triumph for the saltwater kill when they had wearied of raking the French sands with bombs and bullets and bloody death for the unprotected soldiers looking in vain for shelter among the crowded dunes—soldiers who, when a friendly vessel was able to draw near, waded up to their necks in water and stood for hours waiting to be hauled on board the rescue ship, and who returned to the shore to wait another day if their turn for rescue had not yet come.

After three gruelling days the exhausted navies were joined by the most gallant armada in history: the proud Little Ships of Dunkirk, some no more than thirty feet long but with skippers all boasting their seaworthiness when many had never before put out to sea. In response to an earlier broadcast appeal had come the soon-to-be world-famous river craft and pleasure boats, the fishing smacks, the tugs, the private tenders, the lifeboats, the drifters, and the paddle steamers. For nine days the Miracle of Dunkirk endured as not forty-five, but three hundred and thirty-eight thousand men were saved from the blazing hell that was now Dunkirk, brought back to Britain, where they were to regroup and re-arm themselves to fight another day.

The code name for that momentous evacuation plan, graded Most Secret, begun on 26th May, had been Operation Dynamo.

"And Emily Seeton knew all about it on May the twenty-second," said Captain Grange as Cox passed the sketchbook to the man beside him. "How?"

"Coincidence?" offered Cox's neighbour Aylwin . . . but then he saw the sketch. "Oh," he said. "Oh, yes, I do see what you mean. A dynamo, certainly—and wouldn't you say this looks a lot like a circuit board she's doodled here? This sort of trapezoid scribble with lines crossed out and arrows in all directions . . ."

"I thought the girl was supposed to be an art teacher," said Captain Grange to Steptoe, in pardonable annoyance. "You never told us she was a—a blasted radio ham in her spare time. It explains how she gets her messages out, of course, and—"

"What for?" broke in Major Haynes, who until then had been a silent observer, none of the sketchbooks having yet made their way to his place at the table.

"What for?" Every eye was turned on him in amazement. "What for? You must be mad," spluttered Captain Grange. "Or an idiot," he added. "Or worse."

"Or perhaps somewhat less inclined to overreaction," Haynes returned calmly, ignoring the implied slur against his patriotism. "If you will excuse the term. In the circumstances, of course—"

The clamour that greeted this remark was confused, but its meaning was clear. With invasion expected at any moment it

35

was hardly overreaction to be worried about the activities of suspected traitors . . .

"I entirely agree," said Haynes as drifts of ceiling plaster set his colleagues coughing. His seat was closest to the open window, and the draught was in his favour. "All I am trying to point out is that if, as has been suggested, Miss Seeton uses her sketches as a means of passing information, what need would she have for a wireless as well?"

Captain Grange was the first to come up with an answer. "Belt *and* braces, man," he growled.

Chandler interposed before Major Haynes could protest. "Anything is possible, yes—but as Haynes knows, Captain Grange, Steptoe can tell us the watch he's been keeping on the girl has given no indication of any transmitter in the house," he said firmly. "Steptoe, would you confirm?"

"Confirmed," said Steptoe, as if he regretted the fact. "And . . . our friend hasn't shown any signs of wireless activity either."

"Ah, yes." Major Haynes sat up. "Our friend in Hampstead, the fifth columnist. Refresh our memories, if you would be so good, as to how the . . . supposed link with Miss Seeton first came to our attention."

"Damn the girl," muttered Captain Grange.

"She seems a pleasant enough young woman," said Steptoe with some reluctance. "I should rather like to believe in her, I think, now that we've met and talked, but . . . there's still that blackout shutter to explain."

"You didn't ask her about it, I assume." This from the major, who was frowning in thought.

"I was there on behalf of the Ministry of Information, looking for pictures of sandbags," Steptoe reminded him. "I suppose I could have said we'd first spotted her talents on the damned shutter, but if she *is* a wrong 'un we don't want to alert her to the fact she's given herself away, even subconsciously, by plastering this chap's likeness where everyone can see it."

"Girl must be a fool," said Captain Grange. "Why didn't she go back and paint over the thing when she realised what she'd done? I would, in her shoes."

"If," said Major Haynes patiently, "they are in truth the innocent shoes they may yet prove to be, she would have no reason to think the shutter needed repainting—even if the grocer could find the paint, which these days I doubt."

"Don't you know there's a war on?" said Aylwin, and even Captain Grange had to grin at the well-worn phrase before demanding, in his turn, to be reminded of the details of the infamous episode that first alerted the security forces to the possible threat posed to the nation's very existence by Miss Emily Dorothea Seeton.

Chapter 5

"It started with the grocer," said Steptoe. "My landlady, bless her, is a busy little body with the fastest-wagging tongue in Hampstead—very useful, in this line of work."

"Being a grocer?" asked Aylwin, but he was ignored.

"She came home one day just after Christmas," continued Steptoe, "full of the state poor, dear Mr. Robin was getting himself into with worrying about when the rationing scheme would start, and exactly how it would work, and how soon it would be before everything was in dangerously short supply the way it was last time—"

"Blasted U-boat blockade damn near starved us into surrender," growled Captain Grange, whose memories of submarine warfare were not pleasant.

"But this time we were—we are—rather better prepared," Chandler soothed him before nodding to Steptoe to go on with his story.

"We hope," muttered Cox darkly. Major Haynes, at the far end of the table, shook his head and frowned.

"The grocer," Steptoe said loudly, "was working himself into a state. I knew the man, not well, but I knew him—and I know my landlady. She gossips, but she doesn't exaggerate; and Robin always struck me as having his head screwed on the right way when he brought the weekly order round. So I thought it might be worth finding out just why he was suddenly getting hot and bothered about a government scheme that had been in preparation for some time, and that we'd all been expecting any day. Everyone knew we didn't plan to be caught with our trousers down by Hitler the way we were by Kaiser Bill—and Robin ought to have known it, too."

"Some people are born pessimists," said Cox, who after his experience with the widow was himself inclined towards a gloomy view of life.

"Not Robin," said Steptoe firmly. "He told me just a few days after war was declared that he went right through the first lot without a scratch, and he wasn't going to let some jumped-up corporal who should have stuck to painting houses get him down when regular blue blood hadn't managed it twenty years before. But three months later, according to my landlady, *down* wasn't the word for him. So I got to wondering whether someone of a . . . of an unfavourable disposition might not have been working on the little man—"

"Alarm and despondency," snarled Captain Grange. "Damned fifth column!"

"That's how it seemed to me," agreed Steptoe cheerfully. "Once I'd had a friendly chat with Mr. Robin and commiserated with him about the shortages—this was still before rationing had officially started, you understand—"

"On the eighth of January," the irrepressible Aylwin reminded his fellow intelligence officers, in case they had forgotten.

Captain Grange snorted. Chandler rolled his eyes but said nothing. Major Haynes shook his head again, and Cox let out a sigh. Aylwin subsided.

"So I jollied the chap along," persisted Steptoe, "and tipped him the wink I was in the know—showed him my ID as a high-up in the Ministry of Supply, and reassured him the best way I knew how. He was a different man by the time I left the shop—of course, I was careful to wait until there was nobody else in the place to overhear—and because we were alone I was able to do a bit of judicious pumping. And he let slip enough to confirm my original idea that someone *had* been working on him, and on some of the other shop-keepers—about how this was a war for the benefit of the bosses and the rich greedy profiteering Jews who raked in the money earned by the sweat of honest men's brows, hiding behind the skirts of the fighting men—"

Captain Grange uttered a salty oath that brought more plaster from the ceiling. The others echoed his sentiments, though in less immoderate language.

"Exactly," said Steptoe. "He let slip that someone's name, as well, though it took a bit of questioning on my part, and I kept out of Robin's way for a while after. He's a shrewd little devil, for all his fusspot ways. I didn't want him to start thinking about me and . . . getting ideas."

"Nobody's reported you as a fifth columnist yet, you'll be pleased to know," Chandler told him with a grin, before prompting: "You kept out of his way for a while—and then?"

"Then one day my landlady came back burbling about some clever little artist called Seeton who'd been asked by Mr. Robin to paint his blackout shutters to show that, even if there *was* a rationing scheme, his shop was still plentifully stocked with groceries in spirit, as it were, if not in fact. So I strolled along one evening at just about the time to help Robin fasten the shutters—and there he was. Our friend Collins, the fifth-column suspect, slap in the middle of the picture, buying a bunch of grapes."

"And the only customer, so far as we have ascertained, *not* to have passed any comment whatsoever on having his likeness on display for the whole world to see," Chandler concluded briskly on his subordinate's behalf. Steptoe was a good man, but long-winded on occasion.

"Suspicious," said Cox, "when everyone else she painted has, according to you, at least said *something* about it."

"Unusual," amended Major Haynes. "It might be no more than a case along the lines of a person's failing to recognise his own voice when it is heard on a broadcast recording—a well-known phenomenon, I believe."

"Bearded bloke, this Collins?" enquired Captain Grange, thoughtfully stroking his own regulation "full set" of whiskers. The Royal Navy does not allow half measures in anything, and a moustache by itself is as unacceptable as a moustacheless beard.

"Clean-shaven," said Steptoe. He looked at Major Haynes and forestalled him rather neatly with: "And, no, he doesn't go to the local cutthroat man, he shaves himself. There's no excuse for his not knowing what he looks like, even in reverse in a mirror."

"Miss Seeton showed him the right way round, did she?" asked the major with another of his frowns.

"The right way round?" cried Captain Grange. "Good God, man—are you trying to tell us the blasted female

41

might be psychic? The right way, the wrong way—the man's a wrong 'un, and Seeton's fingered him—pah!"

"I'm saying no such thing," returned Major Haynes, for the first time roused from his habitual calm. "What I am saying is that, while of course there are such things as photographs in which a man might recognise his likeness, some people don't care for photographs and never have them taken. And some have a . . . a blind spot about themselves—and Collins may be one of them. You've reported, Steptoe, that since Miss Seeton's picture first appeared in the Hampstead street for passersby to admire, any fifth-column activities in which the man might have been engaged appear to have stopped."

"We haven't caught him out in anything," Steptoe acknowledged. "No wireless activity, as I said—but of course we don't know if that's what he was doing before he . . ." He shot a quick look at Captain Grange. "Before he was fingered by Miss Seeton," he said.

The captain muttered into his beard, but it was the major who replied.

"Why," he asked gently, "should she do that if she's in league with him?"

"She's in love with him," said Cox. "Women are damned funny creatures. The subconscious mind . . ."

Captain Grange muttered wrathfully once more against Miss Seeton's psychic tendencies.

"It's hardly my idea of a valentine," said Aylwin quickly. "To have my face in poster paint on a blackout shutter in the High Street, that is. I'd say if she's trying to get him to propose, she's out of luck."

"Pretty, is she?" Chandler asked Steptoe, whose startled look implied that courtship—by whatever means—and Miss Seeton had not before been brought together in his mind.

"Oh, pleasant enough," Steptoe said after a pause. It seemed that Emily Dorothea Seeton, whatever other impression she might have made on him during their brief encounter, had not slain him with one of Cupid's darts. "She'll be a regular little old lady if she lives so long—"

"If any of us live so long," interposed Cox.

"—because if she's half an inch above five foot," said Steptoe, "I'll be surprised, and sopping wet she can't weigh more than seven stone . . . but nice, neat features, though she doesn't wear more than a dab of lipstick, and not even clear polish on her nails . . . A lady, of course—and a born spinster, I'd say." He looked across at Cox. "You *could* be right, but somehow—"

"Suppose we all stop bothering about the blasted woman's love life," said Captain Grange, "and start asking ourselves just what the devil she meant by doing *this* when she did?" He'd had only half an ear on the discussion around him as he leafed once again through those damning sketchbooks. "Look at the date, for pity's sake! Look!"

They all looked. The page now open for scrutiny showed little in the way of detailed drawing: there was rather a series of swift, swooping pencilled lines depicting a row of men, imperiously posed, on plinths, with their names jotted underneath.

"Pitt," read Chandler aloud. "Palmerston, Peel, Walpole—and 'Walpole' has been underlined, you note, gentlemen."

"*And* with a question mark," added Captain Grange in case they couldn't see this for themselves.

"Gladstone," said Major Haynes, continuing to read aloud the names under the plinths. "Disraeli, Asquith—the girl simply has a bee in her genteel bonnet about British prime ministers, that's all."

"Then why," asked Captain Grange darkly, "has she put so much emphasis on Walpole, damn her? Where does a wise man hide a leaf? In a blasted forest, that's where!" With an effort he controlled himself. "And why," he went on, even more darkly, "did she write *this*?"

He stabbed a furious finger at one word that floated, as it were, to one side and slightly above the swiftly sketched prime-ministerial statues. "*Diamond*," he read in his darkest tones yet. "And the date, man—the date!"

The date was there for all to see in Miss Seeton's neat hand: *11th May, 1940*.

"Whitsun weekend," said Major Haynes at last. "Evidently she didn't take the government's cancellation of the bank holiday too much to heart, if she could find the time to go doodling history lessons around town—but I agree," he went on quickly as Captain Grange again began to simmer audibly. "The coincidence is . . . remarkable."

The others considered this statement in silence. Other words than *remarkable* might well be applied to Miss Seeton's apparent foreknowledge of the stirring events of that Order in Council cancelled Whit Monday, 13th May 1940—events graded Most Secret, and with very good cause. The German invasion on 10th May of neutral Belgium and Holland had sent Britain on full alert. Forces leave, like the bank holiday due on Monday, was cancelled as the nation geared up to face the ever-nearing Nazi hordes. There was fighting in Norway, there were landings in Iceland, there were supply convoys to be escorted against the U-boat menace that lurked unseen under every wave . . . and yet, amid so much busyness and alarm, with every other ship of the Royal Navy preparing to sell herself and her crew dearly, the elderly destroyer HMS *Walpole* received strict instructions to stay away at all costs from the action. Her commanding officer was told on Whit Sunday that he must carry three anonymous male passengers at full speed across the Channel to the Dutch port of Ymuiden, and bring them—together with whatever luggage they might have acquired during their brief stay abroad—back alive the following day.

"*Diamond*," said Captain Grange, once more stabbing at the word where it floated above the statue labelled *Pitt*. "The blasted girl gives me the creeps, the way she seems to *know* what we're up to even before we know ourselves . . ."

The luggage brought back in HMS *Walpole* by the three anonymous men had consisted of an ordinary canvas kitbag, such as any sailor might carry, although no sailor's kit in history had ever been so priceless. A value of two million pounds would be a conservative estimate: two million pounds' worth of industrial diamonds, without which none of the factories engaged in war work could be tooled. Diamond, the hardest substance in the world, was essential for the drawing of wires to an accuracy of a thousandth of an inch; some wires must be thinner still, for use in certain items of electric, electronic, and radio equipment so vital, yet so secret, that even Cox and his Subsection R boffins understood little of their function. Without industrial diamonds, the very industry of war would come to a halt . . .

"Brave chaps, those merchants," said Captain Grange, and cleared his throat. For a moment nobody spoke; there were one or two coughs, and then a general murmur of agreement ran around the table. It was a worthy tribute to those quiet Dutchmen who had handed over their diamond stock to Britain's anonymous representatives in the full knowledge that Nazi intelligence would all too soon discover—if indeed the facts were not already known—what that stock should have been. The German war machine had as great a need for diamonds as anyone else. Punishment for thwarting the invaders would be severe . . .

Yet the merchants had not hesitated. The diamonds had left the country; the handful of craftsmen—perhaps six—who could drill a diamond hole as small as the technically near-impossible triple-O-five required by radar and electronics had gone into hiding, and there were plans to effect a rescue once their whereabouts were known.

"Doubt if we'll be able to send the *Walpole* next time," said Captain Grange, with all the regret of a naval man whose role has been usurped by a different branch of HM forces. "It'll be midnight landing strips and airlifting the poor blighters out of occupied territory, just you mark my words."

Nobody argued with him. Once more there was a brief pause, broken by murmurs of agreement.

"She knew about the *Walpole* operation three days before it happened," said Chandler at last.

"Or so it would appear," put in Major Haynes, who was still weighing the possibilities of coincidence against the likelihood of Miss Seeton's having, if not psychic, then perhaps prophetic powers.

"She also appears," continued Chandler heavily, "to have had some previous knowledge of Operation Dynamo."

"Suspicious," observed the cynical Cox. "Nobody normal could have expected the Belgians to throw in the towel as quickly as they did." His tone implied that even he had not thought so poorly of King Leopold, who had begged for Allied help and then, it seemed, abandoned the struggle without warning and left the BEF to its fate.

"Except Miss Seeton," said Aylwin, who had been struck by a sudden inspiration. "Has it occurred to anyone that if the girl really has allowed Steptoe to requisition every sketchbook she owns, we might—with a spot of judicious study— be able to work out in advance what the hell is going to happen next?"

"The date of the invasion would be useful," said Captain Grange, who like his colleagues was more than willing to fight on the beaches, on the landing grounds, in the fields, in the streets, and in the hills, but who unlike the military men would prefer the chance to fight on the seas and oceans first. "We've been waiting since May, dammit—since June, anyway, after Dunkirk. And that," he went on, snatching up a sketchbook and turning to another of the markers Chandler and Steptoe between them had placed at those points they deemed most worthy of consideration, "brings me to *this*— and all I can say about this is, there *must* be a security leak somewhere. We can gabble about coincidence and—and psychic powers until we're blue in the face, but that young woman is a damn sight too psychic and coincidental for her own good. For the good of the country, blast her.

"Argue it whichever way you want, Haynes," he hurried on as the major looked about to protest. "Seeton is *dangerous*.

She knows too much—far more than anyone who isn't in the intelligence racket has a right to know—and she's playing some damned cunning double game with the knowledge, I'm sure of it." He waved the sketchbook in the air and glowered at every face around the table in turn, quelling all attempted interruption. "What we can't be sure of," he went on, "is whether or not she's telling anyone about it, although from the lack of known contact, it's possible she might not be, just yet—but she's getting in a hell of a lot of practice disguising the important stuff among the rest of it, which is what I meant about wise men hiding leaves in the forest."

"It—" began Chandler, but Captain Grange steamed over his beginning at full verbal speed ahead.

"In my opinion," he said, "she was simply . . . biding her time. Of course, now that she knows we've broken her cover she'll wait to see if we manage to crack her blasted code—which brings me," he repeated grimly, "to *this*, gentlemen. An operation even more vital—even more secret—than the *Walpole* business—and yet Emily Seeton seems to have known about Operation Fish more than a week before it started!"

Chapter 6

Once more the tubby policeman pedalled his regulation black bicycle along the road, his gas mask in its canvas bag bumping against his hip. He reached his destination, propped his bike against the wall, and marched up the short flight of steps to the bell, which he rang in his most official manner. There was a rattle at the lock, and the door swung open.

PC Badgery touched his helmet in salute. "Miss Emily Dorothea Seeton?" he asked in his most official tones.

"Why, yes, of course," said Miss Seeton, with a welcoming smile. "How may I be of assistance, Mr. Badgery?"

PC Badgery glanced warily over his shoulder and then bent forward to whisper, although there was nobody within half a mile of the little porch as far as he could see. "Orders," he hissed, fishing an envelope out of his pocket and again glancing warily around before passing it to Miss Seeton. "Best wait till you're inside before you read 'em," he went on in the same low voice. This was noble of PC Badgery, for his curiosity was very great—but his patriotism was even greater, and the superintendent had emphasised that nobody was to know what any of this was about. A friendly visit from the neighbourhood bobby would probably pass unnoticed: if it didn't, he was to say, if anyone asked, that there had been some complaint about the blackout, unlikely though this was in the case of the Seeton ladies—but it was what he was to say, and all he was to know.

PC Badgery had responded that it *was* all he knew. He didn't have a clue, and hadn't known from the start, what any of this was about, just that they'd wanted him to invite Miss Seeton to the cop shop for a chat and then, when she was out, they'd sent someone else along to chat with her at home. And now, with this letter, he supposed they wanted to chat with her somewhere else . . .

"Don't *suppose* anything," the superintendent told him. "Just do what you're told and forget all about it. Right?"

"Right you are, sir," said PC Badgery, who had a cheery suspicion the super didn't have any more of a clue what was going on than he himself did.

That suspicion was, of course, correct. Secrecy was all-important. Nobody must ever be allowed to forget there was a war on . . .

The envelope was neatly typed, with OHMS in the top right-hand corner, and was firmly sealed. Miss Seeton slit it carefully across the top with a knife so that it could be reused with a sticky label. There was a war on, and it was the patriotic duty of everybody not to be wasteful.

She was rather surprised to find a second, smaller envelope, even more firmly sealed than the first, inside. The direction on the second envelope was in handwritten capital letters, in red ink.

"Dear me," murmured Miss Seeton, whose preference was for a less flamboyant mode of address. She slit the second envelope with the same care she had applied to the first and shook out a folded paper that, unfolded, proved to be—as PC Badgery had said—her orders.

"The Tower of London?" Miss Seeton meditated on this startling instruction for some minutes, but could arrive at no logical conclusion. Had she been told to report, say, to the headquarters of the Women's Voluntary Service, it would have made sense. While there was as yet no compulsory registration scheme for female workers, everyone throughout the country was doing what she could—even her dear mother, who had never been strong, but who was happy to stay quietly at home sewing, or knitting comforts for the troops with wool from unravelled sweaters, taking a gentle stroll twice a week to the local WVS to collect more sweaters because she didn't care to put people to the bother of bringing them to the house when petrol was in such short supply, and when public transport was so . . . unreliable.

Despite the unreliability:

"I'll go by tube," Miss Seeton resolved after reading her letter again and noting the time at which she was required to be at the Tower. "A taxi, could I even find one, would be so expensive, and these days there are so few buses going where one wants. With the new line it should be so much easier than it used to be—I hope . . ."

Her hope was fulfilled. She waited only seven minutes at Finchley Road underground station for a through train to Charing Cross on the Bakerloo Line. As the doors opened and Miss Seeton climbed on board, she glanced back with approval to the platform and the lively young woman in her still-unfamiliar guard's uniform, whistle and flag at the ready to signal the driver it was safe to move off. Really, it was splendid that so many men were being replaced, and with such ready efficiency, by their female counterparts—even if (and here Miss Seeton's smile faded) the men were leaving to join the armed forces. She sighed. Leaving to risk their lives. Leaving to fight an enemy roused to war by an evil madman . . .

Miss Seeton left her train at Charing Cross and hurried up and down stairs and along various tunnels to the District Line, hoping that a change of scene would help to change the direction of her thoughts. One was not normally so—so morbid, and while it might be argued that in such times of national emergency there was every reason to be concerned, it was surely more sensible—so much better for morale—if that concern did not so much remain unvoiced as even . . . unthought. One had one's patriotic duty to remain, or at least to appear to remain, optimistic at all times. What was the phrase? *Spreading alarm and despondency.* There was that new, special Act of Parliament that could send alarmists to prison—perhaps (she supposed) as in the old days to the Tower of London . . .

But Miss Seeton did not (she told herself) seriously believe that a charge of treason was the cause of her summons—and in so curious a manner—to the Tower, although she suspected there might be rather more to it than the theory she had proposed to her anxious mother. Alice Seeton, upon learning what was in her daughter's letter (though Emily had given her only the gist of its contents, for to allow anyone else to read it might be a breach of security), had agreed with her daughter's cheerful assumption that it was probably a mistake: no doubt something to do with the sketches and leaflets Mr. Steptoe had said they might ask her to draw, and in the way of government offices they had used the wrong address.

It would soon be sorted out, as such things always were. When there was a war on, it must come as no great surprise if wires, or rather letters, were on occasion crossed. Indeed, it was surprising that, in such circumstances, more letters than hers did not go astray, but the postmen were so clever . . .

By the time Miss Seeton had reached Mark Lane and emerged into the fresh air, she was smiling once more. Even the somehow unexpected sight—one had of course read about it, but it was the first time she had actually been there and seen it—of the Tower of London's grassy moat turned over entirely to rows of vegetables did no more than moderate her smile to a still-optimistic upward curve of the lips. It was truly splendid, the way everyone was playing his part—even the Beefeaters. Who, perhaps, one might whimsically suppose to have somewhat less cause than others to be interested in a vegetable diet. Miss Seeton's smile broadened again. Or more. Roast beef and two veg was, after all, the traditional English Sunday lunch, and could anyone doubt the traditionally English nature of the Tower of London and its Beefeater guards? For hundreds of years they had watched and protected . . .

"Halt!" cried the sentry as Miss Seeton, still smiling, set foot on the bridge. He snatched the gun at his shoulder to the "present" position. "Who goes there?"

Miss Seeton had not fully emerged from her daydreams of King Henry VII, upon whose authority the Beefeaters—though one should not forget their correct nomenclature was the Yeomen of the Guard—had been formed. She blinked at this modern khaki-clad guard with his gun at the ready, and waited politely for the rest of the traditional challenge. She waited some moments before it became clear it was not to be uttered.

"Who goes there?" cried the sentry again, rattling the bolt of his gun in a purposeful manner. As other khaki-clad figures along the bridge arranged themselves and their weapons in attitudes of readiness, the man confronting Miss Seeton stamped his heavy boots on the flagstone paving and glared through narrowed eyes at the young woman who stood blinking at him in such a peculiar way.

"Friend," Miss Seeton replied with a gasp, startled by the booted stamp out of 1485 and back to 1940 in the space of one quick breath. "Oh, yes, friend—not foe, I do assure you. I—I have this letter . . ."

"Let's see," said the sentry, reaching out with his free hand to take the OHMS envelope even as his other hand tightened on the gun. "Right—wait there . . ."

He took three or four steps back towards his comrades in arms, out of range of any tricks this self-styled "friend" might decide to try to stop him giving the letter the thorough once-over it deserved. He glanced quickly at the young woman before he pulled the letter from its envelope; she was standing meekly waiting as he'd instructed, her fingers idly twisting at the string that tied her gas mask in its cardboard box to the strap of her handbag. Good-quality leather, that looked, same as her shoes. Clothes respectable, apart from the hat, which was—well, like no hat he'd ever seen before—but then, everyone was trimming and refurbishing these days, and perhaps she'd just got carried away once she started. Some women were like that. You couldn't say the same for her makeup—very restrained, that was. A dab of powder, a smudge of lipstick, and her light brown hair looked as if it waved naturally, which it probably did, as she hardly seemed the type for a perm.

Even as his quick eye summed up the meekly waiting Miss Seeton, his study of the letter within the red-ink envelope showed him he had been right to be ready to accept her for what she seemed to be, a conventional young woman of the English middle classes, here at the Tower on official business—and what *sort* of business he knew damn well it wasn't his place to start wondering. He'd heard too many tales of young women applying for what people told 'em would be a routine job—translating from the foreign papers, maybe—and never seen a second time on account of being parachuted somewhere abroad, in disguise, though if anyone asked his opinion, the high-ups'd gone badly wrong with this one, who wouldn't—couldn't—pass for anything but English, not if she tried for a thousand years . . .

"Pass, friend," said the sentry with a grin, returning the letter to its owner and snapping off a ferocious salute. English as they came, and away to fight the Hun on his own territory—why, if it wasn't against standing orders, he'd take off his hat to her!

Miss Seeton's identity was checked, rechecked, and confirmed all along the bridge. At the final checkpoint the sentry asked her to wait while he called for assistance. He retreated into his box, cranked a handle, and spoke urgently into a field telephone.

"Someone'll be down for you in a minute, miss," he said as he emerged from the box. "Lovely day, innit?"

"Oh, it is indeed," said Miss Seeton, thankful for the gambit. After such a display of military efficiency she was starting to feel just a little apprehensive about what might be in store once the Tower gates were closed behind her. So many people had entered the Norman fortress, never to leave again.

She thought of tragic Lady Jane Grey, the youthful Nine Days' Queen, at first ruling from, and then imprisoned in, the Tower, to be beheaded on the orders of Mary Tudor, at just sixteen—Thomas Seymour, Lord High Admiral of England—Sir Walter Ralegh, Elizabeth's gallant pirate, whom her successor James had taken in such dislike, if that wasn't a ridiculous meiosis—Anne Boleyn—Catherine Howard—Sir Thomas More . . . Traitors' Gate, and the courageous behaviour of the young, innocent Princess Elizabeth—

"Miss Seeton?" From the tone of voice it was evident this was at least the second time of asking.

Miss Seeton blushed and once more emerged from history to confront the present day, which stood before her now in natty gents' tailoring, complete with buttonhole rose.

"Oh," said Miss Seeton, blinking. "Oh . . . yes, I am Emily Seeton." She had been expecting she knew not what, but certainly someone in uniform. Except that she supposed one could regard pin-striped trousers and a well-cut black jacket as a uniform, of sorts. Didn't a humorous popular song refer to the Bowler Brigade? Not, of course, that this gentleman was wearing a bowler, but it was not difficult to envisage such a hat on a mahogany stand in his office . . .

"My name is Chandler," said he of the pinstripes and flowered lapel, as the sentry snapped off a salute to the newcomer and then, turning slightly to one side, grinned and winked at Miss Seeton. "If you would care to follow me," went on Chandler, ignoring both the grin and the wink, "I'll take you to meet Major Haynes."

As his victim pattered in his wake—he did his best to shorten his six-foot stride to accommodate her, but he kept forgetting—Chandler wondered, not for the first time in his present employment, at the contrast between vision and reality. Between them they'd all—except Steptoe, who'd actually met the girl—built her up into some sort of . . . genteel bogey woman. They knew her personal details and family background, and on paper she looked about as great a threat to national security as he himself did—but in view of those damning sketches, they still had to play safe. She could yet turn out to be dangerous: even without concrete proof they'd decided she probably was, or at least the risk couldn't be taken that she wasn't without a good deal more investigation. Which is why the interview between her and Haynes would be monitored to the hilt, with hidden microphones and, if it could be wangled, someone watching through a convenient hole—not eyes cut out of portraits on the wall, which was very old hat, and she'd be bound to spot it, art being her speciality, as they well knew . . .

They knew everything about her, yet they knew nothing about her. It was up to Major Haynes, the only one who'd been able to hold a totally balanced position about the girl all the way through that intense discussion the other day, to find out just what made Miss Seeton tick . . .

With the long practice of the intelligence officer who could live life on several levels at once, Chandler was busy pointing out sights of historical interest to his companion even as, on a different mental plane, he continued to wonder about her.

". . . school parties, in happier days," Miss Seeton was telling him as they crossed a small courtyard and headed for a discreet wooden door reinforced with iron studs that after so many centuries were rather more rust than iron. "The children do so revel in all the bloodthirsty stories, you know. I find that once they are back in the classroom they throw themselves with the greatest enthusiasm into the task of drawing whatever has made the most impression on them." Miss Seeton's manner showed that she held enthusiasm in very high esteem. "It's a curious thing," she added as Chandler produced a small, shiny key and applied it to a surprisingly modern keyhole, "but the girls seem to enjoy quite as many beheadings and gory splashes of blood as any of the boys I have taught." She smiled faintly. "Until, that is, they reach a certain age."

"The female of the species, Miss Seeton," said Chandler as he ushered her through the door, locked it behind them, and slipped the key back in his pocket. Was her remark one of the Freudian slips the shrinks and trick cyclists warned you about? Was her subconscious boasting that she, one of your typical English middle-class girls, could be as bloodthirsty— as dangerous—as anyone, if she wanted? She'd retrieved her mistake quickly enough—if it *was* a mistake, of course . . .

"In here, Miss Seeton." They had climbed some narrow twisting stone steps and walked along an even more narrow corridor painted a dull, faded green and lit by electric bulbs that were no substitute for daylight. Now they stood outside one of the many doors—identical, except for the numbers and letters in their metal frames—past which they had walked in the gloom.

Chandler raised his hand, knocked a sharp *rat-tat*, and opened the door without waiting for an invitation from within. "After you, Miss Seeton," he said with a courteous nod; and as she entered, he followed her. "Miss Seeton, Major Haynes," he said, and then said nothing more.

Chapter 7

Major Haynes had been sitting at his desk when Chandler knocked, but was already on his feet as the door opened and Miss Seeton walked in.

For several seconds the two regarded each other in a thoughtful silence Chandler did not break. At last, Haynes nodded and smiled.

"Good morning, Miss Seeton," he said.

"Good morning, Major Haynes," replied Miss Seeton with a shy smile of her own. "It—it *is* Major Haynes, isn't it? I thought Mr. Chandler told me—but without a uniform . . ."

Neither of them noticed Chandler close the door as he retreated to the nearest hidey-hole to join Cox and those others of the team who could be spared to spy on one who might, or who might not, herself be a spy.

"It *is* Major Haynes," the major reassured her, pulling himself together. "But in my job—in this branch of the service—we're pretty easygoing about uniforms." He did not enlarge upon either the nature of the job or the branch of the service, and Miss Seeton, who understood the meaning of security, had no intention of asking. "We all know who we are," the major went on with another smile, "and so long as we do, there are more important things to worry about than spit and polish and hats with scrambled egg on them, as our friends in the navy say." He recollected himself with a start. "Please, Miss Seeton, won't you sit down?"

Miss Seeton sat. Her handbag and gas mask were rather too bulky on her lap for comfort, and she glanced toward the major for permission to put them on his desk, where they could be reached in an emergency. Her glance was distracted by the blotter on his desk—or rather by what lay upon that blotter. Her second glance, followed by a quick frown and then a faint smile, was not the reaction the hidden watchers might have expected. Was she, then, so cool a customer she believed she could talk her way out of anything? Or was she a genuine innocent, honestly puzzled as to how her property had ended up in the Tower?

"Your sketches, Miss Seeton," Major Haynes responded at once to the look of enquiry she turned on him, too polite to ask a direct question. "You may be wondering how they have come into my hands when it was to Mr. Steptoe of . . ." Damn, he'd forgotten the wretched man's cover story. It was that shy, enquiring look of hers that had done it.

"Of the Ministry of Information," supplied Miss Seeton promptly. "At least, that was what he said," she added as the major's shoulders seemed to shake.

His dawning relief faded. "You didn't believe him?" he asked as the quick little frown reappeared, and once more faded into a smile.

"It was hardly my place," Miss Seeton pointed out in her most courteous tones, "to disbelieve a guest in my mother's house, although I confess I thought it a little . . . odd that a government official should concern himself with my

60

poor artistic efforts—but of course at such times as these, many . . . strange things happen. And, naturally, if he was indeed speaking the truth, I would be proud to assist in any way that I could, even though my training is not in commercial art, and I feel sure there must be others better suited to the task than I am. Whatever," she finished with yet another smile, rather less shy, "that task might be."

"Public information leaflets," Major Haynes reminded her as once more she turned that enquiring look upon him.

"Yes, of course," said Miss Seeton, nodding sagely, and with a smile that was almost a twinkle. "Showing people how to fill sandbags, and—and similarly difficult operations." She spoke with an element of control in her voice that made the major give her a sharp look. "Sketches," enlarged Miss Seeton, nodding again. "Photographic reproduction can be so very costly, can it not? Even for government departments."

Major Haynes was suddenly tempted to wipe his brow. The interview, he suspected, might just not go quite the way he and the others had planned . . .

What was it about this girl that seemed to have everything topsy-turvy, for no good reason that he could see? Apart from the hat—*remarkable* was the understatement of the century—you could trip over a dozen like her the minute you walked out of the door.

Or, on second thoughts—that look she gave you was uncomfortably shrewd—perhaps you couldn't. Honesty, he decided, might be the best policy—insofar as honesty was ever possible in the intelligence world.

"It seems," the major remarked with a wry smile, "that it isn't easy to fool you, Miss Seeton."

"I have been a teacher for several years, Major Haynes," Miss Seeton reminded him, and stifled a sigh for those earlier years when she had hoped that her talent might be . . . something more. Those who can, do; those who can't, teach. And the conscientious teacher knows more of human nature—both its depths and its heights—than almost anyone else.

"A teacher, yes, of course." The major's voice expressed his relief as he recognised more familiar conversational territory. He lifted the sketchbooks from the blotter and took up the cardboard folder that had been concealed underneath. "I take it you won't be too surprised that we know your educational record and professional qualifications," he went on. "And your family background."

"In wartime," said Miss Seeton with resolution, "it is as well to be prepared for any eventuality. Should you indeed wish to employ me—and for whatever purpose—a charge of carelessness—carelessness in the extreme—would be levelled at you should you fail to . . . check up on me."

Her clear gaze was almost accusing. "Or even a charge more serious still," she continued sternly. "Treason, for instance."

Behind the walls there was consternation among the hidden watchers. They could mop their brows without being seen—and mop they did. Their quarry was turning the interrogatory tables with a vengeance.

"Your father's daughter," said Major Haynes, "is surely an unlikely candidate for treason." As Miss Seeton's eyes brightened with sudden tears and her gaze fell, he coughed, and opened the cardboard folder. "Major Hugo Monk Seeton," he read aloud. "Volunteer, August 1914—awarded the Military Cross in 1916 at the Somme . . ."

He had been watching Miss Seeton's hands, clasped on her lap. They twitched and tightened briefly before her gaze lifted again to meet his own. He waited for her to speak.

"I do beg your pardon," said the daughter of Major Hugo Seeton, "but it was the Victoria Cross. And Passchendaele, in 1917. I was only a child, but I remember it well . . ." She blinked, and shook her head, and now her eyes gleamed with gentle mischief. "So, Major, are you satisfied that I am who I say I am?" asked Emily Dorothea Seeton.

This time Major Haynes permitted himself the visible luxury of a quick handkerchief across his brow. He tried to believe it was because the room was hot—but his belief in his motives wasn't very convincing.

"I'm sorry, Miss Seeton," he said. "But you understand that we have to be sure."

"My father died in 1919," said Miss Seeton, and once more her eyes were bright. "In the influenza epidemic—he had been badly gassed, as I'm sure you know, and his lungs were never strong . . . and then my poor little sister . . ."

Major Haynes waited again. Either the girl was a brilliant actress, or it would be cruel to test her further.

"Poor Amabel," said Miss Seeton at last with the hint of a sigh. "She was always so frail—they had hoped so much for a second child, and . . . And my poor mother almost wore herself out nursing them both. She refused to have them taken from the house, as my father had such a distrust of hospitals after . . ."

"Yes, of course," said the major quickly.

"I was rather too young," said Miss Seeton, looking back twenty years to her nine-year-old self, "to be of any great help in a sickroom, and of course there was the additional worry that I, too, might become ill. My mother sent me to stay with Cousin Flora in Kent, and—and I never saw either my father, or Amabel, again."

"So after your return you remained in Hampstead," prompted Major Haynes. "You went to school there, attended art college in London, and followed this with various local teaching posts."

"My mother is not strong," said Miss Seeton. "She has had a sad life—and she would, I think, have missed me had I studied away from home. And as I have had but slight inclination towards matrimony . . ." She cleared her throat. "As your files surely explain," she concluded, and once more that mischievous gleam appeared in her eyes.

"Talking of explanations," said Major Haynes, who felt that matrimony and the disconcerting Emily Seeton were indeed improbable partners, "there are one or two of your drawings that are of considerable interest—if you could bear with me a moment . . . This one, for instance." He had closed the folder of personal details and pushed it to one side, pulling one of the sketchbooks towards him and opening it at the first marked page. "It's an unusual composition," observed Major Haynes with feeling.

Miss Seeton studied the sketch for a moment. "The zoo," she said, and then frowned. "At least, that's how it started out—but there was something about the young woman in the refreshment kiosk that reminded me of little Miss Brown at college, who used to make us chuckle with a comic verse during life classes—because it was such a hot day . . ."

The date on the sketch was 19th June 1940.

"After Mr. Churchill's stirring speech the day before," Miss Seeton explained, "I thought it only fitting that the

64

young people of England—certainly, those with whom I had some association—should be given the chance to play their part. To—to bear themselves with as much . . . fortitude, to show themselves as resolute, as their elders. With so many parents taking a stand and refusing to evacuate their children a second time, there is plenty of work for those like myself who are used to dealing with the young, and I have arranged several little trips and outings over the past weeks—as your files no doubt tell you," she finished with another gleam of mischief.

"Well . . ." began Major Haynes, and said no more.

Miss Seeton nodded. "We have been to Hampton Court, and Hyde Park—where I fear several children took strong exception to the Peace League representative at Speakers' Corner, and I had to deliver a—a little lecture about freedom of speech and the right to make up one's own mind before they could be persuaded to listen quietly." Miss Seeton's cheeks were pink as she pressed on: "While any right-minded person must surely agree that peace is preferable to war, there are some wars, regrettably, that—that have to be fought for the sake of—of principle. Bullies," said Schoolteacher Seeton, "must be stopped."

She sat up straight on her chair and shook her head as she tried to find the words. "It is," she said earnestly, "most important, I feel, that young people should learn as soon as possible that we in this country are—are upholders of the right to freedom. And if that right means allowing others to stand on soapboxes in a public place to deliver what I, for one, find a—a most unwise message, then they must be allowed to stand there, or we will be as bad as the Nazis. And so I explained to the children."

"Hampton Court!" cried Major Haynes without warning. Behind the wall the hidden watchers jumped quite as high as did Miss Seeton. He turned hurriedly to one of the other marker slips in the sketchbook and held out the page marked *22nd May 1940* showing what Cox had said was a dynamo, and the trapezoid scribble Aylwin had suggested might be a circuit board. "Would this, by any chance, be your attempt at working out the plan of the maze?"

Miss Seeton twinkled at him. "Have you read *Three Men in a Boat*?" she countered. "Such an amusing book, and of course had I been on my own, it would hardly have mattered, but with the responsibility of so many children I thought it better to try to avoid the experience of Mr. Harris and his cousin—even if my strong suspicion is that the children might have thoroughly enjoyed losing themselves in so spectacular a fashion." She was twinkling again as she went on. "Their parents, however, might with justification have been less than amused had our party returned home in any way . . . reduced in number, and so, as we walked, I tried to sketch out our path."

Major Haynes remarked that it must have been a tricky task, in the circumstances.

Miss Seeton nodded. "Indeed it was, for there were a good many dead ends and false turnings, and then some of the children grew rather excited and started running ahead. Had I run after them I would, of course, have had to leave the slower children behind, and at least I knew that there was only one way out, where they had been told, if they found it, to wait until the rest of us arrived, if we ever did. And only one way to the centre," she added. "If we ever managed to find *that*."

"Er—did you?" asked the major, grinning.

"Eventually." Miss Seeton's answering smile might well have been, in a young woman less genteel, another grin. "And the children were so tired with all the running that they were extremely well behaved on the journey home, even if some of the boys did not allow me to forget that I had promised to take them to see Faraday House—it is not far from the palace, and they are so interested in cats'-whisker wirelesses and electricity and—and so forth."

"And dynamos," murmured Major Haynes, looking with new understanding on Miss Seeton's doodled coils and crossings-out. "Dynamos . . ."

"Exactly. He invented them, you see," Miss Seeton informed him brightly. "The children chattered so much, and of course I looked him up. Michael Faraday, 1791 to 1867, considered by most authorities to be the greatest of all experimental physicists—let me see. Dynamos, and electric motors, and—dear me, I've forgotten—something to do with change . . ."

"Change. Transformers?" prompted Major Haynes, who felt he might be starting to fathom the workings of Miss Seeton's decidedly unusual, and certainly lively, mind.

"Transformers, yes," said Miss Seeton, grateful for the reminder. "And as it would take us only a little out of our way, it seemed a pity not to encourage their enthusiasm by going home from the palace via the green, which I was only too pleased to do."

"You take your duties seriously, Miss Seeton," remarked Major Haynes with approval. "All these trips around and about require time and effort on your part to plan, to say the least of it." Miss Seeton blushed and murmured modestly, but Haynes pressed on with his compliment. "Escorting a bunch

67

of pesky brats who are acting up because they're bored would be my idea of purgatory," he told her with obvious sincerity. "The trick is to keep them interested, isn't it? Which is easier said than done, I know—but a good teacher can interest his or her pupils in anything. Even politics," he added with a smile, and held his breath as he waited for her reply.

It was offered in a tone of wry amusement as Miss Seeton's blush faded. "Speakers' Corner is noted more for its oratory than for—for the sense of its political opinions," she said, twinkling at him again. "Except that even the oratory all too often lacks any sense, if one pays close attention. We only went once, you know, for balance, as one might say. I think it most unlikely they will wish to pay a second visit." She smiled. "I have advised them to listen to Mr. Churchill's wireless broadcasts if they wish to hear oratory at its best . . . for I think," she said with every appearance of sincerity, "that history will mark him down as perhaps this country's greatest-ever prime minister, don't you?"

While the invisible watchers noted that nothing in Miss Seeton's words, tone, or demeanour hinted that she might hope history, as written by Adolf Hitler, would never be given the chance to acknowledge the greatness of Prime Minister Churchill, Major Haynes seized thankfully upon the conversational lead. "Like Pitt?" he asked.

The watchers pricked up their ears.

"Or Palmerston, or Gladstone . . . Or Walpole?"

And once again the major held his breath as he waited for her reply.

Chapter 8

"Walpole," echoed Miss Seeton, as a fleeting pucker appeared once more between her brows before turning into a smile that Major Haynes, who could see it most clearly, thought looked slightly sheepish. The hidden watchers, watching from a less favourable angle, saw it as evidence of guilt . . . or of over-confidence, perhaps, as she tried to spin him another of her remarkable yarns.

If it was anything, it was guilt.

Or embarrassment, at least.

"It's so—so silly," confessed Miss Seeton, with a blush and a second smile inviting Major Haynes to share her wry amusement at her silliness. "One had to learn them all at school by heart, of course, like tables, and weights and measures, and kings and queens. The majority are easy, for naturally Pitt the Younger comes after Pitt the Elder, and there was only one Gladstone—but for some reason I can never remember which is Hugh and which Horace, especially when there was Robert, who really *was*." She frowned again. "Prime minister, I mean," she went on in a slightly less confident tone. "When the other two were both writers—and in different centuries, which ought to make it easier, but for some reason does not . . ."

"Now you come to mention it," said Major Haynes, "I'm not so sure myself. Strawberries come into it somewhere, I think—" He brought himself up sharply. What on earth had the girl done to him, making him babble nonsense almost as convoluted as her own?

"Strawberry Hill Gothic," supplied Miss Seeton happily. "Yes, indeed—which means that *that* was Horace, not Hugh—the same short 'o,' you see, as in Gothic, which should make it easy to—oh, dear."

"The same as in Robert," said Major Haynes, who had been coincidentally struck by the same realisation that Miss Seeton's little mnemonic was not as foolproof as she had hoped. "But never mind that now. What," he went on cautiously, "is the connection with diamonds?"

"I rather think that was his grandfather," Miss Seeton told him with only slight hesitation. History was not, after all, her subject, and her school days were some years behind her. While she would, whenever possible, look things up, she now had so many calls on her time that it was often far from possible.

"Pitt the Elder, that is—or perhaps his father," she amended. "I recall that he bought it from an unscrupulous person who had no legal right to sell it, and sold it in turn to the royal house of France." She stifled a sigh for the current fate of that newly conquered country. "Napoleon." she continued, her thoughts turning automatically to an earlier conqueror, "had it embedded in his sword hilt—which is why he bore the soubriquet of Diamond Pitt—the elder's grandfather, I mean, because he was a nabob, not a politician. If he was not his father, that is," she ended with a hint of breathlessness.

"I see," said Major Haynes, who (to his increasing surprise) did. He wasted no time in referring back to the sketchbook and Miss Seeton's hasty doodle of the British prime ministers—it now made perfect sense to him. He was beginning to understand the way—the undoubtedly unorthodox way—her mind worked . . .

But there remained one more sketch to be explained away, the most frightening of them all. What she seemed to have known-without-knowing in that undoubtedly unorthodox way of hers was another secret belonging to Britain's most secret history, a history that had perforce repeated itself—that had been perhaps an even more desperate secret the second time around than the first . . .

The first time, it had been during the Great War—the so-called War to End Wars, that war whose hope of everlasting peace had been betrayed within twenty years of its ending by the eruption of another war. A war that could well be even more great, more terrible, before it was won.

Or lost.

He would not think of that. He would, rather, try to find out from Miss Seeton just what she had known about the time history had repeated itself, only a few weeks ago.

Operation Fish, it had been called this second time around. It had worked once before: it had at all costs to work again . . .

The collapse of Europe, crushed beneath the Nazi jackboot, and the sudden, final fall of France, had left Britain and her Empire standing alone against the foe. Invasion of the defiant little nation so close to the mainland—at its narrowest point the Channel was only twenty-two miles wide—looked easy, temptingly easy, to the eyes of the triumphant, land-hungry Germans. In those first dark days—days whose darkness even yet continued—Winston Leonard Spencer Churchill had become the voice of freedom. His bulldog roar, reverberating in broadcasts around the world, had dared the enemy to do his worst . . .

A worst that in secret—most secret—conclave even Churchill had to fear might come about at any moment . . .

Invasion.

Invasion, successful invasion, would mean that Britain—that proudly royal throne of kings, that scepter'd isle, that precious stone set in the silver sea—had found the silver sea no longer "a moat defensive" and had been, for the first time in almost a thousand years, defeated.

And, as Churchill feared, the chances were high that the moat would be crossed and the British Isles would indeed be defeated—yet geography was unimportant, for the British spirit would never admit defeat. The fight would continue overseas. The war would be fought from Canada, where money for the fight already waited in the vaults of certain banks in Ottawa and Montreal—two and a half billion dollars' worth of gold as ingots and coin; five billion dollars' worth of shares and securities, stocks and bonds, tied in bundles by Canadian clerks who, sworn to secrecy, had used more than seventy miles of tape to keep the priceless papers in order.

Operation Fish. The gold, transported across the U-boat-infested Atlantic by the fastest of His Majesty's warships, was reckoned to be worth more than all that Cortés had from Mexico—than Pizarro had from Peru—than had been mined in the rushes of the Klondike and California, Australia and New Zealand together . . .

Operation Fish. Securities and gold, whose first highspeed transport, the cruiser HMS *Emerald*, had sailed from beleaguered Britain on the 24th of June . . .

Miss Seeton's sketch was dated June the nineteenth.

Major Haynes turned the book around so that his visitor could take a closer look at her handiwork.

"This is an unusual composition, Miss Seeton," he said, as he had said before. "Almost surreal, one might say."

Miss Seeton smiled. "The zoo," she said again. "It was such a very hot day . . ."

The sketch seemed at first sight to depict a sturdy cage in which a prowling lion, shaggy of mane and fierce of eye, lashed its tail and bared its pointed teeth at the world. (The British lion, defiant to the last, mused Major Haynes.) Closer inspection showed that the bars of the cage were bent inwards, as if by the application of some huge external force. *(The enemy outside, trying to attack the embattled lion? So great was the weight of gold in the* Emerald's *magazines that her angle irons had buckled under the strain.)* Beneath the lion's raised—protective?—paw stood a glass bowl—but it was not a bowl of drinking water. Through the curved sides could be seen a fish—a fish that, despite the lenslike distortion afforded by the curve, was unmistakably a goldfish, swimming with gaping mouth . . .

"It was such a very hot day," Miss Seeton reminisced. "The children were thirsty and so good, on the whole, about not spilling their orange squash, but one felt so sorry for the poor creatures that remained in town, although of course most of the larger beasts had been evacuated to other zoos—and lions, coming from Africa, have less cause to dislike the heat than other animals, as long as they have enough water to drink. Which made me think of the aquarium, you know, and how it had been drained in case it was hit by a bomb and flooded everywhere . . ."

The authorities, on the outbreak of war the previous September, had thought it advisable for London Zoo to dispose of the two hundred thousand gallons of water that might otherwise do untold damage to Regent's Park and surrounding areas if suddenly released. Some fish were rehomed in other zoos; the rest were, like the prized collection of poisonous spiders and snakes, humanely killed, to be either eaten or preserved in bottles and jars for future reference. Many animals, such as pandas and elephants, were sent to Whipsnade Zoo in Bedfordshire; the lions and tigers remained in London, although marksmen with rifles were always on hand in case a dropped bomb should release the carnivores from their enclosures to add to the public's danger.

"Gold," murmured Major Haynes as Miss Seeton sighed for the folly of it all. "Fish," he added with barely a pause.

She looked at him and smiled. "It was the girl in the kiosk," she said again, "who sold the children their drinks. She reminded me so much of little Miss Brown at college—not a great, though undoubtedly a gifted, artist . . ." Miss Seeton, who saw little merit in her own artistic gifts, stifled another sigh and hurried on:

"Miss Brown was an excellent mimic, you see, and one of her favourite turns was Sandy Powell—"

"Can you hear me, Mother?" cried Major Haynes before he could stop himself.

Miss Seeton chuckled at his imitation of the wireless comedian's catchphrase, and nodded. "Exactly so," she said. "And his poem about the goldfish in winter always used to make us laugh, for she recited it in such a very lugubrious way." Miss Seeton chuckled again at the memory of Sandy Powell's unfortunate goldfish "swimming round, and round, and round" with a "tail full of chilblains and chaps on his fins" and wondering what he could have to live for in his bowl, forever going round, and round, and round with no hope or prospect of ever going anywhere, or doing anything, else.

Haynes found himself laughing in sympathy. Even the hidden watchers had to suppress their mirth, and a snigger from the irrepressible Aylwin would have betrayed their presence had not the major's right foot kicked the side of his desk as he tilted his chair backwards.

With a thump Major Haynes returned four airborne feet—two of his own, and two belonging to the chair—briskly to the ground. He had made up his mind. He glanced at the clock on the office wall, and checked it against his watch.

"Miss Seeton," he said, "I wonder if you would care to have lunch with me?"

The goldfish-inspired smile in Miss Seeton's eyes turned into one of surprised delight. "It would be a pleasure," she replied without hesitation. "If, that is, you are sure you can spare the time." Now surprised delight turned to a mischievous twinkle. "Of course, as my dear father used to say, time spent on reconnaissance is never wasted. Is it?"

"Er—well—no," was the major's response. Once again the girl had wrong-footed him. "I mean . . ." He found that he wanted to loosen his collar, which felt suddenly tight. "I assure you, Miss Seeton, the pleasure will be all mine," he said firmly, and rose to his feet.

As Miss Seeton gathered her belongings together, her glance fell on the major's desk, and the three sketchbooks he had made no move to return to her.

From her tone it was hard to tell whether or not she was laughing at him. "You will let me know, won't you," she said gently, "when the sandbag information-sheet idea is—forgive me—somewhat more concrete than it appears to be just now?"

Major Haynes cheerfully groaned as expected and rendered silent thanks to the gods of military intelligence that she had given him so adroit an escape route. "Sandbags and concrete—Miss Seeton, that was awful. If you promise not to come out with any more puns like that, I might make it dinner as well as lunch."

Miss Seeton smiled as he took his umbrella—a sturdy black, crook-handled, neatly furled gamp with a well-polished ferrule—from the mahogany stand in the corner of the room. "Thank you," she said, "but perhaps it is a little short notice for an evening engagement, wouldn't you say? When there is my work at the canteen—although after your letter arrived I did tell them that I could not say when I should be able to return to duty . . ."

As he tucked the crook handle over his arm and prepared to open the door for his luncheon guest, Major Haynes paused to give her a slow, appraising look. Miss Seeton, who had been admiring the neatness of the bulky brolly's black silk furls, raised her eyes to meet that look with one quite as thoughtful before lowering her gaze with a smile and a blush that might have been modest . . . and might not.

Mopping his brow, Major Haynes opened the door. "After you, Miss Seeton," he said, and the pair left the room.

Chapter 9

Major Haynes returned, alone, from an extended luncheon to find his office full of impatient colleagues, their voices clamouring to know where he had been, what he'd been doing, and why it had taken him so long.

"Gentlemen—please, gentlemen!" He silenced the clamour with a swift flourish of his umbrella, which he hung with his usual care on its mahogany hook. "One at a time, please," he begged as he made for the chair behind his desk, which was being smartly vacated by young Aylwin, who had established squatter's rights only until its lawful owner should arrive, and had no wish to trespass further.

"Now, then," said Major Haynes, seating himself and directing a courteous nod towards Chandler, his nominal superior. "If you'll let me explain—"

"You'd better," said Chandler.

"If you can," muttered Cox.

"We thought you'd eloped," offered Aylwin with a grin.

"Never in a million years," said Steptoe as the misogynist Cox snorted at his side. "Though she's a pleasant enough young woman," he added.

"Indeed she is," said Major Haynes, taking advantage of the momentary lull before they all got their second wind. "And with more common sense than any of us had realised," he continued. "I tried her out with some of the best rumours going round at the moment, and she squashed the lot of them without a second's thought. We could do with a few like her in Duff Cooper's crowd—no, seriously," he went on as the startled jaw of Steptoe, who had used that Ministry of Information cover to make the initial contact with Miss Seeton, dropped. "It must be teaching that does it," went on the major as Steptoe retrieved his jaw and could only blink at him in silence.

"If," enlarged Haynes, "you spend your time having to cope with hundreds of somebody else's youngsters frolicking and larking about and trying it on every blessed minute of the day—*and* you manage to keep 'em under control, whether it's in the classroom or on a trip to the zoo, or Hyde Park, or Hampton Court . . ."

"We take the point," said Chandler as Haynes paused for effect. "Common sense, coupled with imagination—thinking up myriad ways of keeping the little dears interested so that they don't run out of control . . ."

"Exactly so," said Major Haynes.

"It's her imagination," Steptoe reminded them, "that's the whole trouble with Miss Seeton. Those sketches . . ."

"Exactly so," said Cox in triumph, looking sideways at the major he had mimicked so viciously. "If you ask me," he went on, though nobody had, "Haynes has fallen for the girl, and it's warped his judgement. Great heavens, the future of the whole country's in the balance, and here he is, seeing everything out of focus through rose-tinted spectacles!"

Major Haynes tried to restrain his wince at the awkwardly mixed metaphor—and at the unfair accusation—and homed in on the one part of that accusation that was of particular interest to him.

"Miss Seeton doesn't wear spectacles," he said. "But if," he added with emphasis, "you ask me"—and here he looked sideways at Cox—"she does have a—a remarkable, if not unique, way of seeing things."

"Seeing things," echoed Chandler grimly while the other men began to mutter, and Aylwin, who had perched himself on the corner of the major's desk, opened the topmost of the three sketchbooks still lying on the blotter.

"Seeing to the heart of things, if you prefer," amended Major Haynes.

"The *heart* of things," scoffed Cox, irritated by even so feeble a hint of romance.

"It wouldn't be easy to pull the wool over her eyes, is what I mean," said Major Haynes. "I . . . think," he found himself adding. Apart from the occasional shrewd remarks that made him feel uneasy, as they had during the interview in the Tower, it had been an enjoyable lunch. He'd been impressed by much of Miss Seeton's conversation, convoluted though some of it had been. But the overall impression had been of a young woman with, yes, common sense, as well as unshakable patriotism . . .

"Her imagination . . . doesn't work that way," he pressed on. "I asked her what she made of the idea that enemy parachutists were likely to use transparent parachutes and wear blue uniforms so that they'd be invisible against the sky until it was too late."

"And?" barked Cox as Chandler and the others were happy to wait for the rest of it.

"And she said the current run of fine weather was hardly the norm for an English July, and that not even the Germans, efficient though they are, could arrange for the sky to remain completely free of cloud for the length of time needed to invade." The major chuckled before appending Miss Seeton's remark that the only way round the problem would be to have a change of uniforms (sky blue and rain-cloud grey) and equipment (parachutes either transparent or cumulus white) in each invading plane, which would be costly in both time and money and would take up twice the space.

"And she said," he concluded, "that the Nazis seem to be so—so attached to their jackboots, the black was bound to stand out against whatever colour background they might have on the way down."

"Good thinking," said Chandler with approval. "And she could well be right, at that."

"Let's hope she is," said Steptoe.

"I asked her next," said the major, ignoring another snort from Cox, "what she thought of the idea that the Nazis were about to tow huge submersible tanks of compressed poison gas across the Channel to render the populace of the coastal regions helpless in the face of a seaborne force."

At this, Chandler had to arch his eyebrows. "Tactless," he observed.

"Catch her off balance," said Cox, prepared at last to regard the major with some approval.

Haynes shifted on his chair at the memory of how he had inadvertently reminded his lunch companion of the long-drawn-out sufferings that had ended in merciful death, but had deprived the young Emily of her father.

He saw no need to mention that at the gleam of sudden tears in her eyes, he had ventured to pat her hand—and that she had not withdrawn it at once. "She said," he said hurriedly, "that the Germans had no more control over the wind than they had over the rain, and given the way the Channel behaves, they were quite as likely to gas themselves as us, if we didn't finish the tanks off with bombs as soon as they came to the surface."

"She's right again," said Chandler. "Miracles of calm weather like Dunkirk happen once in a lifetime."

"And those nine days used up several lifetimes at one go," said Aylwin. "If you ask me," he added, looking from Cox, silently scowling, to the major, hiding a smile.

"Then," said Haynes, "I asked her opinion of the ban on church bells, and she said the trouble with only allowing them to be rung in the event of invasion was that there was no guarantee those with sufficient authority to allow the ringing would be able to find at short notice anyone able to ring them. She also pointed out that very few churches were likely to be connected to the telephone service, which would mean an inevitable delay while whoever took the message hopped on a bicycle and pedalled off, looking for someone who wasn't going to break his neck tugging on a damn great rope with a lump of metal clanging on the end of it."

"She never said that," protested Steptoe.

"Not in so many words," admitted Major Haynes, "but the sentiment was exactly as I've reported it—and, really, she has a point."

"The LDV are too busy patrolling to keep men on permanent ready alert on bikes," agreed Chandler. "You know, I'm starting to like the sound of your Miss Seeton, Haynes. Common sense, indeed. What else?"

"She thinks taking down the signposts and removing the milestones and so forth is fine in theory, though she said seeing the war memorials defaced was a shame, but it was a small sacrifice compared to the sacrifice made by those with their names on the memorials . . ."

Major Haynes coughed. "She said some might see this war as a betrayal of that sacrifice, but that bullies had to be stopped . . ."

"Consistent, at any rate," said Chandler, who, like the others, could recall eavesdropping on the first time Miss Seeton had voiced this opinion.

"And she thought," said the major, "that anyone taking the trouble to invade and who really had no idea where he was—which, in view of the proverbial German efficiency, she thinks improbable—would have enough sense to get into the nearest bank or post office and check the address headings printed on the forms and writing paper and so forth."

"An answer for everything," said Cox, sourly.

"You must have had a lively meal," said Aylwin. "I bet the ears of the people sitting near you were out on stalks. I bet the reports about fifth columnists and spies will come flooding in any minute now."

Major Haynes shook his head. "We lunched on board *Chrysanthemum*," he said, referring to one of the two divisional ships of the Royal Naval Volunteer Reserve moored in the Thames within easy reach of Tower personnel. HMS

Chrysanthemum, like her sister HMS *President*, had seen much in her long lifetime, and the ships' crews were famed for their discretion. "Oh, they argued a bit at first," conceded the major, "but I'd phoned Captain Grange on the way out of here, and he had them fix her a temporary pass, so in the end it was fine."

"You must have pleaded a highly convincing case," said Chandler. "I wondered why Grange sent a message that he saw no need to attend this meeting."

"Miss Seeton strikes again," said Aylwin brightly, looking up from the sketchbooks as Cox rolled his eyes and Steptoe shrugged.

"Miss Seeton," said Major Haynes, pressing on with his narrative, "doesn't think much of the suggestion that there should be wholesale drainage of certain easily recognisable reservoirs and basins in the immediate London area. While she concedes that not everyone has the artist's eye, she feels sure that enemy pilots will have been well trained in aerial reconnaissance, and that if they can't follow the course of the Thames, with its famously distinctive shape, they have no business flying at all."

"The idea of drainage," Cox reminded him, "was suggested to prevent the landing of enemy seaplanes on the aforesaid reservoirs and basins."

"Miss Seeton," returned the major promptly with a twinkle in his eye, "saw no sense at all in draining reservoirs when any seaplane pilot worth his salt—her little joke, I fancy—would have the whole surface of the Thames on which to land. She admits that her knowledge of such matters is nil, but she finds it difficult to conceive of any way in which London's main waterway could be closed to hostile aircraft without at the same time closing it to what I suppose should be called legitimate domestic traffic."

"That lot at PLA would have had something to say if we'd told them to start stringing booms and setting booby traps all over the show," agreed Chandler. He and his team had endured more than one security tussle with the doughty sea-dogs of the Port of London Authority, whose majestic grey building with its pillared portico loomed reproachfully in the distance at the Tower staff as they emerged from Mark Lane tube station on their way to work.

"I suppose," said Cox, "Miss Seeton had her own ideas about that fishing ban in Scotland, too."

Major Haynes cleared his throat. "I, er, did ask what she would think of a civic authority that refused to allow its anglers to fish on the reservoir banks in case they were disguised fifth columnists armed with poison, but she said she thought it unlikely anyone could carry sufficient poison on his or her person—except that she thought women would have more sense—to do more than effect the odd upset tummy among the more vulnerable of the populace such as the sick, or children, or the elderly."

The major grinned. "She was pretty annoyed at the very idea of poisoned drinking water and could see why Edinburgh imposed the ban, but she still thinks they were overreacting because—well, that's not the sort of thing the British would do, she said. Fair play, and so on. If wars *have* to be fought, she thinks it wrong to inflict them on the—the non-professional fighters at home."

He sobered. "She rather gave me the creeps, in the end. She said she was very much afraid that, given Hitler is a raving lunatic, only she put it more politely than that, we have no way of telling just how far he's going to turn on the non-professional fighters at home. She thinks"—and his voice was grave—"that Churchill wasn't exaggerating when he told us it was going to be blood, toil, tears, and sweat for all of us in this island. She thinks it's going to be the first civilian—the first people's—war in history . . ."

"I'd say she's right," said Chandler. "It's what we've been expecting ourselves, after all."

"*I'd* say," said Cox, "that if *that* sort of talk isn't spreading alarm and despondency, then I don't know what is. Great heavens, man, you should have arrested the girl, not—not filled her with lobsters and champagne and encouraged her to babble her ridiculous nonsense for everyone to hear!"

"In fact, it was grilled sole—" the major began, but Chandler interrupted him with an upraised hand.

"Haynes was only doing his job," he said, with a frown for the unrepentant Cox. "Miss Seeton was, prior to this morning, a—an unknown quantity. Now, thanks to Haynes, she isn't. Be fair to the girl. She was asked a direct question. Was she supposed to fudge her way through an answer? The very fact that she didn't—that she came right out with plain, straightforward replies, no matter how unpalatable some of them might have been, makes me as inclined to trust her now as I—well, as I admit that I wasn't so inclined before. A properly trained fifth columnist would have fudged. Miss Seeton's downright honesty is a definite point in her favour."

"Like her common sense," said Steptoe. "And her imagination, or lack of it—that blackout shutter of hers . . ."

"She saw through Collins without knowing how or why," said Major Haynes. "You, Steptoe, have confirmed that the man's as good as retired since she drew attention to him. If you ask me, Miss Seeton is one of the kind that knows things without knowing how—or why—or even, as in the case of those sketches, that there's anything to be known."

"You mean she's a sort of . . . psychic coincidence," said Chandler as Aylwin closed the sketchbooks through which, as the debate raged about him, he had been leafing.

Major Haynes shrugged. "I doubt if she'd care to be called psychic—she probably wouldn't think it respectable—but there's something there, some quality . . . And if we can harness it—well, why not? Even if nothing came of the experiment, what harm could she do with a few sketches or doodles or cartoons or whatever they are?"

Cox, who had been about to argue, changed his mind. "*If* the girl is psychic—and if she isn't a wrong 'un, there's no other rational explanation that I can see—then you're right, we ought to try turning it to our advantage. If we can," the pessimist added. "Don't forget, they say Hitler believes in astrology and witchcraft and hocus-pocus nonsense of that sort. You say Miss Seeton has her own queer hocus-pocus, and she's supposedly on our side—which would be fighting fire with fire, wouldn't it?"

Everyone considered this in silence for a while before Chandler nodded slowly.

"Fire," he said, "or . . . Spitfire?"

"Ah," said Major Haynes. "Yes . . . Miss Seeton would be the first to tell you her mechanical abilities are limited. Even using a hand-cranked sewing machine for anything fiddly is beyond her, from what she says, and she leaves that side of things to her mother, which sounds like a good idea. Mrs. Seeton has turned out dozens of chintz bags since hospitals started asking for them, while she—Miss S.—had me in stitches—sorry!—with the sad tale of how she tried to knit a pair of seaboot stockings in oiled wool . . ."

"That's why she works at the King's Cross canteen," said Steptoe, recalling PC Badgery's caution that he might be asked to hold skeins of wool for winding if Alice Seeton was alone at the house when he arrived.

"We wouldn't ask the wretched girl to work on the factory floor," said Chandler irritably. "For one thing, even if she'd be any use, which from what you say she won't, it would take too long to train her to build aeroplanes. The sabotage—if sabotage it is—has wasted quite enough time already. And, sabotage or bad luck or sheer bloody incompetence, we need action—and we need it now!"

Chapter 10

This time the letter was brought, not by PC Badgery, but by the postman. Two days after Miss Seeton's lunch aboard HMS *Chrysanthemum*, another brown envelope marked OHMS in the top left-hand corner clattered through the neat brass oblong in the Seetons' front door to land on the inside mat.

This envelope, like the first, was addressed to *Miss E. D. Seeton*, but in contrast to the previous missive, the illegible signature at the end was a name she now recognised: G. Haynes, Major. Fleetingly Miss E. D. Seeton wondered whether G might stand for Gordon or Gregory or . . . but there were more pressing matters to consider.

"They want me at the Tower again, Mother," she said to Alice, who smiled vaguely at her daughter before returning to her own correspondence, which was mostly bills and made her frown. Emily blushed.

Perhaps this was because she believed her mother's frown to have been inspired by the somewhat melodramatic way she had paraphrased the contents of the major's letter . . .

"Major Haynes suggests the day after tomorrow at half-past ten, if that's convenient," Emily went on in as prosaic a tone as she could achieve. "Dear me. I'll have to see if anyone will change her canteen shift with mine . . ."

Fifteen minutes' telephoning resolved the little difficulty, and Miss Seeton was able to set out with a clear conscience on that day's excursion, even if the next day's must be cancelled. Today, however, she would accompany a dozen or so children to Kew Gardens, there to learn something of the mysteries of plant life and how marmalade might be made from green walnuts, or paper from stinging-nettle leaves and artificial silk from their stems.

"And," she informed Major Haynes when he greeted her at the Tower entrance (no sending Chandler as an escort on this occasion) by asking what she'd been doing with herself since their last meeting, "there are experiments being carried out to ascertain whether potato eyes will work as well as seed potatoes, which, if that is the case, will save both fuel and space. Potatoes are so bulky, aren't they? The children were most interested by it all."

"I should think they were," said the major. "And you, Miss Seeton? Bored to death, of course. Putting up with it just for the sake of the brats, eh?"

Miss Seeton twinkled at him. "Enthusiasm is always to be encouraged," she reminded him. "In moderation, that is, and of course it is always a pleasure to watch an expert at work. The botanists were so very informative, and without ever once appearing to lecture, that I believe several of the children have made up their minds to find some form of horticultural or agricultural employment when they are able. Even I—who know almost nothing of gardening and have no need to do so, as it is one of my dear mother's greatest pleasures—was tempted to consider offering my services

89

to the publishers of biology textbooks. As an illustrator, that is."

"Ah," said Major Haynes. "Yes." Not for the first time he had cause to wonder about Miss Seeton's psychic—or in this case telepathic—powers. She'd as good as handed him on a plate his lead-in to the purpose of her visit.

"Stinging-nettle paper's quite a way in the future," he said grimly. "And if this war lasts only a couple of years, we'll be running short of the regular stuff—there will be smaller newspapers and far fewer books—"

"Of course," said Miss Seeton with a decided nod as he paused for breath. "The ration of paper pulp, if that is the correct term, will be saved for more important things. Such as public information leaflets."

His collar felt tight around his neck, and Major Haynes raised a hand to loosen the knot of his tie. "Public information leaflets," he echoed dully. "That wasn't quite what I meant to say, Miss Seeton. It was more in the nature of a—a friendly warning that there might not be so many textbooks published in the future."

"Meaning," prompted Miss Seeton, "that my—shall we say 'proposed career change' might perhaps be unwise at this particular juncture?"

"Oh, *damn* it!" burst from the major before he could stop himself. Miss Seeton arched her brows but said nothing. Was that another faint twinkle at the back of her eyes? Major Haynes couldn't be sure. He wished he had loosened his collar as well as his tie.

"Look, Miss Seeton," he said, leaning across his desk and meeting her gaze levelly. "You're an intelligent young woman and your father's daughter. You know what national security

90

means. You know the sort of sacrifice any one of us may be called upon—at any minute—to make in the interests of this country's safety. I wasn't being entirely . . . frivolous when I mentioned the likely shortage of paper pulp and your chances of getting a job illustrating textbooks." He drew a deep breath, and laid his hand upon the sketchbooks neither he nor his visitor had mentioned since the interview began.

"You've shown here that you're a—a more than adequate artist," he went on. Miss Seeton failed to hide her quiet amusement at this remark. The major felt hot. "I didn't," he emphasised, "mean that as a backhanded compliment, Miss Seeton—but you said yourself that you have talent, not—not genius." Not, he added silently as Miss Seeton nodded amiably, genius in the normal sense of the word, that is. "What I meant," he persisted, "was that—well, there are quite enough competent artists around who could supply botanical publishers with cross sections of a nettle stem, or whatever else was wanted."

"Sandbags," murmured Miss Seeton with a smile.

Major Haynes coughed. "There is," he went on with a wary look at the young woman who watched him with such quiet interest, "a certain . . . immediacy about your sketches that would do very well—very well indeed—for a series of public information leaflets—but, really, once you've done the initial sketches, the same comment must apply. Any competent artist could copy them—amend them—to suit the particular intention of the time."

Miss Seeton nodded. "I understand," she said helpfully as he loosened his tie a little more. "You wish me to produce sample sketches, as it were, for others better qualified to modify—to improve—to the required publication standard when my training, of course, was never in commercial art. I quite understand," she said again, as he looked at her with an air of surprise and she herself was surprised (and, indeed, perhaps a little disappointed) that she had apparently been mistaken as to the friendly sympathy she had thought was growing between herself and the major. From his remarks it now seemed that he had supposed her to be one of those temperamental Artists with a capital "A" who resented any criticism, no matter how justified, of their work; and she was not.

Yes, disappointing . . .

Miss Seeton pulled herself together. This was no time for indulging in the temperament she had only just now been telling herself she did not possess. She might have been called to service by His Majesty's Government for the sake of her "more than adequate" artistic abilities, but she was a realist. The major's kind words had been a gentlemanly courtesy, not a compliment: her head would not swell as a result of his remark. Nevertheless, in Miss Seeton's view the Ministry of Information, in choosing her, had made a wise choice. She was not vain about this: she knew her limitations. Ministry leaflets were distributed to every household in the country. Their message must be clear, not confusing; must be both informative and precise. Hers might be the original creative inspiration—if this was not an immodest way of putting it—but when it came to the imparting of accurate facts, there must be no possibility of error.

And yet . . .

And yet she was uncomfortably aware that sometimes—it didn't happen very often, but she was no longer disconcerted when it did—sometimes her sketches—and especially those drawn (or altered) from memory—her sketches did not always accurately differentiate between what was really there and what was . . . well, not. Between what she thought she saw, or had seen, and what she . . . well, hadn't. Or didn't. Which would be hard to explain to the major when . . . well, he hadn't seemed to understand that she really didn't mind being told her work wasn't exactly what was wanted, even if there was no question of her being so foolish to object to as many changes as the experts might think necessary. There was a war on, after all . . .

"I quite understand," she said again, firmly, banishing all temperament to oblivion. "And naturally I will be only too happy to provide the basic ideas"—which sounded far less immodest than *inspiration*—"once you have given me some idea of . . . well, of what it is you really need. After the sandbags, that is."

The sandbags were becoming their private joke. Major Haynes met her twinkling smile with a broad grin. He sat back in his chair with a sigh.

"I'll be frank with you, Miss Seeton," he said, trusting that she had insufficient experience of the MI mind to know that when an intelligence officer proposes to be frank, he intends to be less than fully honest. Major Haynes would be as honest as the situation allowed.

"You're a teacher," he said, "and used to youngsters—to keeping order, and so on. How do you feel about youngsters who are barely out of school?"

"Children mature at different rates," said Miss Seeton, having considered the question for a moment or two. "Many are ready to leave school at fourteen, or even twelve, while others seem sadly incapable of leading an independent life as late as twenty-one." She sighed. "And of course some, even more sadly, are forced by—by biological necessity to become adult far too soon. There was, of course, nothing of the sort with any of our school pupils, but once they were evacuated and had met some of the sturdy, one might even say lusty, young country girls, it came as something of a shock for them to have the theory shown so blatantly in practice."

"Er—ahem," said Major Haynes, shifting on his chair and hoping he wasn't blushing. Discussing unmarried motherhood among the infant peasantry was not the way he'd planned to lead into the subject . . .

Or had Miss Seeton, yet again, helped him out without realising the fact?

"Suppose," he began, "we were to ask you to become a—a kind of lady almoner, a workers' welfare officer, for the young women and girls working in one of our aircraft factories." *Whatever you do*, Chandler had warned, *don't tell her it's Most Secret experimental work. What she doesn't know won't hurt her—or anyone else, if our "experiment" goes wonky and she turns out to be a wrong 'un after all . . .*

"We've been having a spot of bother at this particular factory over the past few weeks," went on the major. *Not a word about possible sabotage, Haynes. Nothing about the engine coolant leaks that for some reason always seem to spray the ignition wires—nothing about how every petrol leak seems to be in just the right place to splash the windscreen. Nothing about the ailerons out of kilter, never mind how very odd it is they fit the wrong number of balance weights as often as they do. And if they* really *have to walk across the wings, contrary to common sense and every order you can think of, why is it always between ribs five and eight, so the wheels won't lock in the "up" position?*

*Nothing dangerous, exactly—any fool can recognise dissolving
wires or perspex or ailerons out of adjustment or wheels that
won't quite lock—but it's the damnable delay. Spitfires are being shot down faster than we can build them, and there are
far too many that can't go straight into service when we have
built them. And nothing about the equipment breakdowns. Of
course, we're driving it all harder and faster than the manufac-
turers ever dreamed, but. . . No, nothing about any of that. Fob
the girl off with any damned excuse you like. Just get her there,
and find out if this crazy idea of yours that she'll see right to the
heart of the problem is worth the strain on everyone's nerves.*

And on your head be it if it isn't . . .

"A spot of bother," echoed Miss Seeton with a nod and
a faint smile. Evidently her casual remark about the early
maturity of country girls had disconcerted the poor major.
One must suppose a military man to be acquainted with the
facts of life, but—accustomed to plain speaking among her
colleagues as she was—she had forgotten that her spinster
status might render such topics somewhat embarrassing in
mixed company, whether the major was a father of ten or . . .
a confirmed bachelor.

At this final thought Miss Seeton knew herself to blush.
She hoped Major Haynes would interpret this as a display of
fellow feeling for his gentlemanly embarrassment.

She suspected that perhaps he might not.

The blush grew more intense. "A spot of bother," said Miss
Seeton once more, and firmly. "For which a welfare officer
is needed—one who has some knowledge of girls and young
women." She nodded at him and managed a smile. "You haven't, I hope, forgotten that I have not been blessed by nature
with a mechanical mind?"

"I haven't forgotten," said the major with a grin. "We won't ask you to *make* the things, just to keep an eye on the ones who make 'em—on what's happening there."

"But surely," ventured Miss Seeton, "there must already be someone at the factory who—"

"An outsider's eye," the major hurried on, for once forgetting his manners. Miss Seeton subsided. "It's because," persisted Haynes, "you'll be an outsider—because you won't understand most of what's going on on the factory floor— that you might well notice things that—don't quite fit the usual pattern, Miss Seeton. You have the artist's eye, and you'll bring a different perspective to things—if I have the terminology correct."

Miss Seeton intimated that (depending on what exactly he was trying to say) she believed he had.

Major Haynes grinned. "Good. So that's settled. You can keep your eyes open on our behalf, and report back when— if—you notice anything that isn't quite right. Anything nobody else seems to have noticed—I'm not explaining this terribly well, am I?"

Miss Seeton murmured that she was only too happy to go where she was sent and to do what she was asked. Even so indifferent an artist as herself could play her part, given her experience of schoolgirls, always provided that she was asked to act only within her capabilities of—of a supervisory nature, rather than—as it were—tutorial . . .

"Exactly," said Major Haynes as she hesitated and once more subsided. "You're a teacher, specialising in art: so we'll call you a Civilian War Artist. We won't ask you to wear a uniform . . ." ("That spooky young wench in the armed forces? Great God forbid!" had been the reaction of Captain Grange and the others when the question of Miss Seeton's official status was being discussed.) ". . . and we'll pay you as such, but we hope you won't object to combining two roles in one. You'll be there as nominal assistant to the welfare officer, but with a brief to sketch on our behalf what you think might be of interest to us, in such spare time as they allow you."

He did not add that at this stage the factory was working round the clock, and Miss Seeton's spare time was likely to be limited. He was banking on the way she seemed to know without knowing the important from the trivial, and to show this in her sketches; he was hoping that whatever was going so badly wrong would somehow draw—draw!—itself to her attention above the desperate work of aeroplane assembly.

"Civilian war artist." Miss Seeton tested the term once or twice and nodded. He wanted her, of course, to sketch enough of—of whatever happened in an aircraft factory to be adapted for use in Ministry of Information leaflets. It was surely not—she felt a blush rise in her modest cheek—surely not immodest to say that she, Emily Dorothea Seeton, was in truth a wise choice for such a task. Someone like herself, lacking all mechanical knowledge—one had, over the years, viewed several documentary "shorts" at the cinema before the main feature film, but these, while interesting, were necessarily of general rather than *specific* interest . . . someone like herself would have no idea of what she was sketching, and would therefore be incapable of endangering the security of the nation. Anything she might draw that was of vital importance would be recognised and—before it could cause any harm, no matter how unwitting—be speedily removed by the authorities to whom her sketches would be sent, while an artist with expert knowledge of what she saw would not be able to help letting something slip—and in more detail than a nonknowledgeable artist could achieve—no matter how much care was taken to control the conscious mind. The subconscious, as Miss Seeton knew all too well, would always find a way, which could only result in wasted time for everyone concerned. And time, in war, was one of the most precious commodities in the world.

"If you need me," said Miss Seeton, "I believe I could be ready by the end of the week. There are the children, you see, and the canteen. It would be unfair to abandon them at short notice without having at least tried to make alternative arrangements . . . and then, there is my mother." Her eyes as she looked at the major were now sad. "There are no aircraft factories in Hampstead, or within easy reach of home," she said. "Which is one of the sacrifices we have agreed must be made, is it not? For me to leave my mother on her own . . ."

"I'm afraid so," said Major Haynes. Without thinking, he reached across the desk to pat her hand, and without thinking, Miss Seeton smiled at him before gently withdrawing it.

"My mother," she said firmly, "will understand. It is no more than my dear father would have expected of us both, I'm sure." She blinked away another tear and sighed.

"I'm sure, too," said the major sympathetically. "From what I've read of him, he was a true-blue patriot—and that reminds me, Miss Seeton." From beneath her three as-yet-unclaimed sketchbooks on the blotter he pulled a sheet of printed paper, headed by an embossed miniature lion and unicorn supporting the mantled shield and imperial crown of the royal coat of arms. Underneath this achievement was the motto *Dieu et Mon Droit*—God and my right—and surmounting the whole were the letters "OHMS."

"We've agreed we'll appoint you a civilian war artist," said Major Haynes. "It sounds good, will satisfy the most curious gossips, and covers a multitude of possibilities. You could be sent anywhere in the country, you could be asked to work at almost anything—but whatever you do, the main thing will be for you to keep your eyes open and sketch what you see and let us have the sketches when we ask for them. Understood?"

"Yes," said Miss Seeton, who thought she did, and was grateful for the major's implied assurance that she would not be required to travel abroad in these uncertain times. Her heart, she suspected, could never be fully engaged in her appointed task if she was overanxious about her mother, alone in London and concerned, as she was bound to be, for her daughter's welfare. Realistically Miss Seeton knew that sacrifice in war was always necessary, and she was happy to play her part . . . if, that was, no one else could be found to play it better—which she felt sure, in most instances, would be the case, although of course if it was her duty . . .

"Parachute drops," she murmured, hoping it would never come to that—which (should she remain in England) seemed unlikely—although in time of war, of course, one never really knew . . .

"Ahem—we'll send you by train," said Major Haynes, suppressing, despite the gravity of the moment, a hurried laugh. "We'll issue travel permits and so on—but before we arrange all that, you, Miss Seeton, have to sign this." He brandished the OHMS paper embossed with the Royal Arms. "After," he added, "reading it through carefully, making sure that you understand it."

He passed the paper across the desk, and Miss Seeton received it with due ceremony. Her quick eye had caught the heading printed under the Royal Arms: *The Official Secrets Acts 1911-39.*

She settled herself to read.

DECLARATION.

My attention has been drawn to the provisions of the Official Secrets Act which are printed overleaf . . .

Miss Seeton turned the document over and studied it with extreme care.

I am aware that serious consequences, including prosecution, may follow any breach of these provisions by me.

I understand that, amongst other things, I must not:

(a) communicate in any form to another person information about the work carried out (directly or otherwise) for the Government, by my employer—

"That's us," said Major Haynes, who had been watching her closely. "Section G." He saw no need to add that the government department of which "G" was but one section was military intelligence.

"Section G," echoed Miss Seeton. Graham? Geoffrey? She pulled herself together, and read on.

—nor discuss this work with any other person;

(b) retain or remove drawings, notebooks or other documents or things relating to this work;

(c) photograph or otherwise make copies of or extracts from drawings, notebooks or other documents or things relating to this work;

unless in respect of any of these matters I am expressly au-
thorised, requested or required by [name of Senior Company
Official]—

"That's me," said Major Haynes helpfully.
Miss Seeton glanced at him, and smiled.

—to do so for the purpose of my work.
I also understand that the Official Secrets Acts apply to me
both during and after the completion of the work in question,
and that these provisions apply not only during the period of
my appointment but also after my appointment has ceased.
I also understand that I must surrender any documents, etc.
referred to in Section 2 (1) of the Act if I am transferred from
one post to another—

"We'll supply you with as many sketchbooks as you need,"
translated Major Haynes, "but you won't be able to let the
children have them to draw on the back of the sheets."

—save such as have been issued to me for my personal retention.

"We'd rather you didn't keep any souvenirs," said Haynes
apologetically. "No scrap paper, no rough notes."

I confirm that my attention has been drawn to the continuing
effect of the provision of the Official Secrets Acts and to the
Declaration made overleaf by me.

Miss Seeton, after noting the space for her signature,
turned back.

. . . and I am fully aware of the serious consequences which may follow any breach of these provisions.

Signed.

Date.

Witness.

"You sign," said Haynes, "and I'll witness. And once we've done that, Miss Seeton, you're in. You're mine." He coughed. "That is to say, you're ours—for the duration . . . however long that might be."

He leaned forward and gazed at her. "However long that might be," he repeated slowly. "Winston has hopes that the British Empire and its Commonwealth will last for a thousand years. Well, as things stand right now, we have no way of knowing if they'll last a thousand minutes, Miss Seeton— but however long they last, you, like me, will remain bound by the Official Secrets Act. If you decide in thirty years' time to write your autobiography, you won't be able to write a word about what you did in the war."

"I shouldn't wish to," said Miss Seeton with resolution. "The very idea that I should make a display of myself, when there is no good reason to do so—I lead such a quiet life, you see, and cannot imagine why anyone should be the least interested in my affairs . . ."

"That's the spirit," said Major Haynes with approval. He opened the top drawer of his desk and drew out a slim, gold-plated fountain pen, unscrewing the top to reveal an elegant nib.

"You first," he said, and Miss Seeton duly signed.

Chapter 11

The Rattling Rhythm of the wheels of the train—*diddly-dum, diddly-dah, diddly-dum, diddly-dah*—would have soothed anyone to sleep, even if the July night had not been so hot and the carriages so stuffy. Behind the heavy blackout blinds, each window of every carriage had been methodically suffocated against attack from the air by fine-meshed wire net; these essential air-raid precautions had made it so great an effort to move the glass even an inch up or down that nobody had done so—with the inevitable result that, to those inside, *ventilation* was nothing more than a word to be serendipitously encountered near the end of the dictionary.

Miss Seeton felt her eyelids droop, despite all her attempts to keep awake. Lack of fresh air, no doubt. And she did not dare leave her seat to find the guard and ask him to tell her when they reached her destination. For one thing, she could not easily move from that seat without disturbing a large number of people; for another, it would be unwise to do so even if she could. In peacetime (she reflected sadly) there would have been no cause to worry that, on her return, the seat would have been taken: but this train, like all trains now, was so crowded that its very corridors were full of people balanced on suitcases or slumped, trying to sleep, in corners on the floor, while in nearly every side compartment five backsides had been squeezed by their determined owners into the space designated officially for four. Not for the first time in her life Miss Seeton found herself thankful that she had inherited her mother's dainty frame rather than her father's splendid physique.

Diddly-dum, diddly-dah, diddly-dum, diddly-dah . . . Miss Seeton's eyes closed. *Diddly-dum, diddly-dah, did-did-did-dah-di-dah-di-dum-dum-dum* . . .

Miss Seeton's eyes flew open. In the sickly light from the solitary blue bulb, she blinked round at her fellow passengers, all shaking and stretching themselves as the train clattered and clanked and rolled and swayed its way onward over the points.

The points! Two tracks merging or separating—that was all it was, and not the rattle of hostile machine-gun fire, or the thunder of shrapnel from antiaircraft guns blazing at the enemy as he swooped overhead—nothing more sinister than the points.

Nothing . . . yet.

But one had heard such dreadful tales from Europe, and with invasion still expected any moment . . .

Miss Seeton shivered. The elderly gentleman sitting next to her smiled vaguely, patted her hand, and nodded back to sleep again without a word.

The others in that cramped, airless compartment shifted awkwardly on the horsehair-prickled seats and tried not to meet one another's gaze in case they saw their own fears mirrored or—far worse—magnified there. Miss Seeton, reminding herself that a soldier's daughter should display no fear, lowered her eyes. Faces that in daytime, at the start of the journey, had looked normal and healthy, now looked grotesque and unnatural, almost unearthly, in the pale blue light, as one might imagine a band of troglodytes in their underground fastness, clammy and cold and like to shrivel into horrified dust should the sun's rays even touch their livid skin.

Or a railway carriage full of corpses . . .

Miss Seeton's lids no longer drooped. At the thought of what she might see should she fall asleep again, she had come wide-awake. She stared at her hands, clasped on her lap; she stared beyond her hands to her knees, veiled from sight by decorous tweed. She stretched her legs in their discreet lisle stockings—perhaps, in such hot weather, a mistake, but so hard-wearing compared with silk when, war or no war, she could not quite bring herself to go bare-legged—and saw two small feet laced in well-polished leather swing into view. She sighed as she wondered how long it would be before shoe polish became a luxury of the peacetime past. Her mother had pored over the pages of *Enquire Within Upon Everything* (which invaluable vade mecum had been a wedding present) and warned that they must set aside a small stock of ivory black, treacle, olive oil, vitriol, vinegar, glue, soft soap, and isinglass against that evil day. "But of course, Emily dear, no more than our fair share," Alice had added as her daughter dutifully noted down the ingredients for Paste Blacking and French Polish for Boots and Shoes. "We wouldn't wish to take advantage once such things were rationed, would we?"

Miss Seeton sighed again as she swung her feet back to the floor. Pale blue light on gleaming brown leather had produced a strange illusion of pearls under moonlit water—poisoned pearls that had killed the people whose dead eyes she would meet if she glanced around the carriage . . .

She was tired—that was all. She must banish these grim visions by pondering some problem that would turn her thoughts—would make her concentrate—in a less uncomfortable direction.

Uncomfortable made her consider her journey. The pale blue light and the blackout blinds were, she felt, rather pointless. Not that she knew anything about the railways, but one couldn't help noticing the signals, and especially the signal *lights*. Red and yellow lights that could surely be seen as well by overhead enemies as by engine drivers on the ground. Did not rays of light travel in straight lines in all directions? Which must mean upwards as well as horizontally. And surely an enemy who wanted an English train to attack had only to see the flicker of a railway signal from the air and then to . . . home in on it? If that was the phrase. Sparks from the funnel—steam, billowing out behind, glowing silvery white in the blacked-out darkness under the treacherous stars . . .

Miss Seeton sighed. These thoughts, like her previous idle musings, were far from comfortable. She frowned at her clasped hands. She would—she *must*—think of happier matters—of her mother's pleasure that her daughter had found, or rather had been given, war work that made good and proper use of her abilities and experience. Young women en masse could not, Miss Seeton supposed, be so very different from schoolgirls. And of course her information leaflet sketches were such a tactful justification for her presence at the aircraft factory. She had no wish to cause distress to the current workers' welfare officer, who might reasonably feel it insulting on the part of outsiders to impose on her an assistant for whom she had not asked.

Except that she felt sure, even from their few meetings, that Major Haynes would never insult a lady.

Major Haynes . . .

"Now, remember," he had said as he issued his final instructions. "You're to keep your eyes open for anything out of the ordinary and sketch it when you see it, and let us know when you've done so. Phone this number"—he handed her a slip of paper—"and, er, someone will be in touch." There was a note in the major's voice that made Miss Seeton suspect she would easily recognise that someone when he presented himself.

"But if," he went on, "there's anything in the nature of an emergency—we know we can trust your common sense and initiative to judge what's important and what isn't—you're to phone *this* number"—he handed her a second slip—"and give the password." His eyes twinkled in response to her own quizzical smile. "Yes, it sounds on the melodramatic side," he said cheerfully, "but in wartime you can't be too careful about the smallest detail. Think of it as along the lines of taking care of the pennies, and the pounds will take care of themselves."

Miss Seeton's smile approved the analogy, and the major smiled back at her.

"All you do," he said, "is ask the operator, 'What goes up a chimney down, but can't go down a chimney up?' and she'll put you through to me—wherever I am, whatever I'm doing, whatever time of day or night it is."

"What goes up a chimney down," echoed Miss Seeton with a pucker between her brows, "but can't go down a chimney up?"

"That's right." Major Haynes seemed amused by her failure to solve the riddle—but it was kindly amusement, and at his smile Miss Seeton smiled again. "Memorise both numbers," he went on without explaining, "and then, please, burn the pieces of paper—yes, I know, more melodrama. I would apologise, but I'm sure you understand."

"Of course I understand," said Emily Dorothea, daughter of the late Major Hugo Monk Seeton, VC.

And, of course, she had.

Miss Seeton blinked, then stretched herself. The elderly man lifted his head from her shoulder, where it must have rested for some time without her noticing. He was rubbing his neck and smiling apologetically at her. She smiled as apologetically back. Had she been asleep? Dreaming? Well, at least—if she had—they had been pleasant dreams . . .

The train began to slow. Others woke, stretched, checked their watches, and either closed their eyes again or looked about them, wondering what had happened to their luggage. Miss Seeton glanced upwards at the overhead rack to which her neighbour, despite his years a good foot taller than she, had kindly lifted her two small cases to rest beside the battered carpetbag he had thrown up into the net just as she appeared at the compartment door. He had not, then or later, told her where he was going: Careless Talk Costs Lives, as government posters and leaflets reminded everyone all the time. Now he had stopped rubbing his stiff neck and settled back to sleep. He was not, it seemed, about to help her lift her cases down if the station into which the train was slowing proved to be the one she wanted.

Miss Seeton stifled a sigh for the easy days of peace. How much they had taken for granted! Now, for fear of helping the invader, no railway station could by emergency law—by Order in Council—reveal its identity to the puzzled traveller except in letters no more than three inches high; and only then if the station was more than a certain number of miles from the coast. As no lights were permitted to shine where enemy eyes might see them, the letters, for all the good they did in the dark, could have been three feet high, or thirty: and they would have been just as much use as three inches. Or as little. Especially when one took into consideration the tiny diamond-shaped hole in the mesh through which they had to be viewed . . .

"Aardvark! Aardvark!" The station porter's informative roar was accompanied by the hiss of steam and the squeal of brakes as the train drew alongside the platform. "Aardvark! Change here for Broccoli, Starfish, and Plunge! Aardvark!"

Miss Seeton wondered if she was still dreaming, but as some of her fellow passengers grabbed gas masks, cases, and bags and prepared to leave the compartment, she decided she wasn't, and rose to her feet with an apologetic smile for her drowsy neighbour. The porter's accent was, certainly, strong: there was undoubtedly room for misunderstanding; but she recalled a remark of Major Haynes to the effect that the factory where she was to take up her new appointment had been erected, at great speed, in an extremely out-of-the-way spot for reasons of national security. *Extremely* out of the way, mused Miss Seeton, as in the distance the porter's bucolic roar continued to warn of the necessity of changing for Broccoli, Starfish, and Plunge—places of which she had never heard, and which she could not hope to interpret. But *Aardvark* sounded sufficiently like her intended destination for her to take the risk of alighting: she did not dare ask anyone where she really was. Careless talk, as the government posters warned, costs lives . . .

"Let me give you a hand," offered a burly, clean-shaven man of her own age whose pinstripe suit and solitary black, bulging bag gave him the air of a medical man. "You'll do yourself an injury if you're not careful," he added as Miss Seeton, with a smile and words of breathless gratitude, lowered herself from her tiptoe stance and stopped trying to reach her cases.

"Don't worry, the train always waits ten minutes while they take on water," the doctor reassured her. His bedside manner had its public application, too. "These yours? Well— fair exchange is no robbery. Hold this." He thrust his own, smaller bag into Miss Seeton's startled grasp, swung her cases down with minimal effort, and, still carrying them, headed for the door, avoiding as many feet and outstretched legs as he could, and nodding apologetically to the owners of those he couldn't.

Miss Seeton pattered gratefully in his wake, her shorter legs more nimble than the burly doctor's pin-striped limbs. She tripped only once, and recovered herself with barely a squeak when what in the pale blue light's uncertain shadow she had supposed part of the floor proved to be the skirt of someone's coat.

She must be tired. Her eye was usually quicker than her hand—or her feet. Miss Seeton smothered a yawn. It had been a long, long day . . .

"Going far?" asked the doctor genially as he assisted his companion down from the train, warning her that the step was rather high and in the uncertain twilight she should take extra care.

"I'm . . . not sure," said Miss Seeton, taking quite as much care herself not to cost lives with any idle talk. She must not let it be known, for instance, that there was a map in her handbag and—had the sky not been darkening even in the west, where the blurred silhouettes of trees marched across a ridge of black hills—she had been ready and more than willing to walk . . .

"Being met?" came the next question as the pair began heading for the exit.

Miss Seeton replied that she thought not. There had been that delay when they pulled into the siding to let the troop trains past, and even the most kindhearted landlady could not be expected, when there had been no possibility of a telephone call . . .

"Ah, a landlady." Miss Seeton's new friend held out his ticket as they reached the barrier. The collector shone a perfunctory torch on it with a cheery "Evening, Doctor"—or so Miss Seeton believed him to say—before studying the young woman's travel warrant with far greater care, holding it close to the gap in the torch's paper mask and squinting at the smudged ink, repeatedly peering, shaking his head, and muttering to himself what sounded to Miss Seeton grave suspicions of her bona fides.

The doctor had already made his diagnosis. "You must work at the factory," he told Miss Seeton, who saw no easy way of (and little point in) denying this. Only those on official business would travel with official documents, and as far as she knew, there was no official establishment other than the aircraft factory anywhere in the neighbourhood.

The ticket collector stopped his peering and muttering to favour Miss Seeton with a long, thoughtful stare.

"And lodging with Mother Beamish," the doctor went on, directing the remark more towards the suspicious one than at Miss Seeton, who barely had time to confirm the accuracy of his guesses before her self-appointed guardian went on:

"That's where several of the girls are billeted. Let me warn you, Tilly's a fair cook and won't cheat you on your rations, but she talks the hind leg off a paddock full of donkeys if you give her half a chance. Keep your diary locked in your case—and don't let the keys out of your sight, if you value your privacy."

The ticket collector abandoned his thoughtful staring to emit a lengthy chortle from which Miss Seeton, whose ear was growing accustomed to the local accent, disentangled the words *slander* and *libel* and *lucky for the doctor he wasn't no tattletale, Tilly Beamish being the sort of woman she was, ha-ha.*

"Get along with your nonsense, Janner, or I'll double my bill before I send it," returned the doctor. "Tilly Beamish is right on my way," he told Miss Seeton once Janner—his suspicions evidently lulled by the doctor's acceptance of the stranger—had (though grudgingly) waved her through the barrier and the two were standing on the station forecourt. "Tricky, these shadows," muttered the doctor. "Hang on a second while I dig out the flashlight . . ." Miss Seeton heard the click of an opened bag and sounds of rummaging. "Got it." There was another click, and a paper-muffled glimmer appeared on the ground at her companion's feet. "Now," he said, "you wait here with the luggage, and I'll fetch the car."

Miss Seeton waited, watching the muffled glimmer as it moved away to be swallowed by the gloom. Waiting was, of course, her most sensible course of action. In an unknown place, in deepening twilight—indeed, it was almost dark— with only a pocket torch to guide her and its battery on the wane (there had been a shortage of the essential number-eight size this past few weeks), one was all too likely to stumble. A broken arm or leg, even with a doctor on hand to deal with it—Miss Seeton smiled in the darkness—would *not* be a good start to her wartime work for Ministry Section G.

Gideon? Gareth?

Miss Seeton, yawning, wondered idly what the doctor's name might be . . .

The rumble of a motor vehicle, its yellow headlamps slitted like the eyes of some enormous beast of prey, drew near and woke Miss Seeton from her weary reverie. Above the rumble the doctor's voice spoke from the blacked-out gloom.

"Hop in," he invited, himself hopping out to throw Miss Seeton's cases in the car beside the bag he had carried away with him on his torchlit progress across the station yard. Miss Seeton, groping her way to the door handle by using the white blackout paint as a guideline, duly hopped, and had settled herself in the passenger seat before the doctor was back in the driver's.

"We ought to introduce ourselves," said the doctor, "if we're going to be neighbours, which we are, with you at the factory . . ." He cleared his throat. "And me," he went on, "the medical man who deals with their bumps and bruises as well as with every other ailment suffered by anyone in this benighted village. Er—my name's Huxter—and in case you were wondering, my parents did indeed have me christened Samuel, though I doubt if either of them ever read a word of Thackeray."

"I'm Emily Seeton," said Miss Seeton, who had. "I fear that *Pendennis* is not one of my favourite books, Dr. Huxter. Such a selfish young man, and so very foolishly indulged by his mother . . ."

She remembered Alice, alone at home in London, and fell silent.

"First time away, Miss Seeton?" Dr. Huxter's guess was not so very remarkable. "During the war, I mean," he added kindly. "Quite a different perspective from peacetime, eh?"

Miss Seeton agreed that it was, adding that even when attending college, she had lived at home. Then it dawned on her that revelation of her identity as an artist might come under the heading of Careless Talk, and she quickly changed the subject by asking how many other girls lodged with Mrs. Beamish and whether they all worked at the factory.

But then it dawned that the doctor's answers to these questions might also be information helpful to the enemy, and she begged him just as quickly not to tell her. She would (she explained) find out for herself very soon.

"Tricky, isn't it?" said Dr. Huxter as he leaned over the steering wheel gazing at what he could see of the way ahead. On either side of the road Miss Seeton could just make out the passing ghostly rings of white paint that hovered in mid-air around the poles of war-blinded streetlamps that would not be lit again until the present conflict was over.

Whether it was won . . .

Or lost.

"And what on earth," went on Dr. Huxter, "we can talk talk about that *couldn't* help an invader, were he of sufficiently devious mind, I've yet to resolve to my patriotic satisfaction." The way he uttered this phrase told Miss Seeton it was far from newly minted. "What's more," he said, as if it were a personal insult, "with our national standby, the weather, a taboo subject for the duration, how *are* we inhibited English to make polite small-talk with strangers? Except." he added before she could reply, "that I doubt if you and I will remain strangers for long, Miss Seeton. This isn't a big place. I don't know what you're going to do at the factory—and you'd better not tell me . . ."

There was a note of constraint in his voice as he hesitated, then went on with more confidence: "But whatever it is, we're bound to run across each other either there, or in the shops or the street or somewhere."

"I look forward to it," said Miss Seeton politely.

It was, after all, no more than courteous to respond to the conversational lead of someone who had so kindly given her a lift . . .

In the darkness, Emily Dorothea Seeton blushed.

Chapter 12

Dr. Huxter slowed his car towards where Miss Seeton supposed the kerb to be, misjudged the distance of the white painted marks, and cursed as the sound of scraping was followed by a thump and a faint hiss.

"That's another puncture, or I'm a Dutchman," he told Miss Seeton after making hurried apology for his language. "I'm always doing it. Whisper it low, but my night vision's not so hot, and of course in a job like mine I can't afford to stop driving." There was almost a laugh in his voice as he continued, "Our local garage must have made a fortune out of me since this blackout nonsense began—excuse me, that's always a bit stiff—" He leaned across in front of Miss Seeton as she fumbled with the door handle and clicked it open. "All gas and gaiters, they call it," he went on with another chuckle as he straightened. "Compressed air in the inner tubes and special patches on the tyres," he translated as Miss Seeton politely essayed a chuckle in response, but failed because she couldn't see what *Nicholas Nickleby*'s Gentleman in Small-clothes had to do with punctured tyres. "Mind you," the doctor added in a noncommittal voice, "I imagine they think of it more along the lines of making hay while the sun shines . . ."

Miss Seeton peered into the unknown dark. "Certainly there must be fewer accidents in sunlight," she murmured with some relief. So much, at least, of what the doctor said she could understand, although what concerned her most was not so much the conversational courtesies as general etiquette. A truly nice (in the original sense of the word) problem had presented itself with the scrape, the thump, the hiss, and the doctor's muttered oath. It had been a golden rule of her up-bringing that a gentlewoman never discussed politics, religion, or money . . .

Money. The conscience of Emily Dorothea, true daughter of Alice, would not let her forget that if Dr. Huxter hadn't so kindly given her a lift to the house of Mrs. Beamish, he wouldn't have run into the kerb and sustained the damage to his tyre—expensive damage, to judge by the force of what he said when it happened, although of course that might just be the doctor's way. Miss Seeton had no idea how much it would cost to repair a puncture—nobody would even dream of buying a new tyre or tube (or whatever might be needed) in wartime—but, no matter what it cost, she had a moral obligation to offer to share some part of that cost. A doctor, especially a village doctor with so many new and extra calls upon his services—the workers at the factory, the mothers and children evacuated to the country from the city—could not afford to remain long without his car.

But—and here Miss Seeton felt her maiden cheeks grow warm with embarrassment—was he likely to take offence at any suggestion that she might defray part of the costs of repair? Would he feel that her offer of recompense held the implication that she saw his original gentlemanly kindness as no more than a routine taxi service? He was, she must remember, a professional man . . .

Or was she worrying about nothing? There was, she must likewise remember—as must the doctor—a war on. Everyone—the newspapers, the wireless, people in shops and in the street—had repeatedly warned that things would be very, very different in the future.

"Dr. Huxter—" she ventured, but the doctor did not hear her brave beginning.

". . . because," he continued his explanation at exactly the same time, "after most private motorists laid up their cars last Easter for the duration, there's really only the key personnel like doctors and farmers and tradesmen left on the road." Miss Seeton blushed again at this reference to matters financial. "And if," he went on, "the U-boats do as well with their blockading as the rumours say they might, it won't be long before even the likes of us are off the road for good."

Miss Seeton felt a sudden stiffening of her spine. "If you will excuse me, Doctor," she said firmly, "there are some who might regard such words as—as defeatist. Which, with all due respect—"

She broke off, once more remembering his kindness and the inconvenience—and expense—it had cost him.

"Sorry, Miss Seeton." The doctor chuckled again. " 'We are not,' " he intoned in the words of the popular slogan, " 'interested in the possibilities of defeat.' Are we?"

"We are not," said Miss Seeton, stiffer than ever. She was her father's daughter as well as her mother's. "Even if—if the worst comes to the worst . . ."

"You can always take one with you?" She could not see his expression, but from his tone it seemed he was smiling as he quoted yet another of the slogans that were meant to inspire the nation to resist to the end—and beyond it. "With—ah—all due respect, Miss Seeton, if German troops invade, they are going to be large, muscular, highly trained, and extremely determined gentlemen. Don't let's delude ourselves. I think we should amend that phrase to 'You can *try to* take one with you'—wouldn't you agree?"

Miss Seeton's innate honesty acknowledged that she, for one, at five foot nothing in her bare toes and a mere seven stone fully clothed, would stand little chance of resisting—let alone despatching—a Nazi paratrooper. "But we certainly have to try," she said, still firm; and with this the doctor could not argue.

"Let me throw a little light on the subject for you," he offered as once more Miss Seeton began to swing herself out of the passenger seat into the blackout gloom. "That is—you can," he amended once she was safely on her feet. "You stay there, and I'll fetch your things." He hopped out of the car—for so large a young man he was surprisingly agile—and Miss Seeton could hear him rummaging on the back seat for her belongings. At least he was unlikely to confuse her two small cases with his one bulky Gladstone bag . . .

"You'd better go in front with the flashlight," he said as he materialised out of the darkness at her side, dropped her cases within half an inch of her toes, and ducked back inside the car to produce the same large torch that had guided him across the station forecourt. "I wouldn't want you signing on with a broken leg before you've signed Mother Beamish's register, now would I?"

Miss Seeton, who had taken a swift step backwards when the suitcases arrived, thanked him for his kindness, but begged him not to waste his battery on one whose eyes, adjusting (if a little slowly) to the dark, were—if he would forgive her—perhaps rather sharper than his, to judge by his earlier remarks about poor night vision.

"I'll have to watch what I say with you, Miss Seeton." Was that a note of amusement in his voice? Impossible, in a virtual stranger, to be sure. "Quick as a wink, you are," he went on after she had opened the gate and begun a careful advance up the Beamish front path. "If anyone tries the odd tall story on you, I bet you'd spot it straightaway. Not a schoolmarm, are you, by any chance?"

Miss Seeton admitted that she had, in the days of peace, been a teacher. In deference to her employment by Section G (Gervase?) as an information leaflet artist, she did not enlarge upon what subject she had taught.

"And now you've volunteered for factory work," said Dr. Huxter, his voice this time holding a clear note of admiration. "If my hands were free, I'd take my hat off to you, Miss Seeton. It'll be quite a shock to your system, I've no doubt-just as I've no doubt you'll cope wonderfully, once you've found your feet."

"Without breaking a leg," said Miss Seeton as the beam of the flashlight fell upon a low stone step, much worn in the centre by generations of rustic feet. Dr. Huxter chuckled at her neat capping of his previous warning, and set her cases down by the step before retrieving his torch, mounting to the door, and rapping briskly on the knocker.

"The Nine O'Clock News is long over, so Tilly will be at the back, in the kitchen," he told Miss Seeton when there was no immediate answer to his rapping. "Doing the dishes, or wondering what she can contrive with half a pound of offal and a few spuds from the garden—ah!"

Miss Seeton, too, had caught the noise of feet approaching the door along what sounded like an uncarpeted passage. There came a swish and the rattle of rings as the blackout curtain was drawn back, and then a suspicious query through the letter box.

"Who is it?"

"Your newest lodger, Mrs. Beamish," Dr. Huxter told the letter box. "Miss Seeton."

"Is that you, Doctor?" asked the letter box.

"It's an imposter," returned the doctor promptly. The letter box snorted and fell shut with a clunk. Once more there came a swish and rattle as the blackout was replaced, and then the door swung open.

"You and your nonsense," said the massive female form that now appeared on the threshold. "Take no notice of the doctor, Miss Seeton. A regular humorist, he thinks he is. You come on in—mind the step—them two bags all you've got?—right—and wait while I shut the door."

"I'll be off," said the doctor. "It's only a slow puncture, from the sound of it . . ." His chuckle suggested that he knew and understood the problem only too well. "And I ought to make it home without too much bother," he went on cheerily. "I leave you in Mrs. Beamish's capable hands, Miss Seeton. Good night—but we'll be meeting again before long, I've no doubt." He flicked the torch quickly upwards so that Miss Seeton could see him tip his hat, and then lowered the beam and headed off back down the path. When she heard the gate click shut behind him, Miss Seeton felt as if she had lost a friend.

"A shocking bad driver, he is," said Mrs. Beamish as, having observed the courtesies, she drew Miss Seeton inside and closed the door. "You'll have met at the station." she went on, pulling the blackout curtain so that her guest could step through into the light, "and being the gentleman he is he'll have brought you here with your heart in your mouth every inch of the way, or so I'd guess."

She gave Miss Seeton no time either to deny or to confirm the guess, but hurried on: "You've come from London, haven't you? And a fair old way you've travelled—all day long and half the night—and you'll want a bite to eat before you take to your bed. Talking of which, I'll show you where everything is, and you can let me have your ration book so's I know how much I'll have and for how many."

"How many—?" Miss Seeton managed to slip in as Tilly Beamish stopped talking to inhale, bending down and taking—above the protests of her guest—the two suitcases in her large, capable hands.

"Five altogether, with you, and most of them good girls—this way, and try to be quiet on account of them that are asleep—but young to be away from home," was the reply. Miss Seeton wondered about *most of them*, but said nothing as she followed her landlady up the narrow, uncarpeted stairs and did her best not to clatter.

"You," Mrs. Beamish told her as they reached the top, "oughtn't to have too much bother fitting in, being not so much older, but . . ." She lowered her voice, and Miss Seeton suspected that this was not entirely in deference to the sleepers. "But there's one calls herself an actress."

"Er—oh," said Miss Seeton as it became clear that an answer was expected. Was it the actress to whom Mrs. Beamish had objections, or the claim? Did she suspect her lodger of immorality or of falsehood? Not (Miss Seeton hastened to remind herself) that actresses were any less moral than anyone else. Or—well—

any *more*. They were people: good or bad like everyone else, some with talent, some without, and if the girl in question had been a poor actress, then—well—as Dr. Huxter had said, one took off one's hat to her for having volunteered for war work in a factory when she could have wangled (if that was the word) her way into one of the forces entertainment groups such as ENSA—Every Night Something Awful, as Tommy Trinder so amusingly had it—which would have been . . .

"A cushy number," murmured Miss Seeton, unsure of the slang but feeling it suited her requirements, as Mrs. Beamish threw open a bedroom door.

"Glad you're pleased," said Mrs. Beamish, preening herself. "But then, I look after all my girls, as anyone in the village will tell you, without fear or favour." The gentle emphasis on *all* was clearly the landlady's way of reminding this new arrival that not everyone in the house was, in her opinion, necessarily as respectable as her fellow lodgers.

In her opinion. Miss Seeton, who always tried to keep an open mind, decided that much of the landlady's suspicion arose from the country's lack of knowledge of the town. Not that she, Emily Dorothea Seeton, would call herself exactly cosmopolitan—the life of an English gentlewoman, whether in Hampstead or Herefordshire, was always quiet and uneventful—but one did, from time to time, attend theatres and the opera, and read about the "doings" of the stars in the newspapers and, occasionally captive under the hairdresser's dryer, the magazines . . .

"Stars," murmured Miss Seeton, stifling a yawn. It had indeed been a long, tiring day.

"Lovely clear night," agreed Mrs. Beamish, dropping the cases beside the bed and dusting her hands together. "For a change. So let's hope they don't take it into their heads to bomb us—I must show you where the shelter is in case they do—but even if they don't, there'll be no stargazing for you, Miss Seeton, until you've had a bite to eat. After which you'll be more than ready for bed, I've no doubt." She coughed. "The bathroom's back along the passage to your left, and the whatever's right next to it, with another in the garden if you're desperate, only it doesn't flush so well, being—excuse me—earth, see. I'll show you when I take you out to the shelter." She coughed again and then pointed sternly at the window.

"If you're still awake enough when all's done, you know not to open the blackout until you've switched the light off, don't you? I'm having no air-raid warden—or anyone else— knocking on my door in the middle of the night, and this always a decent house. Don't you ever forget, Miss Seeton, there's a war on."

Chapter 13

Miss Seeton was anxious not to oversleep on her first day at work. She had finished in the bathroom and was downstairs, fully dressed but yawning, before anyone in the house except Mrs. Beamish was properly awake.

"Did you sleep well, dear?" asked Tilly, once the morning salutations had been exchanged and she could return to her domestic duties. From above came the sound of shrill, muffled giggles and pattering feet as other sleepers began to bestir themselves. "Them bombers—and wasn't I right to say they'd come?—didn't disturb you, did they?"

"Er—yes, thank you. And no, they didn't," replied Miss Seeton, somewhat startled to learn that she had slept right through an air raid. The journey from home must have taken rather more out of her than she had realised.

"I'd have woken you if they looked like coming close," Tilly told her, "but they didn't—well, they never do. It was that factory again, and I shan't rest until them night shift girls are safely back—but we're tucked nicely out of the way here. Them devils haven't hit more than a couple of houses on the outskirts of the village since they started bombing—and even then there was nobody killed, which is a mercy."

"Oh," said Miss Seeton, and sat down. "Yes, of course." Tilly's calm disdain for the enemy set an admirable example she would do well to emulate. "Of course, it really is a most comfortable bed," she said in a voice she was pleased did not tremble. "And a very pleasant room."

Mrs. Beamish nodded amiably as she poured boiling water into a large brown teapot, and then started the egg timer. "That's right," she said with pride. "It was good enough for my Beamish to die in, that room, which until the billeting officer insisted, I wanted to keep in his memory, war or no war." With her gaze fastened on the tumbling grains of egg-timer sand she did not notice Miss Seeton's startled expression.

"Not that I'd dream of putting kiddies in there, and so I told her when the evacuees came—but oh, he made a *lovely* corpse," enthused the relict of the late Beamish. "Mind you—he'd had a cruel time of it, poor man: his chest, it was—but he laid out lovely, and the wreath was worth every penny I paid for it, as everyone said when they came to see him. Young Dr. Huxter's dad, he was still with us then, and of course he did what he could, but this is a terrible area for chests, being a valley, and the hills so high all around."

"I'm very sorry," said Miss Seeton, hoping this would be an acceptable response. Mrs. Beamish had not volunteered the date of her husband's demise, and it seemed impertinent to inquire, though she had to concede that the widow seemed remarkably . . . cheerful about her loss.

Cheerful she was. "Oh, well, it's an ill wind," philosophised Mrs. Beamish. "It wasn't yesterday he went—and of course it's why they built the factory here, on account of the fog. Comes up real sudden, it does. Last night with all the

126

stars and the bombs—you take it from me, Emily, that's not what it's usually like . . ."

Once more she missed Miss Seeton's start of surprise. Miss Seeton hoped that she was not so foolish as to mistake informality for deliberate discourtesy; the world she knew was changing—changing fast—and if survival depended on one's ability to adapt to change, then she, Emily Dorothea Seeton, would adapt with the best. It was, after all, only what Dr. Huxter had tried to tell her—warn her—about last night. Miss Seeton silently thanked him for the warning, but trusted to her native common sense not to need it.

". . . like a bowl of whipped cream, sometimes." Mrs. Beamish sighed as the last grains of sand trickled through to the lower glass compartment. "Though dear knows how much longer they'll let us have cream, whipped or not." She put the egg timer back on its shelf, picked up a spoon, lifted the teapot lid, and embarked on a bout of loud and vigorous stirring. "You mark my words," she said above the clatter of metal on earthenware. "It won't be so very long before cream's on the ration, too."

Miss Seeton said that she supposed not, but looking on the bright side, for proper enjoyment of a cup of tea one only needed milk. And could she help by fetching the jug from the larder?

"It's there on the table, thanks for asking, but them girls need to get a move on, or they'll miss the bus as well as the News. You might give 'em a shout while I warm up the wireless, seeing as if they miss it, so will you, and them supposed to be showing you the ropes this first day until you find your way around." Tilly Beamish favoured Miss Seeton with a long, appraising look as the newest lodger prepared to alert

127

her unknown mentors that they were likely to be late for work. Miss Seeton, sensing that the older woman had something of significance to add, waited a few moments to hear it before she went to the kitchen door.

Whatever it might have been, Mrs. Beamish thought better of saying it. "But don't *shout*," she begged, waving Miss Seeton on her way. "It's my head. What with them devils keeping me awake half the night, I tell you, Emily, if Hitler don't watch out, he's going to make himself very unpopular around these parts."

Miss Seeton approved this meiosis, but was still wondering how to answer when she realised there was no need. The giggles and pattering had grown suddenly louder, and even as Mrs. Beamish poured tea through a strainer from one pot to another, two young women erupted down the stairs and ran side by side along the hall to the kitchen.

"Morning!"

"Morning!"

The two spoke almost as one. For Miss Seeton (who did not know them) this came as no more of a surprise than it did to Tilly Beamish (who knew them well). Family likeness—the set of the ears, the shape of the eye sockets, hairline, colouring, the overall build—could be neither missed nor mistaken, by an artist; and such likeness was, as often as not, far more than merely physical. For one thing, they seemed to share—Miss Seeton sniffed—a strange taste in perfume . . .

"Morning, you two," said Mrs. Beamish, still busy with the straining. "Sleep well? Them bombers didn't wake you?"

Miss Seeton, about to introduce herself, recalled that she was not the hostess, and compromised with a welcoming

128

smile. The sisters smiled back at her and told Tilly they had slept like the dead as, her delicate task complete and the leaves set aside to be dried and used again, their landlady made the introductions.

"This, girls, is Miss Seeton—Miss Emily Seeton, your new assistant almoner or what d'you call it at the factory, so just you watch your step or she'll have you sent home in disgrace." Miss Seeton opened her mouth to deny the charge, but just in time realised from the girls' smothered giggles that it was Tilly's idea of a joke. "Emily," Mrs. Beamish continued, "this here is Beryl, and this is Ruby."

"We're not twins," said Beryl, "though everyone thinks we are."

"But there's only ten months between us," said Ruby.

"And we do everything together," said Beryl.

"Which is why we're here," said Ruby.

Miss Seeton expressed her pleasure at meeting them and hid a twinkle of amusement in case it should encourage them in their quick-fire cross-talk. They were hardly more than school-girls—and children did not always know where the boundaries were. As she was to have some (admittedly small) authority over them, it would not do to let matters get out of hand so early in the working relationship.

Beryl and Ruby, who had spotted the twinkle, twinkled back. A lively conversation might have ensued had not Mrs. Beamish intervened.

"It's nearly time for the news," she said, "so you three sit yourselves down and get your breakfasts inside you while we listen, or that blessed bus will go without you—and on Miss Seeton's first day, too. Emily, this will be your butter . . ." Tilly handed her newest guest a small, pale green bowl that had a yellow saucer for a lid. "It'll stay with the others in the pantry outside mealtimes," the landlady continued as her lodgers meekly took their seats. "And I'm sorry I forgot to ask last night, only you were so tired, what you wanted doing about the marge. We've been pooling it for cakes and so forth up to now, but you might be of a different opinion—though never you mind, we'll sort everything out this evening when there's more time, you being a bit pushed as you are at present." Miss Seeton hurriedly swallowed the reply courtesy had been prompting her to offer. "You girls," Mrs. Beamish concluded, "can do all the chattering you like, once you're out of the house—so long as it's not giving anything away . . ." She favoured Ruby and Beryl with the same appraising look she had earlier directed towards Miss Seeton. "Walls," came the stern reminder, "have ears."

"And you never know who's listening," chirped Beryl in the words of one of the most famous propaganda posters.

"No, you don't," said Mrs. Beamish, using the bread knife for emphasis. "Not never, you don't—so just you watch them tongues of yours and save wagging 'em until you're out of the house—and even then you think twice before you get talking, you hear? And now all of you, keep quiet, and make haste—or that bus will go without you!"

Everyone settled to eat and listen at the same time as the newsreader delivered the first official bulletin of the day. The destroyer HMS *Brazen* was reported lost under tow, having been put out of action during a bombing attack; the full ship's complement had been saved. Enemy bombers made wide-spread attacks across Britain the previous night, losing three aircraft in the process. The latest war budget would increase income tax to eight shillings and sixpence in the pound; the cost of beer would go up by a penny a pint. Following Mr. Churchill's broadcast, the Local Defence Volunteers were in future to be known as the Home Guard; with nearly one and a third million men registered since Mr. Eden announced the formation of the LDV on the fourteenth of May, recruitment was closed . . .

Despite their enforced silence, it was easy for Tilly's guests to mime requests for salt, pepper, milk, or bread. No need to ask for butter: each guest had her week's ration in an individual dish beside her place. Miss Seeton was pleased to note that her two companions were of similar habits to herself, which boded well for the future in what (she supposed) one might call a cooperative domestic establishment. Butter, thinly spread or (in the absence, so far, of rationed jam) spread not at all, would with care last the requisite seven days and leave a little spare to put with the margarine for the "cakes and so forth" Mrs. Beamish had mentioned earlier. It hadn't taken Miss Seeton long to decide that if everyone else *chez* Beamish cheerfully surrendered her weekly two ounces of margarine to the mutual benefit of the household, then she, Emily Seeton, would do likewise. It wasn't that she had an especially sweet tooth; cutting down on confectionery and drinking unsugared tea for the duration would be no great hardship; but the very idea that Hitler and his "Nahzee gang," as Mr. Churchill called them, could try to stop the people of Great Britain enjoying a fruitcake or a Madeira when they wanted one made her . . . well, indignant on the nation's behalf, if not necessarily on her own.

"Time to go, Emily!" cried Beryl, gulping down a final piece of toast, pushing back her chair, jumping to her feet, and heading for the hall almost in one movement.

"Now, don't you forget my sweepings," called Mrs. Beamish as the others followed Beryl out of the room. "On the table in the linen bag."

"Now, don't *you* forget your identity card," Ruby warned Miss Seeton as Beryl called back that the sweepings would be remembered. "They won't even let *us* into the factory without checking, and they ought to know our faces well enough by now."

Miss Seeton, quickly gathering together her gas mask, bag, and other belongings, agreed that the sisters' non-twinnish resemblance was not only remarkable, but (she would have supposed) unforgettable.

"But it is understandable that they would err on the side of caution," she said with a gentle smile for her two young companions. "There is a war on, remember."

"Can we forget it?" said Beryl, winding a flowered head-scarf into a turban that expertly concealed all of her hair except a wisp of golden fringe.

"It's why we're here," said Ruby, tucking her own wavy locks inside an equally expert snood. "Beryl, we've *got* to try that new style this evening—we look such a mess!"

"Mess?" Beryl went to pick up a faded navy-blue linen bag from the hall table, and blinked as she saw what lay beside it. "Oh . . . yes." She coughed. "We—we were 'prenticed straight from school to a—a milliner," she went on as Miss Seeton took her hat—such a hat!—from the table and patted it automatically in place without wasting time at the mirror. In Beryl's hand the navy-blue bag jingled and shook with her suppressed laughter. "They let—they let Ruby leave a bit early on account of I'd be with her, see, and learning a useful trade," she brought out with only a slight tremor in her voice.

"But when That Man went into Poland, we could see what was coming," said Ruby, seizing the conversational initiative at the same time as the doorknob. "We wanted to *do* something—something more useful than hats."

"That's right," said Beryl, recovering as the door opened and the little procession trotted down the steps. "I ask you, what use are fancy titfers when there's a war on?" She brandished the blue linen bag in the air, and again it jingled with a metallic, martial sound.

"We're good with our hands, we told the lady at the Employment Exchange," said Ruby.

"And we said," said Beryl over her shoulder as she reached the garden gate, "that if they wanted things doing neat and tidy, we could do them as well as anyone."

"Only we didn't want to sew uniforms—or parachutes," Ruby added darkly as the gate clicked open.

"Uniforms," explained Beryl, "are awful hot and heavy to work with, like the stuff they make barrage balloons out of. And parachutes is—is defeatist, that's what it is." With a defiant bang she closed the gate and began a brisk march to the other end of the street.

"We are not," Miss Seeton found herself quoting as she hurried along, "interested in the possibilities of defeat."

"We wanted to *do* something," reiterated Ruby, before her slightly breathless companion could add that parachute precautions against . . . well, mishaps in the air might perhaps be considered not so much defeatist as, sadly, realistic.

"So we got our parents to sign for us," said Beryl.

"And here we are!" Ruby rounded off the narrative with a triumphant giggle. "Beryl does the ailerons, and I do the rudders—covering them, I mean."

"Which is harder than it sounds," said Beryl. "You have to pin the canvas tight and turn it inside out and blanket-stitch along the seams, eight in a row and then a double knot to stop it running too far if it splits—"

"And," broke in Ruby, "the dope—the varnish! Ugh!"

"That's what makes the smell," said Beryl. "Pear drops— you just can't wash it out, and it gets into everything."

Miss Seeton, trying not to sniff, felt herself blush.

"Your clothes," said Ruby. "Your hair . . ."

"And it's not as if it pays as well as the other jobs," said Beryl. "In fact, it's about the worst."

"But we don't really mind," said Ruby. "Because it saves having the men make fun of you."

"Some of the girls," Beryl explained, "are aero detail fitters—don't ask, but they make special bits, I think—they've been trained and everything, with certificates to prove it for them that don't believe it, but—"

"But some of the blokes," said Ruby, "you wouldn't believe the way they carry on!"

"But they showed them," concluded Beryl with a giggle as she turned to Miss Seeton. "Are you good with your hands, Emily?" The ex-apprentice milliner could hardly ignore The Hat and its extraordinary trimming. "Can you sew?"

Miss Seeton modestly confessed that—while she could indeed hem a seam, make buttonholes, patch, and darn—lack of both talent and inclination had encouraged her to leave anything more elaborate than the basics to her mother, who was a needlewoman of some repute.

"Well, that's good enough," was Ruby's comment as Beryl hid a smile. "She doesn't," the younger sister reminded the elder, "need to read patterns or anything—not if she's going

134

to be looking after us girls, and in an office most of the time."
She turned to Miss Seeton and tried to explain. "You see, uh,
Emily . . ."

With Miss Seeton taking no particular umbrage at this
boldness, Ruby looked pleased. "You see," she explained,
"you'll have had a dressmaker come in, or bought off the peg
in posh shops . . ."

Though Miss Seeton was moved to deny the charge, Ruby
paid no attention. "But the likes of me and Beryl," she went
on, "we've made our own clothes since we could hold the
scissors to cut out—with Mum keeping an eye on us to start
with, of course—so it's like second nature to make sense of a
paper pattern, and anyone can do blanket stitch."

"It's doing it properly that's the difficult bit," Beryl reminded her sister sternly, and Ruby giggled before adding
that the men didn't see it quite the same way, did they?

Miss Seeton, above the sisters' renewed giggles, was
heard to remark that this denial seemed, one had to say,
somewhat shortsighted on the part of the men. While,
from the purely physical point of view—height, weight,
muscular structure, and so on—there were, undeniably,
some tasks better suited to males rather than to females,
for her part she could see no good reason why neatness
of hand and quickness of eye should not render a young
woman quite as capable of—of reading a paper pattern as
any young man.

"Or any older man," supplied Beryl, which had her sister
giggling again.

They had reached the end of the street and were nearing
a group of a dozen or so other young women, all chattering
together in and around a telegraph pole on which Authority

had fastened a wooden sign painted with four crisp, informative words: WORKS BUS STOP ONLY. In the true Au-
thoritarian manner, no hint was given as to where nonworks
passengers might hope to board, or even to find, a bus better
suited to their needs. Miss Seeton supposed that those who
ought to know would know already, and that those who had
no business knowing would keep their own counsel. There
was, she must never forget, a war on . . .

"Girls!" cried Beryl as people began to point and wave in
the direction of the newcomers, "this is Emily Seeton, our
new assistant welfare lady—"

"And this," cried one of the girls, "is the bus!"

And it was.

Chapter 14

The welcome given to Miss Seeton was friendly but muted, as she had suspected it might be. The impersonal smiles, nods, and sideways glances surprised her no more than the various muffled exchanges she was not supposed to hear. Nobody's voice, nobody's expression, was unkind; there was no overt hostility: but there was the inevitable wariness of any close-knit group when a stranger makes an appearance. She hoped that she would not long remain a stranger, but for now even the casual wartime introduction offered by Beryl and Ruby hardly constituted a licence to join in—even had she wished so to do—the giggles and gossip enjoyed by the other girls (who were somewhat younger than she) once they were all inside the bus and bumping briskly along the road.

Miss Seeton hid a smile. She couldn't help thinking of school excursions in happier days: the noise was quite as deafening; she felt sorry for the driver. His ears must be ringing with the exuberant shrieks and squeals as girls who hadn't seen one another since they left work the previous afternoon caught up on the latest items of essential news. Those who had heard the evening's wireless programmes repeated for the benefit of their friends who had missed it the unmitigated nonsense broadcast from Germany by the renegade whose strangulated, plummy accent and ridiculous manner had caused his irreverent audience to bestow upon him the soubriquet of "Lord Haw-Haw."

"Jairmany calling. Jairmany calling. Jairmany calling," intoned a young woman with curly red hair, whose green eyes held an infectious twinkle in their depths. "Where," went on the redhead darkly, "is the *Ark Royal*?"

Howls of girlish laughter greeted this wicked imitation. Miss Seeton (who with a small party of canteen colleagues had attended a recent performance of the revue *Haw Haw!* at London's Holborn Empire) smiled more broadly as she savoured the moment. With such spirit and courage to support them in their endeavours, how could the British be beaten?

"The church clock in Grantchester," enunciated the redhead, whose ear for mimicry was almost perfect, "is stopped at ten to three. Ten to three precisely!"

Sitting quietly amid the renewed howls of mirth and applause for red-haired Muriel, Miss Seeton reflected that Rupert Brooke had said the same thing, and said it with far greater elegance, a quarter of a century before. Between the poet and the Nazi there could really be no choice . . .

Out of the village rattled the bus, stopping from time to time to take on more workers. Houses and cottages gave way to hedgerows, beyond which could be seen newly harvested fields dotted with overturned carts, heaps of old tyres, and random bales of hay—fields on which no enemy aircraft would easily land. Around most of the obstacles there were tractors and horses already busy preparing for the next crop of the year. A small island nation under U-boat siege must use every available square inch of earth, or starve . . .

The brakes groaned, the indicator flicked out, and the bus turned to the left. After a few hundred yards, hedgerow metamorphosed into a high chain-link fence topped with stout barbed wire; at intervals along the fence the sun baffled camouflage to glint on the barrels of antiaircraft guns, manned by day and night. After another hundred yards, barbed wire became tall metal posts on which hung heavy double gates, resolutely closed. In front of the gates, evidently waiting for the bus, milled a restless, weary crowd. Overlooking the crowd, by a smaller, open gate, was a little wooden hut, outside which a uniformed sentry stood watching as the bus disgorged its cargo and the weary crowd pressed forward, eager to embark.

"Got your identity card and pass, Emily?" Beryl and Ruby, her official escorts, closed in upon Miss Seeton and led her up to the hut. "Hello, George!"

"Passes!" snapped the sentry, ignoring the greeting and holding out his hand. Beryl and Ruby nudged Miss Seeton in a meaningful way, and giggled. George glared at them— and continued to glare even after he was forced to acknowledge that the sisters were indeed who they claimed to be.

When it was Miss Seeton's turn to be identified, he gave her a long, hard look that she was able to return without blinking. Years of quelling refractory pupils from the far side of a classroom had left their mark.

George grunted, briefly lowered his gaze, and then returned to the attack. "New, ain't you?" he challenged, and drew himself to an imposing height.

"Absolutely brand spanking new," said Beryl before Miss Seeton could reply.

"The very latest thing," chirped Ruby.

"I am Emily Seeton—" began Miss Seeton as the girls were overcome by further giggles.

"Yes, I can read," growled George. "Can't I?"

Miss Seeton felt her cheeks grow warm. She hadn't meant to imply—

"Oh, never mind him." Beryl snatched Miss Seeton's pass and card from the sentry's sullen hand. "Come on!"

"Yes," said Ruby. "Quick." She tugged at Miss Seeton's arm and pulled her through the little gate. "You'll have to report to the welfare lady—and we've got to hurry."

"To clock in," Beryl explained as they bustled their charge down a concrete path towards a brick building that was relentlessly utilitarian in design, and (to an artist) of even more incredible ugliness because of its camouflage paint. Miss Seeton reminded herself, not for the first time, that There Was A War On . . .

"We'll have to leave you here," said Beryl. "If we miss the clock, they knock off a quarter of an hour's money, and it's always such a rush—but through that door, and ask for Mrs. Morris."

"That was certainly the name in the letter—" began Miss Seeton. But it was not her morning for finished sentences.

"She'll look after you," said Ruby. "But we'll be late!"

"We'll see you!" cried Beryl; and with a hurried farewell, the sisters were gone.

Their departure left Miss Seeton suddenly aware that she was on her own. She took a deep breath, reminded herself that she was a soldier's daughter, and with an almost steady hand pushed open the door of the relentlessly ugly building. She stepped inside and paused to get her bearings.

"Yes?" A man's head popped out through an open hatch. "Who're you, and whatcher want?" Once more Miss Seeton was subjected to a long, hard stare.

This time she could not meet it as she had done before. She was indeed all too aware that she was entirely on her own in the strange, new, industrial environment. Beryl and Ruby, who had been so kind, must at this very minute be—what was the phrase?—clocking on for work. "I have to—that is, I should like to speak to Mrs. Morris, please," said Miss Seeton meekly.

The head, still staring, advanced through the hatch and brought with it a uniformed body with broad shoulders but—Miss Seeton caught her breath—only one arm, which extended a muscular hand to seize the papers she obediently offered in response to an unspoken command.

"Ah," said the uniformed man. "Yes." Head, hand, and papers promptly retreated behind the hatch. A loud, suspicious rustling was followed by the tinkle of a telephone and a muttered one-sided exchange of which Miss Seeton, mindful of her manners and moving a few steps away, heard nothing beyond the single syllable *hat*—which in full, she knew, could have referred to almost anything.

"Awright," said the uniformed man, reemerging from his retreat with a suddenness that made Miss Seeton jump. "Here you are." The muscular hand waved the papers in her direction. "You shouldn't have to show 'em again after Ma Morris has checked 'em, but keep 'em by you all the time, just in case." Now that the newcomer's legitimacy had apparently been established, the custodian of the hatchway was willing to impart useful information. "Third door on the left, and go in as soon's you've knocked."

141

"Thank you," said Miss Seeton, receiving her assorted credentials with a shy smile. "The third door on the left, and I'm to go in after knocking. Er—thank you."

"Time enough to thank me when you come out again . . . if you come out again." The hatchway's custodian grinned as he uttered this ominous warning. "There's some folk whose bark is worse'n their bite, but our Mrs. Morris ain't one of them. She can be a holy terror if she takes a dislike to you, not that you look the sort to go giving trouble."

"Indeed I'm not," Miss Seeton assured him with a startled blush. It was true there had been those at art college who preached—and lived—the bohemian lifestyle, but Emily Dorothea, daughter of Alice, had never been of their number; and, so many years later, she had hardly thought herself to resemble (even by association) the sort of young woman who might Give Trouble. Which was of course the uniformed man's tactful way, as he must know from her identity card that she was unmarried, of saying Getting Into Trouble. Which, even had she ever been so inclined to do, at her age, thirty next birthday, which was closer than she cared to think, whether there was a war on or not—

"Off you go, then." The one-armed man's encouragement was brisk. Looked terrified out of her wits, and going to be a welfare officer—'strewth. Those girls would eat her for breakfast if she didn't buck up her ideas, and dithering in the corridor wasn't exactly a good start. He hoped Mrs. Morris would set the poor girl straight, he really did, but if he knew the woman, she'd make mincemeat of this one.

"Off you go, duck," he urged. "Third door on the left." Then he winked. "And give her my love!"

142

Miss Seeton, unsettled by the wink—one had to suppose he was joking, but in these uncertain days, when the whole world seemed upside down, who could tell?—nodded politely at him, blushed again, and hurried to the third door on the left, where she knocked and waited a courteous five seconds before turning the handle and going in.

There was a grim, grey-haired woman standing by the window—would there ever again (mused Miss Seeton) come a day when windows were free of their brown paper tape?—holding a cardboard folder in her left hand. Even from the doorway Miss Seeton could not fail to notice how white her knuckles were, and how deep the lines of tension on her face as she looked at the newcomer, hesitated, and tried to force a smile. She tried in vain. "You must be Emily Seeton," she greeted her visitor, who could not deny it.

Nor was Miss Seeton's attempt at a smile any more successful than that of the grey-haired woman. On both sides courtesy had fought with nerves, and lost.

"You'd better let me see your papers." The grey-haired woman moved away from the window and threw the folder on her desk with an irritable slap.

Once more Miss Seeton held the documents out for inspection. Mrs. Morris (that air of authority required no formal introduction) was not so much casual in her manners, she decided, as preoccupied. The war, no doubt . . .

Mrs. Morris hesitated again after studying the papers, then tossed them across the desk towards Miss Seeton, and sighed. "Sit down," she instructed, following her own instruction as she spoke. Quietly Miss Seeton collected her papers, pulled out the visitors' chair, and seated herself in front of one she must now regard as her new superior.

"They told me to expect you," said her new superior in noncommittal accents. "You are Emily Seeton, sent from the ministry—and I'm Mrs. Morris."

"How do you do, Mrs. Morris," said Miss Seeton.

Mrs. Morris waved the courtesy aside. "We've no time for the niceties, Seeton. We've a war to fight—aeroplanes to manufacture—and you may as well know right now that I didn't want you." Miss Seeton blinked. "There's no time," Mrs. Morris informed her crisply, "to waste on training you. Some kind of teacher, they told me?" She gave Miss Seeton a sharp look as she opened her mouth to explain. "Art, of all things," went on Mrs. Morris with scorn. "That's no use on the factory floor, believe *me*."

Miss Seeton would have liked to agree with her superior that, without training, she would indeed be of no practical use on the manufacturing side, but Mrs. Morris continued her scornful denunciation of the younger woman before the latter could draw breath.

"You're still wet behind the ears for a job like this, Seeton. We're not dealing with schoolgirls sitting in nice neat rows with their arms folded while you stand in front of a blackboard hurling order marks and detentions at anyone who misbehaves. This is the real world, not the Never-Never Land. Here," said Mrs. Morris, "we've had to grow up."

"There *is* a war on," said Miss Seeton as Mrs. Morris sat forward on her chair preparing to emphasise her next point.

The interpolation, quietly though it had been delivered, startled the welfare officer. Her prim, grim curls trembled under their steel-grey net as she shot upright and for the first time regarded Miss Seeton with—grudging—respect.

Miss Seeton met her gaze calmly.

"Yes," said Mrs. Morris at last, the first to blink. The silent confrontation had been swift, but (to her surprise) decisive. She wondered that she was not more tempted to begrudge Miss Seeton the honours: but she was now strangely willing to concede that there might—just might—be more to the young woman than her appearance (that hat!) and her personal history (an art teacher!) suggested. "Yes," she said again. "There *is* a war on, and the most unexpected people have shown the stuff they're made of when they've been given the chance . . ."

She recovered herself, and once more leaned forward for emphasis. "But I warn you, Seeton, I've no time to see how, or whether, you exceed expectation. There are nearly a thousand people in this factory, working round the clock, all of them knowing what they're doing—and doing it. You don't, so you can't, without a lot of people taking valuable time to show you." Her eyes challenged Miss Seeton to argue the point, but Miss Seeton, incurably honest, said nothing.

Mrs. Morris sighed and nodded. It was almost a gesture of approval.

Almost.

The tone in which she concluded her welcoming remarks was slightly—slightly—less brusque than before. "The ministry," said Mrs. Morris, "sent you here—heaven knows why—as a war artist, so that's what you'd better be. Orders are orders: I can't get rid of you without a lot of paperwork for which I haven't the time: but I want you out of my way. You've had no experience of office work and keeping files in order—I have. You don't know the first thing about industrial work and workers—I do. Keep from under everybody's feet, scribble quietly in a corner and don't interfere, and the ministry will be happy." Another attempt at a smile had more success than when she had first set eyes on Miss Seeton: it did not reach her eyes, but the curve of her narrow mouth was less angular.

"The ministry will be happy," she reiterated, "and so will I. You can call yourself my assistant, as that's how you'll be listed in the records, but for pity's sake *don't* try to assist me. Someone like you will be more hindrance than help until you know the ropes . . .

"By which time," concluded Mrs. Morris, "we could have been invaded."

Chapter 15

What Mrs. Morris said was, indeed, all too true: but Emily, daughter of Major Hugo and Alice Amabel, could scarcely approve of her having voiced the defeatist thought aloud. Yet Mrs. Morris—dislike the arrangement as the elder woman might—was Miss Seeton's professional superior. It would be discourteous to challenge her—and so short an acquaintance could only compound the discourtesy. In traditional British fashion, Miss Seeton compromised: saying nothing, but making her disapproval known with a frown.

Mrs. Morris cleared her throat and shifted on her chair. "Yes . . ." she said uneasily. "Yes—well . . . I suppose we may as well start, as you *are* here, by taking you on a quick tour of the factory."

Miss Seeton nodded politely, murmured her willingness to do as she was told, and waited for further instructions.

"And I suppose we'd better find you a tin hat," said Mrs. Morris, "if you're going to be wandering about the place by yourself . . . But we'll do that later. Don't let me forget—though I really haven't the time to spare," she reminded the younger woman as she left her desk and headed for the office door. Mrs. Morris was regaining her self-possession. She had mistaken Miss Seeton's quiet acquiescence for the dumb-struck dismay of one thrown in suddenly at the deep end; one who would all too soon find herself helpless in an alien environment. *Seeton would have to remember, just like the rest of them, that there was a war on—first day or not . . .*

Mrs. Morris, pointedly leaving her steel helmet on the table, unhooked her gas mask from its peg and slung the strap across her shoulder. She watched without comment as Miss Seeton, selecting (also without comment) a discreet corner of the room in which to deposit those of her accoutrements she deemed unnecessary, followed her example.

"Of course," said the welfare officer as Miss Seeton presented herself for duty, "I can't take you to any of the high-security areas. And of the areas you *will* be allowed to visit, I'll only show you where the *girls* work." That thin smile again crooked her mouth into an angular curve. "We might as well," said Mrs. Morris, "go along with the ministry as far as we can—but I assure you that even if you *were* my assistant I would never dream of asking you to deal with the men until you've found your feet." She said no more, but the implication was clear. In the opinion of Mrs. Morris, spinster school-teacher Emily Seeton, war worker for the duration, was unlikely ever to find her feet among the female of the factory species, let alone the male.

Miss Seeton, still polite, nodded again and smiled. Like the nod, the smile was polite: but there was a gleam at the back of her eyes that—had she noticed it—might have warned Mrs. Morris her new assistant was not as helpless as first appearances might suggest. Miss Seeton accepted and understood the irritation of one who had had imposed on her by a government department an assistant—herself—who, nobody could

148

deny, was untrained . . . but she did not regard herself as completely *inexperienced* in the ways of young females, even if she could also accept that factory girls must be different from schoolgirls in some ways—just as she supposed that in other ways they must resemble them. Or students, in whose ways she was similarly experienced—if only as an onlooker. And did not the onlooker, after all, see most of the game?

Fun and games. Miss Seeton continued to smile as she recalled some of those she had met, both male and female, during her student years. How odd that Mrs. Morris should suppose (or so it seemed) she would be helpless in mixed company and be perplexed by its mysteries. She had, after all, been to art college, where she had seen enough male (and female) bodies, both alive and dead—although the latter had been in hospital—

"Well, come along!" Mrs. Morris barked out the command, and Miss Seeton blushed. This was no time for reminiscence: there was a war on.

"If I *must* leave my office," the welfare officer went on, "I want to get away *quickly*." Miss Seeton's blush grew more pink and guilty. "Before the phone rings," Mrs. Morris condescended to enlarge. "Or people take five minutes out to come here to complain, which they *will do*, about anything—even in wartime."

"Time," murmured Miss Seeton, composing herself as she followed the older woman out of the room into a corridor lit by flickering fluorescent light. "Oh, indeed, yes, I know—slipping away when they say they're going to the lavatory, which I imagine must cause difficulties with the foreman, or whoever is in charge—which is no doubt why they do it, if that is what they do."

Mrs. Morris shot a startled look over her shoulder.

Miss Seeton was calm. "Girls," she said, "have quite as lively a spirit of mischief as any boy, and will always try to take advantage if one is insufficiently firm—and, of course, if they try their excuses with a male supervisor, one can well imagine that he would find it embarrassing to deny them, as they will find it amusing that he should. When, that is, they are supposed to be working round the clock—or rather in shifts, as my fellow lodgers told me."

Mrs. Morris looked at Miss Seeton again. What else had her fellow lodgers told this young woman? There was something about her . . . did she know more than she was, in her apparent confusion, saying? Yet there was, indeed, *something* about her that hinted the ministry might—perhaps—have been not entirely wrong about young Seeton . . .

"Tea breaks," said Mrs. Morris after a few thoughtful moments, "were often the excuse—before things got so— so frantic . . . although I imagine that at school you always knew when the breaks were going to be, which would rule *that* one out for even the most enterprising pupil."

"You might," remarked Miss Seeton as she accompanied her preceptress along the corridor, "be surprised, Mrs. Morris."

"Or I might not," said Mrs. Morris dryly, after another few moments spent in thought. "Feeling faint is another good one, though a burnt feather under the nose can often work wonders."

"And so much less messy than a glass of water in the face," agreed Miss Seeton, her footsteps clattering on the bare concrete floor. "For myself," she continued, "I found smelling salts to be even more convenient, as they did not require matches. I don't smoke, you see."

Mrs. Morris grunted. Perhaps it was merely shortness of breath as they hurried on their way. "Well, stay here long enough," she said, "and you'll smoke like a chimney—everyone does. Sometimes it's the only way to keep awake."

Miss Seeton replied with a noncommittal murmur, and Mrs. Morris sighed.

"To be fair," she conceded—she grudged the concession, but she made it—"the girls don't try it on half as much as in the early days, when things didn't seem so—so urgent." She glanced at Miss Seeton and stifled a sigh for those early days of the Twilight War, as Mr. Churchill had called it. Others—except sailors, who knew only too well that the war at sea was far from boring—had called it the Bore War: but since Dunkirk that term was no longer in use among the peoples of the United Kingdom.

"Most of the faints we have now," Mrs. Morris continued as the two turned a corner, "are the genuine article." Her tone was still grudging, but she had to be fair. "It can really get *very* stuffy, with every window in the place permanently boarded up. Each time they bomb us I wonder if our luck will run out because an incendiary has blocked a main exit route. Without the windows . . ."

Miss Seeton pondered these remarks for a few moments. "I suppose," she ventured at last, "that it would take too long to install and remove the blackout each day over so large an area as you must have here."

"It would," Mrs. Morris agreed with emphasis. Yes, she might just have second thoughts about the wisdom of the men from the ministry . . . "With those huge skylights in the roof it would be far worse than painting the Forth Bridge. You wouldn't so much have to start as soon as you'd finished as start *before* you had finished, and that's not counting the windows in the walls. Mr. Coleman—he's the works manager—insisted that all the glass came out and the boards went up right after Dunkirk." She lowered her voice, and for the first time slowed her walking pace so that Miss Seeton could, without too much effort, move closer. "Mr. Coleman knows all about bombs, you see. His son—his only son—was killed in Spain."

"Oh," said Miss Seeton. Grim visions of dusty rubble and shards of glass, broken limbs and bloodied flesh, swam before her inward eye. "Oh—I'm so sorry."

"Mr. Coleman said *we'd* be sorry if the roof blew in on us," said Mrs. Morris darkly. "Sticky brown paper and wire mesh would be no use at all, he said. It might just stop the windows being blasted sideways, but there would still be the risk of splinters and in any case it wouldn't hold up the roof—so out the whole lot came."

"And in," supplied Miss Seeton, "went the boards. Yes, I see. But during the day, I suppose, the factory doors may stand open to allow whatever draught there might be to bring a little fresh air from outside?"

Mrs. Morris almost laughed at this. "Remember how hot the weather has been, these past few weeks?" She gave Miss Seeton no time to say that she remembered very well. "Every building on site was a positive oven after the first day," she said grimly. "All the overhead ventilation systems burned out within hours—the heat rose straight to the top of the roof, and of course with the blackout it couldn't escape—and with everyone so busy, you just try asking for repairs or replacements and expect to see anything happen! Believe me, Seeton, Lord Beaverbrook himself couldn't do it." Now Mrs.

Morris did laugh, albeit briefly. "And I'm sure he *wouldn't* do it," she added, "no matter who was brave enough to ask him—or foolish—if anyone was, which even Mr. Coleman says he isn't."

"The works manager," Miss Seeton reminded herself, as Mrs. Morris hesitated, and seemed lost for words.

"One of the kindest—most considerate—men on earth," the older woman brought out at last. In someone less world-weary the tone in which this accolade was spoken might have been accompanied by a blush. "Which is why you're here," she went on quickly as Miss Seeton turned an enquiring look upon her. "Or so I imagine. Mr. Coleman's no fool. He knew how much my job was growing—and likely to go on growing—with the increase both in workers and in the rate of production, and I know he said that at least he could do something about *that*—although why they sent *you* . . ."

"An unskilled worker," supplied Miss Seeton before Mrs. Morris could say it,

"Exactly." Mrs. Morris was by no means mellowing, but she was undeniably less hostile than when they first met. "Unskilled—at least, unskilled in terms of what's needed here." It was yet another concession. "No doubt," she went on with a creaking attempt at humour, "if Lord Beaverbrook found out you were here, he'd have you enrolled on a training course as soon as look at you—which would in my opinion be a total waste of time, because he wouldn't have had a proper look at you. They say the man does everything at double speed, and never rests. He eats, sleeps, and dreams fighter aircraft and expects everyone in his factories to do the same—which takes me back to the blackout and the fainting fits. Heaven help anybody who even thinks of wasting time on—on non-productive jobs like extractor fans when he could be fixing a lathe, or a drill, or anything else that's broken down because it's in constant use making Spitfires, and there's never been a chance for anywhere to cool down during the night, with every machine in the place working virtually round the clock and all the doors closed to stop the light showing. And according to the locals there's no such thing as a draught in this wretched valley. They say the hills are too high to let a breeze through in summer or to let the fog out when it settles in winter . . ."

"Things," said Miss Seeton with a firmness she did not feel, "could be worse, Mrs. Morris."

Mrs. Morris stopped in her tracks. Once more she turned a startled look upon Miss Seeton. Was this young woman a witch? How had she so contrived to get under the guard of Susan Morris and encourage her to . . . to reveal more of her worries than she had shared with anyone since the factory had opened? Even Mr. Coleman—

"Come on," she snapped, cutting that final sentiment briskly short. It would never do to let Seeton suspect—"Through here." They had reached the end of the corridor and would soon be outside. "Hurry up!"

In an uneasy silence the smaller of a pair of double doors was opened, and the two women emerged into a world that was far from silent, filled as it was with the roar of a Spitfire on a test flight—looping the loop and tying a knot around the sun with its white vapour trail. Miss Seeton, who knew she really should have been following Mrs. Morris along the concrete path to the next building, stopped and stared, transfixed, into the sky.

"Hurry up!" cried her superior, to whom the sight of a Spitfire was no longer as arresting as the young art teacher found it. "I told you I've no time to waste!"

"View halloo, Morris!" cried a cheery female voice from the shadows. "And who's your friend?" the voice continued, drawing closer.

Miss Seeton, half-dazzled by the sun and the Spitfire's swooping beauty, blinked as she tried to focus her gaze on what at first, before the figure spoke, she would have taken for a willowy youth with hair that (to an art-college graduate) was only a fraction too long and wavy for conventional taste.

"Miss Wilkes." Mrs. Morris received the newcomer with a stiff nod. "This is Miss Seeton, who has been sent by the ministry to—to provide sketches for information leaflets. And," she conceded as she caught Miss Seeton's eye, "in her spare time, to help out in the Welfare Office."

"A usurper in your precious kingdom, eh?" Miss Wilkes, a tall young woman whose slender build was of the whip-cord-fitness kind, chuckled richly as she extended a competent hand for Miss Seeton to shake. "How d'you do, Miss Seeton? Jemima Wilkes, at your service. Pay no attention to Old Sourpuss here. She disapproves of almost everyone, so you mustn't take it personally that she doesn't sound so very keen on you."

"I'm Emily Seeton," returned Miss Seeton. who thought it wiser to ignore most of this unconventional greeting.

Miss Wilkes shook her briskly by the hand a second time, and grinned down at her. "Well, Emily Seeton," she went on, "let me inform you that she's *not* keen on you, especially if you've been sent by the ministry without waiting to be asked. Sourpuss Sue is far too conscious of her own worth ever to admit she might need anyone to . . . what was it, Sue? To help her out. *She* doesn't want strangers interfering—she knows her job backwards. Right, Sue?"

"I have no time, Miss Wilkes, to waste on levity." Mrs. Morris, all signs of mellowing gone, studiously ignored the younger woman's ever-broader grin. "There is," she reminded her, "a war on. However"—this with a sniff—"as you seem to have nothing better to do with *your* time at present, you might give Seeton some idea of what your job, when you condescend to do it, entails. And a tour of the works would be helpful, too. Good morning."

She nodded to Miss Seeton in a way the latter could interpret as she chose: *Good morning and good riddance*, or *Good morning for now; I will see you later*—and turned on her heel to march stiffly back, without another word, to the double doors of the office and administration block.

"Boohoo, I've hurt her feelings." Miss Wilkes made a face in the direction of that ramrod spine as it vanished from sight. "Don't worry," she added to Miss Seeton, who couldn't hide her surprise at so juvenile a gesture from one who was obviously an intelligent adult. "It won't make it any worse for you that Sourpuss has her knife into me and I always take mine out and scratch her with it when we meet. She's like that with everyone—with a few honourable exceptions. Mr. Coleman, now—he's a widower. And if *he* dropped the handkerchief in front of Sourpuss, she'd be quick enough to pick it up."

Miss Seeton, who from her reading understood the old-fashioned reference to an offer of marriage, said nothing.

Miss Wilkes chuckled again. "I've shocked you, Emily. D'you mind if I call you that? We're all in this together, and it seems silly to stand on ceremony when we could be blown to Kingdom Come any minute without warning. And what price etiquette then?"

"What, indeed," Miss Seeton found herself replying.

"Splendid!" cried Miss Wilkes, once more shaking her by the hand. "And my pals call me Jem." She let out a peal of laughter. "Jem and Em—it sounds like a music-hall act, doesn't it? Too ridiculous!"

Miss Seeton's native common sense saw no objection to informality, and could never suspect Jemima of deliberate ridicule. She smiled up at her new friend and chuckled politely as Miss Wilkes continued to laugh.

"Oh, Lord," the young woman said at last with a gasp, bending over and rubbing her side. "I've got a stitch. Sourpuss would say it was a judgement on me, of course."

Miss Seeton recognised a hint when she heard one. While she could not bring herself to ask a direct question, which might smack of impertinence, she favoured the side-rubbing Jemima with a quizzical air that betokened her willingness to learn more.

"Mrs. Morris," said Miss Wilkes, straightening to her full height after a briskly friction-filled thirty seconds, "doesn't approve of me—of most of my crowd—because she thinks we don't take the war seriously enough."

"Oh," said Miss Seeton.

"We don't walk round with gloomy faces all the time," Miss Wilkes translated, "and we enjoy a bit of a laugh with the factory people once in a while."

Miss Seeton briefly pondered this heinous crime and then replied that, as long as nobody was being distracted from his or her work, which must of course take priority in this time of national crisis, she saw no particular reason why anyone should object to expressions of the lighter side of life. "Because, of course, even in wartime there is one," she concluded, and Jemima grinned at her.

Emboldened by the grin, Miss Seeton appended that it was, after all, one's patriotic duty not to give in to gloomy thoughts, which would not only spread the alarm and despondency against which they had all been warned, but which would also be—well—self-indulgent, would it not?

"Well said, Emily!" cried Jemima, and clapped her on the back. "I wish you could get Morris to see it our way. I'm sure that sourpuss face of hers does as much damage to the general morale as—as hearing about any number of planes shot down when—when the pilots were friends of yours."

There was a note in her voice as she uttered the final phrase that made Miss Seeton look at her. The laughter was gone from the tall young woman's eyes.

"He bought it three weeks ago," was all Jemima said, and she needed to say no more.

"I'm so very sorry," murmured Miss Seeton, venturing a gentle pat on the other's arm.

"Thanks," came the reply, from a hastily cleared throat. "Yes." Miss Wilkes cleared her throat again. "Just one of those things. His plane was shot up, and he bailed out, but the Hun came back to make sure and—and machine-gunned him on the way down. Our chaps saw what was happening and got the blighter, but it was . . . too late . . ."

"Oh," said Miss Seeton, shivering.

Jemima took a deep breath. "Well, you're a sitting duck under a brolly, of course," she said. She caught Miss Seeton's puzzled look. "Sorry," she said with a faint hint of laughter. "Slang for parachute—and that's another reason Ma Morris doesn't approve of us. If it's not the slang"—she slapped herself on the thigh—"it's the slacks—so fearfully unladylike, don't you know."

"Oh?" said Miss Seeton, whose personal preference was for skirts, but who saw nothing wrong with the dungarees and overalls sported by many of the factory girls. Given the unladylike bending, crawling, climbing, and scrambling that must surely be part and parcel of constructing a Spitfire, some form of slack or trouser was, she felt, a highly practical solution to the requirements of modesty.

"Catch any of our crowd," said Jemima, "even thinking of bailing out with our unmentionables on public display just because Sourpuss thinks women should still be in crinolines! Oh—I should have explained," she added, as Miss Seeton's bewilderment was plain. "We're the ferry pilots. We fly the planes from the factory to the aerodromes—once they've been built, that is. And—and tested okay . . ."

She shrugged. "Which *might* be some sort of excuse for Suzy Morris's sourpuss face," she conceded. "Once they've been built—*and tested* . . .

"You've heard about the sabotage, of course?"

Chapter 16

"You mean you haven't heard?" Jemima was startled by Miss Seeton's obvious surprise. "I know everyone's been warned not to gossip about it—careless talk, you know—but . . ."

"I have heard nothing about any sabotage," said Miss Seeton. She honestly believed this. Not for a moment did she connect the "spot of bother" Major Haynes had mentioned with something so despicable as this. "The girls with whom I travelled on the bus were, I agree, somewhat guarded in their behaviour—their conversation—but of course I took it for no more than their natural unease at the appearance of a stranger."

Jemima favoured Miss Seeton with a swift, head-to-toe survey. The appearance of a stranger? Well, you could take *that* more than one way. It was probably the Hat that would have made the girls wary about gossiping too much to soon—but you had to hand it to them. They'd been told not to talk, and they hadn't—and, goodness knew, there was more than enough to talk about . . .

"Of course," echoed Jemima, smothering a smile, "you've only been here five minutes, haven't you? Still, if Sourpuss and the ministry vouch for you, I can't see that it matters if you know. Good grief, everyone else does."

Miss Seeton, while understanding fewer than one word in five of the story now poured out by Jemima Wilkes, was an excellent listener. She heard of problems encountered by some of the test pilots: *Switch on the fuel pump at twenty-five thousand feet for a boost, and what happens? Nothing happens, that's what! Just a loose wire, they're told—but what good will that be when they're out looking for Jerry? Without the pump you can't climb much higher than twenty-five—and if you can't climb, then Jerry's going to be higher than you, waiting, and you a sitting duck. You might as well give up and run right back to base.* She heard of undercarriage problems: *First thing you check when you climb inside—but what do you do if the hydraulics say it's down and the electrics say it isn't? While you're on the ground there's no question—if it wasn't locked down, the damn plane would fall over—but what if they decide to disagree when you're coming in to land? You just can't risk finding out by taking off in the first place—so back she goes to the factory again.* Even the delivery pilots themselves were complaining: *Those gun sights, now. They're reflectors, so they need a lightbulb—bright in the day, dark at night. So in daylight the bulbs burn out in no time, and the pilots have three spares to save having to return to base. Well, there was I delivering a kite the other day when I happened to look at the rack of spares—and they were all duds—all three blown already!*

Miss Seeton said that, of course, while she didn't understand how a gun sight worked, she could certainly see, as it were, that a pilot with no spare bulbs wouldn't—well, see, either—or rather, would see he had no spares but wouldn't see the gun sights . . . and she could also see that there did seem to be—well, something wrong, from what she had heard.

"Indeed," she cried, "what you say—what you imply—is disgraceful!" Her technical knowledge might be nil, but she was no fool. "Why, it's—it's treachery! It ought to be stopped!"

Jemima smiled sadly for her new friend's indignation. "Stop it?" she said. "We don't even know how it started—or how it's been able to continue for so long. The only thing we know . . ." She paused. "The only thing we think we know," she amended, "is that it must be one of us. Someone on the factory payroll, I mean, not someone from outside—not even from the village—because nobody from outside is allowed on site. You must have seen that for yourself," she added as Miss Seeton stirred and seemed about to speak. "I'll bet George on the gate was pretty careful—thorough—about letting you in, wasn't he? Not to mention Old George in the admin, block!"

She grinned at Miss Seeton. "No, your ears don't deceive you," she reassured her. "We're a very patriotic lot in this factory, apart from—well, anyway, it's a weird coincidence, but half the men on site seem to have been named after the royal family. There's Day George on the gate—the night chap is Albert—and Old George with his arm, or rather without it, not forgetting George Watkins, the head electrician—but never mind all that. What I'm saying is that nobody from outside gets in here without a very good reason. You'll have seen the ack-ack positions around the perimeter, but do you know about the patrols?" Miss Seeton intimated that she did not. Jemima chuckled.

"They call them the Beaver's private army," she said. "All the aircraft factories in the country have their own LDV, except we have to call them Home Guard now, thanks to Churchill, and I do think it sounds better, because they *will*

162

guard us, if and when the occasion arises. Rumour has it that Beaverbrook somehow . . . intercepted a shipment of weapons from America before it left the docks, though they were meant for the public LDV—and we have the guns as well as our armoured cars—the Beaverettes. Every ministry property is guarded night and day . . ."

"Which is why you suspect the—the guilty party to be an insider," said Miss Seeton, who disapproved of melodrama even at a time like this, but who could think of no better way of putting it.

"Security's as strict as they can make it," said Jemima. "But it's not strict enough to stop the sabotage, if it *is* sabotage—though it does stop outsiders coming in, which is how we know . . ."

"I see," said Miss Seeton after a pause. "If, as you say, it is indeed sabotage, then one is in the uncomfortable position of having to suspect everybody—and, with everyone concentrating so hard upon the task at hand, there can be few opportunities for what could be called the—the normal bouts of wandering attention, which is when one might expect to notice anything that was—was out of the ordinary. Or anybody," she added thoughtfully.

"You've got it," agreed Jemima. "It's the very devil of a problem, and until he's caught . . ."

"Yes," murmured Miss Seeton. She frowned. "Not an outsider, then . . . But . . ." It was, she knew, her patriotic duty to suggest the possibility, although she felt wretched at pointing the finger of suspicion towards one who had been so kind—so helpful . . . "But has anyone considered, for instance . . . the doctor? He gave me to understand that he is a—a not infrequent visitor here, and I wondered—that is, was it not Mr. Chesterton, in his clever short story, who showed how a man may be visible and invisible, seen and unseen, at one and the same time? Or the laundry man, or the plumber, or other visitors of that sort," she concluded, a little breathlessly.

Jemima nodded. "It's a thought . . . But he would need to outsmart an awful lot of people—and don't think we haven't jumped through the same hoops as you! On the rare—very rare—occasions when outsiders have to be let into the factory, the security crowd makes sure their access is carefully restricted." She grinned again. "Your Dr. Huxter, Emily, has to wait at the gate while George phones for an escort to the sick bay—he's never allowed on the floor."

Miss Seeton dismissed her immediate vision of the burly doctor vanquished by a muscle-man in a wrestling bout. *On the floor*, it seemed clear, must be a collective reference to the factory buildings.

This was confirmed by Jemima's next words. "Talking of which," she went on, "perhaps we should start the guided tour. It'll keep Sourpuss Morris off your back—and mine— if we can tell her you've checked a few things out—and, who knows? You might spot something out of the ordinary that will give us a line on this damned saboteur."

"I would think it unlikely," said Miss Seeton as Jemima led the way down the road towards the nearest brick-and-breeze-block edifice with its camouflage paint, shuttered windows, and, on closer inspection, Air Force wings moulded into the guttering and downpipes. "I know nothing of industrial work, and—"

"Didn't Sourpuss say you were some kind of artist?" her companion broke in with an impatient gesture. "Well, there you are! Keen-eyed, alert—it's worth a try—so let's get going, so you can see for yourself."

They reached the double doors that stood open and from which, as they drew closer, Miss Seeton had begun to hear an indescribable clamour bursting forth. Indeed, from the level of noise that assailed her ears as they went inside, she was amazed that she had caught even a syllable of what Jemima had been saying as they headed in that direction. Now that they were well inside she saw—and heard—that it was a huge, high-roofed, echoing, whirring, rattling, banging, clanging cave lit by stark white lights, crowded with people and machines and movement, and smelling of heat and dust and oil and perspiration.

Jemima, grinning at her evident confusion, grabbed her by the arm and, as they walked down the central gangway, set about a running commentary in a voice she projected above the general hubbub of the factory floor in a manner reminiscent of Miss Davidson, games mistress at Miss Seeton's old school. "Daisy" Davidson's lungs had been developed to maximum capacity by years of galloping about hockey fields, shinning up and down ropes at speed, and vaulting wooden horses with style, aplomb, and considerable vigour. It was with equal vigour that, as they moved from building to building at a pace that gave Miss Seeton no time to think, Jemima Wilkes held forth on such varied topics as Vernier gauges, watchmakers' lathes, rivets, power presses, draw bench dies, blanking and dishing tools, fly presses, drilling jigs, and flat-bottom forming. Miss Seeton's head began to spin with both the barrage of manufacturing sound, and the barrage of mostly unintelligible information.

While they were in the Machine Shop, a loud and sudden clanging rent the air. Nobody except Miss Seeton took any great notice of the clanging, though it was evident from the demeanour of those working at the nearby capstans, lathes, and drills that it was welcome.

"Tea trolley's on the way," said Jemima, as Miss Seeton glanced about her in case it was, after all, a fire alarm. It had sounded so like the bell at school . . . "Can't waste time letting everyone trot off to the canteen," Jemima said with another grin. "But—talking of wasting time, d'you think you've seen enough to be going on with? I'd hate to overwhelm you all at once"—Miss Seeton, tactfully, said nothing—"and if I know Sourpuss, she'll be expecting you back with your report even though she's trying to pretend you don't work for her really . . ."

This, Miss Seeton decided, as she hurried in Jemima's wake from the Machine Shop, was her new friend's diplomatic way of explaining that she had now spent (if not, indeed, wasted) an hour of her valuable time with Miss Seeton when she could have been better employed elsewhere. As to what, exactly, a ferry pilot did when not ferrying, Miss Seeton could only guess, but it was sure to be more important than sketching people at work making fighter aircraft when, truth to tell, she would—had she but the skill and the training—have preferred to be making the fighters herself . . .

Miss Seeton's brain, as she stood catching her breath in the outside air, was awhirl with the many and varied industrial sights and sounds and smells she had never encountered—had never expected to encounter—in her life before. Was there talk of *time*? It would indeed take time for her to absorb all she had just seen and heard and smelled: the various buildings—no, shops—of the factory had been a riot (though on close inspection an organised riot) of urgent rhythm, ringing echoes, and (except in the Drawing Office, where it was almost peaceful, and the Sewing Shop, where peace ended when Beryl and Ruby spotted her) an all-pervading hot, metallic, oily, dusty, acrid reek so pungent she wondered how Miss Wilkes—Jemima—had been able to inhale without choking, never mind delivering that crisp, efficient commentary on what was happening, and why.

Miss Seeton breathed again, more slowly. Major Haynes had asked her, on behalf of Section G (Godfrey? Gilbert?) to record her impressions: did he realise the magnitude of the task with which he had presented her? Yet in time of war each must perform to the best of his or her abilities. If sketches were what the ministry required of her, then she would sketch—although whether her official, as she ought (she supposed) to call them, employers would be able to make use of the flurry of images now crowding her senses, she did not know. All she now knew was that she would be thankful to return to the peace of her—no, *their*, she supposed, since Mrs. Morris had tacitly agreed that they should share it . . . to the peace of *the office*, Miss Seeton compromised, with an uneasy blush.

Besides, had she not left her sketching block and pencils in the discreet corner she had chosen for her own? As a welfare officer, she might not be able—or, by Mrs. Morris, allowed—to play a useful part in the war effort, but, pedestrian though her artistic talents might be, they could not be denied. She would start work at once.

Yet Miss Seeton's resolution was more easily formed than fulfilled. Mrs. Morris, already busy at her desk when her new assistant slipped quietly back into the Welfare Office, threw herself at once into updating her files and began a series of telephone calls Miss Seeton did not care to interrupt. Mislaid and/or damaged and/or wrongly stamped ration books, complaints from landladies about lodgers and countercomplaints from lodgers about their billets, lost or damaged laundry, and the transport problems of female staff until recently refused permission to sleep overnight on factory premises, were far more important than a request (however briefly worded) for a plan of the site so that she could wander and sketch, within the limits appointed by security, at will.

Miss Seeton's continued quietness, as Mrs. Morris continued to talk, was not stillness. The younger woman was unable to sit for long as a mere observer. The competence of Mrs. Morris much impressed her: Miss Seeton always liked to watch an expert at work, and she approved of the enthusiasm with which her superior tackled the job in hand, even if she suspected that the other's concentration might not be as thorough as first appearances would suggest. Her years in school staffrooms had left Miss Seeton fully conversant with manifestations of professional jealousy, but, as she knew herself to be no serious threat to Mrs. Morris, she felt sure that Mrs. Morris would, in time, come to know it, too. She must, meanwhile, do nothing to disturb her superior further. She must remain silent, unobtrusive, and without motion . . .

It was her fingers that betrayed her. More restless than she, they selected a pencil, opened the sketchbook, and presented Miss Seeton with a tempting blank page that she very soon filled with swift strokes and skilful hatchings of light and shade and movement to produce a not unflattering likeness. There was Mrs. Morris, neat and trim in a steel-grey suit that matched her sober curls—a suit from whose jacket pocket a starched white handkerchief peered with a prim, triangular eye. Mrs. Morris was making hurried yet detailed notes on a scrap of paper . . .

Mrs. Morris was looking—glaring—at her. "Seeton," said Mrs. Morris tightly, "is that by any chance *me* you have been—have been doodling in such a ridiculous and impertinent and—and distracting fashion?"

Miss Seeton, with a guilty blush, confessed her fault and, as Mrs. Morris did not relax the glare, meekly passed to her the sketchbook her outstretched hand demanded. There was a thoughtful silence.

"I don't care to have my photograph taken," said Mrs. Morris at last. "Heaven knows, Seeton, I am sufficiently stiff in my manner not to want it . . . preserved in black-and-white to make me feel—But never mind." She cleared her throat. "This isn't bad—it's not bad at all. Why, just by looking you can tell how busy I am—how many burdens a job of this nature lays upon those of us who do it properly—conscientiously . . . And this is what the ministry wants you to show the rest of the country, I suppose. That we are working—working hard—on their behalf. Am I right?"

Miss Seeton murmured that such was her understanding.

A dry chuckle creaked at her from the far side of the desk. Mrs. Morris was almost smiling as she said, "But where you got the idea I had a handkerchief, I can't imagine. Are you a mind reader? No, you must have been here while I was arguing with the laundry. They've lost more than a batch or two of overalls in the past fortnight—I haven't a handkerchief to my name anymore, and I'm not the only one—still, it's a good likeness. If this is your usual standard . . ."

She took the younger woman's blush for one of pleasure at having her skill appreciated, her presence approved. She did not realise that Miss Seeton had suddenly recalled the remarks of Jemima Wilkes about Mrs. Morris, Mr. Coleman the works manager, and the dropping of handkerchiefs . . .

As Miss Seeton coughed, Mrs. Morris creaked out another chuckle. "You're hinting that you want to be off about your business," she deduced. "Well, I've no objection—but do you think you can find your way around without bothering people? Assuming the Wilkes girl did as I asked her, you shouldn't find it too much of a problem."

Her mention of Jemima had Miss Seeton blushing again for that unfortunate handkerchief, but she covered her confusion by putting her request for a site plan, if such a document existed, so that she would need to trouble as few people as possible as she moved around the factory and sketched.

Mrs. Morris looked at her again. She hesitated. "You're not to remove it from the premises," she said at last. "You must keep it with you at all times, and let nobody else see it. You must sign for it each time you take possession, and you don't leave here until I have countersigned that you've returned it—is that clear?"

Miss Seeton assured her that it was.

"Good," said Mrs. Morris. "We must never, never forget that there's a war on!"

Chapter 17

The end of her first day at the Spitfire factory found Miss Seeton as weary as she had ever been in her life. Not even standing for hour upon hour at the King's Cross canteen, repeatedly washing cups or pouring tea for servicemen in transit, had been so draining; and as she had not (she sadly reflected) started work until the day was half over, she only hoped she could cope better on the morrow.

But there had been so many new impressions to absorb— so much noise and bustle and urgency wherever she went— not that on this, her first day, she went far . . . so many new faces to remember—so many strange words and phrases of a technical nature with which she must quickly familiarise herself if she was to understand anything of aircraft manufacture and, in her sketches, to depict—to interpret—it for the ministry's leaflets and the national morale . . .

Mrs. Morris examined the floor plan closely when, just before six o'clock, Miss Seeton brought it back. Whether or not she suspected some attempt at illicit tracing on the younger woman's part, the welfare officer did not say; but at last she nodded, refolded the plan, and produced from a locked drawer the small black receipt book in which she and her assistant would sign and countersign each time the document was entrusted to a different custodian.

"You haven't worn your pencil to a stub, I notice," said Mrs. Morris, having consigned both plan and receipt book to the drawer and returned the key ring to her jacket pocket. "Wasn't there enough going on to catch your interest?"

Miss Seeton smiled a little ruefully as she answered that there had been rather too much going on for her to be anything other than interested. "It is," she explained, "always a pleasure to watch experts at work—but with my sadly limited understanding of—of exactly *what* was going on, I fear the number of useful sketches I have drawn is likewise limited, although I hope to do better tomorrow, once I have asked a few questions. One cannot, of course, disturb people at their work—such vital work—but *after* work I might perhaps—"

"Careless talk costs lives!" The eyes of Mrs. Morris flashed as she slapped an insistent hand on her desk and made Miss Seeton jump. "The girls have been strictly forbidden to chatter about their work, particularly in public—and especially on the bus, and—"

"I was not talking about the bus!" Miss Seeton's eyes, too, could flash in anger: so much anger that, despite her upbringing and background, she had been moved to interrupt. "I trust, Mrs. Morris," said the daughter of Major Hugo Monk Seeton, VC, "that I understand the meaning of security as well as anyone. I would, however, be greatly surprised if Mrs. Beamish's house, where I am billeted with several other of the female factory staff, is a hotbed of—of spies and fifth columnists." She disliked the melodrama, but really: how else could she make this woman see her point? "What

172

I had intended," she went on more calmly, "was to take one or two of the girls aside this evening and ask for advice, no more than that, as to which parts of the factory, and which processes, I might most usefully observe tomorrow."

"Oh," said Mrs. Morris. She could not bring herself to apologise for the misunderstanding: there was a war on, and vigilance was a national watchword. "Yes, I see. Which of the girls—?"

This time the interruption came from a tap on the door. Mrs. Morris frowned, but then sighed as the door failed to open, and called for whoever it was outside to enter.

"Excuse me, Mrs. Morris, it was Miss Seeton I was looking for," said Beryl once her turbaned head, peeping round the door, had been followed by the rest of her. "Hello, Emily," she added as Miss Seeton smiled at her in some relief. "All done? Ready to go home?"

"Thank you, yes." Miss Seeton smiled again, glanced at Mrs. Morris, received another of the older woman's nods, and took it as a licence to depart. She gathered up her belongings and glanced once more at Mrs. Morris. "Until tomorrow morning," said Miss Seeton, and thankfully took her leave as Mrs. Morris achieved a final, still-silent nod.

"She's a dragon, that one," said Beryl, giggling as she led the way back down the corridor, past one-armed George in his uniform behind the hatch, and out into the fresh air. "A holy terror," went on Beryl, hurrying her companion down the path to where the surly Day George stood on guard in his wooden hut. "I bet she's been giving you a hard time!"

Miss Seeton thought it tactful to change the subject. "Where is Ruby?" she enquired as George waved them through the gates towards a cluster of young women whose faces, and certainly whose voices, she recognised from the morning. "I thought you girls did everything together. I trust she has not been taken ill?"

Beryl giggled again. "We tossed for it, and I lost," she said, and then blushed. "Sorry, Emily, that didn't come out like—it sounds so—I mean, I didn't mean to be rude, honest. What I should've said is that it's more Ruby won than me losing—about which of us came to fetch you for the bus, see, and which of us got to fetch Tilly's bag of sweepings from the cleaner."

Miss Seeton recalled Mrs. Beamish's remarks that morning as her lodgers left the house, and a faded blue linen bag that clanked. "Sweepings from the cleaner?" she prompted as they attached themselves to the outskirts of the cluster, which greeted them with vague smiles and carried on talking. Now that they were not such complete strangers, Miss Seeton had time to notice that several of the girls carried faded blue bags of their own.

"He's new," said Beryl. "Been here a couple of weeks, I suppose. Quite old—he must be forty if he's a day—but ever so good-looking, for all he's a conchie . . ."

Miss Seeton wondered why being a conscientious objector should preclude the possession of good looks, but had the wisdom not to voice the thought aloud.

". . . or else," Beryl chattered on at her side, "there's something wrong with him—that doesn't show, diabetes or something—because if he was healthy you'd think he'd want to do his bit at a time like this, wouldn't you? And he'd look smashing in uniform, I'm sure he would."

Miss Seeton murmured a noncommittal reply to which her companion paid no attention.

"I suppose," conceded Beryl, "somebody has to sweep the floor—but it just seems such a waste of a bloke like him. Not that he isn't doing a valuable job, Emily, don't think he's a passenger on this ship! We all do our best not to drop things, but often you can't help it, and if there's rubbish left lying around we might have a fire, what with sparks and all from some of the processes, and everything so crowded. And *they* go for sorting when the rest is thrown away—nuts and bolts and rivets and screws and things. Tilly and the other old dears in the village, we take them the bags and they give 'em back next day, all labelled and everything ready to be used again."

"Which," offered Miss Seeton as Beryl came to a halt, "must result in a considerable saving of metal and—and manufacturing effort—and, indeed, of money, too." She considered her own neat-fingered talent—basic stitchery, a little sculpture and collage work—and decided that, with her sketching necessarily limited to factory hours, she was not doing nearly enough for her country. As soon as they were home she would ask Mrs. Beamish if she needed an assistant; and she hoped her landlady would be more amenable to that assistance than Mrs. Morris had seemed to be.

Above the laughter and gossip from the others they heard the patter of approaching feet, accompanied by clanking that Miss Seeton, following Beryl's explanation, knew at once for the sound of nuts, bolts, rivets, screws, and similar metal items being shaken together as whoever carried them hurried on her way. She looked towards the sound, and saw Beryl's not-twin sister.

"Why, here is Ruby," she said.

"And there's the bus," chorused the others, who had been looking in the other direction. Red-haired Muriel, Lord Haw-Haw's mischievous echo, waved at Miss Seeton.

"Keep well back," she warned, "until the night shift has got off, or you'll be trampled in the rush!"

Pink-cheeked and breathless, Ruby joined her sister and friends. "Just made it," she said as the night-shift workers began pouring off the bus and the day shift waited to climb on. "I wouldn't have wanted to walk in this heat! But he kept me talking . . ." She caught Beryl's quizzical grin and giggled. "Well, it would have been rude to hurry away," she finished with another giggle.

"He's too old for you, young Ruby," said Muriel, who had spotted Ruby's clanking linen burden and brandished her own faded blue in sympathy. "Beryl, you ought to keep a closer eye on this kid. She's still wet behind the ears—and you know what they say about men who prey on innocent girls . . ."

"They say they give them a ruddy good time!" shrieked someone who then collapsed in howls of laughter in which everyone except Miss Seeton, who managed a smile, joined.

With minimal pushing and elbowing by its passengers, the bus was soon filled. Seats were claimed in an orderly fashion that surprised Miss Seeton, until she realised that all the workers except herself had had several months to learn the ropes. She had been too bewildered to notice much that morning, but the system had no doubt been the same: she was thankful to Beryl and Ruby for having again squeezed her between them into a bench made for two. She might have committed some shocking faux pas had she been left to her own devices.

The jokes about Ruby's youth and the chances of her se-duction by an older man soon palled, and the girls turned to other matters: wireless programmes, what was on at the cinema in the nearby town, and the difficulty of obtaining lipstick, powder, and nail varnish to impress men of whatever age were discussed in a shrill fortissimo gabble that must, Miss Seeton reflected as she had before, have made it hard for the driver of the bus to concentrate.

Ruby nudged Miss Seeton, and jangled her blue linen bag. "I wasn't going to say so in front of the others, Emily, but he might do for you—being a bit older than the rest of us, no offence meant."

Miss Seeton, her cheeks pink—although this could have been caused by the heat inside the crowded bus—assured her that no offence had been taken. One could hardly argue with the fact that she was, indeed, by several years senior to most of the other girls who worked at the factory . . .

"That's what I thought," Ruby said. "And if you haven't got a chap of your own—well, you could look farther and fare a lot worse. Couldn't she, Beryl?"

Beryl agreed that she could, and both sisters giggled. Neither of them noticed that Miss Seeton's cheeks had grown pinker as she murmured something they did not hear.

"I've already put in a word for you," said Ruby, once the giggles had subsided. "Told him there was a new girl just started—well, I didn't think you'd mind, 'cos if I'd said you were one of the bosses, not that you act like it, but he's not to know—well, it might have scared him off, him being just a cleaner for all he speaks so posh. He's got a lovely voice," she ended wistfully.

"For a conchie," added Beryl. "She's right, Emily, he has—he sounds far too healthy for someone who's not joined up, but if you didn't mind that, he'd suit you a treat."

Anxious to divert her young friends from this kindly but embarrassing interest in her love life, Miss Seeton slipped into schoolteacher mode and reminded them that this was (she was proud to say) still a free country, which was why they were fighting the war; and whether or not one felt that pacifism, against an enemy such as Hitler, was justified, one had (she felt) to respect the right of others to hold the opinion that it was. Especially (she went on) as, from what Beryl had told her earlier, there was no indication other than his lack of uniform that the gentleman under discussion was in fact a pacifist. There were many people who, for one reason or another, had not received their call-up papers on the outbreak of war, or who had personal or—or family reasons for not volunteering at once . . .

Miss Seeton blinked and fell silent as a sudden vision of Alice, giving her daughter a farewell hug and trying to smile, drove all other thoughts from her mind.

Beryl glanced at her and glared at Ruby, who took the hint and at once began to sing again the praises of the man who swept the floor. His name was Raymond Raybould, which sounded (and was) daft—only not the way *he* said it—and he was tall, with brown hair and a lovely smile to match his voice, and when he smiled his eyes twinkled, and they were as blue as any she'd ever seen . . .

Miss Seeton found herself admitting to a preference for brown eyes, at which Beryl and Ruby squealed with glee.

"Oh, Emily! *We* know who drove you from the station last night," cried Beryl.

"And aren't you a fast worker?" exclaimed Ruby with one of her giggles. "But come to think of it, Dr. Huxter might just do for you, at that—being the right age, and ever so sympathetic when you're poorly."

"And a doctor's a good, steady job," added Beryl. "Mind you, he's nowhere near as handsome as Ray . . ."

Both girls sighed. Squashed between these two romantic chatterboxes, Miss Seeton also sighed: but hers was not the enjoyable distress of teenage daydreaming. She was thinking that a doctor's job was indeed a steady one; she feared for what the future might bring, and how much more busy in his work poor Dr. Huxter could very soon become—

Miss Seeton stopped herself right there. *Alarm and despondency!* She, being older than these children, should be setting an example, not . . . *wallowing*. It wasn't as if she had voiced her pessimistic—her sadly realistic—thoughts aloud, but it was the principle that mattered.

She knew she was unpractised in the art of badinage, but she had to say *something*.

"Perhaps," she suggested with an attempt at a twinkle, "I should look at Mr. Raybould first, to see if I—if I like him? Then, should I do so, he might be persuaded to . . . to change the colour of his eyes by means of one of the cosmetic tricks that are, I believe, not unknown among film stars—if more than a little expensive—but of course, if he is as good-looking as you have given me to understand, he would consider it money well spent . . ."

The sisters were giggling again. Miss Seeton smiled for their merry innocence, and they giggled even more, mistaking her smile for one of mischief shared.

"I'll tell Ray tomorrow that you're sort of keen on the doctor," promised Ruby, giving the bag of metal sweepings a little shake. "When we fetch another lot for Tilly—make him a bit jealous, see?"

"That's a good idea," chimed in Beryl. "Mustn't let him think he's the only pebble on the beach, you know."

"No," agreed Miss Seeton absently, and set the sisters giggling all the more.

"Or the only fish in the sea," said Ruby.

"Or the only horse in the race—gee up, there!" cried Beryl, bouncing on the badly sprung seat. "Gee up!"

Miss Seeton smiled again. Gavin? Guy?

Miss Seeton, despite her silent strictures on romantic daydreaming, drifted off into a world of her own . . .

Chapter 18

Miss Seeton's second day at work went noticeably better than her first. There was only a brief altercation with George on the gate; uniformed George waved his one arm and grinned at her through the hatch as she hurried by; and Mrs. Morris was almost cordial as she unlocked her desk and extracted the floor plan without which her unwanted assistant would remain under her feet all day.

As the hours passed, Miss Seeton, armed with her sketch-book, her pencils, and the plan, grew ever bolder, ranging farther and farther afield in her search for suitable information leaflet sketches. Yesterday she had elected to stay in the relatively familiar territory around which Jemima Wilkes had guided her, but now she took heart and began to slip through doors she had never opened before. Here her questioning of Ruby and Beryl the previous evening proved its worth, for after asking her business and (having checked with Mrs. Morris) accepting her answers, none of the foremen tried to throw her out, but let her settle herself in some unobtrusive spot to watch—and to draw.

While she acknowledged that there remained large gaps in her understanding of what went on, Miss Seeton felt reasonably confident that she had grasped the basics of Spitfire man-ufacture, and felt sure that Major Haynes would not find her work entirely useless. She was rather less certain that she would grow accustomed to the noise, the smell, and the bustle wher-ever she went. Even in the canteen there was no relief. People began gobbling their meals as soon as the plates came into their hands: nobody settled for more than five minutes at table, and Miss Seeton shuddered for their digestive systems. King's Cross and Euston had never seemed so urgent. She asked the helpers when she could sketch the room empty, for contrast.

"You can't," they told her. "It never is. We're working round the clock here, remember! If they aren't eating, then we're clearing the tables or mopping the floor or getting the next lot of grub ready . . ."

By the end of the afternoon, Miss Seeton, even using both sides of the page, had filled well over half the sketchbook. She had also blunted her pencil three times. She wondered what would happen once the blade of her pocket sharpener was likewise blunted. There was a war on: metal was in short supply: salvage was all important, as witness last night's sort-ing labours of Tilly at the kitchen table, though Mrs. Beam-ish had refused her help on the grounds that this was expert work. Miss Seeton, hurrying to return the floor plan to Mrs. Morris, resolved that at the earliest opportunity she must find a shop that sold penknives. Or might she be able to obtain a supply of small blades from Major Haynes? This drawing job was, after all, for the government . . .

Miss Seeton blushed.

Miss Seeton stopped as a voice called her by name: the voice of a man, hailing her from a distance so that she did not—could not—recognise it.

No doubt the warmth in her cheeks was caused by her hurry to return the plan of the factory to the custody of Mrs. Morris and the safety of the locked desk drawer.

"Miss Seeton?" The voice—the man—drew closer.

Miss Seeton braced herself and turned back in the direction of the voice and the queer, clanking footsteps that accompanied it.

"Oh," she said as a man—tall, brown-haired, wearing khaki dungarees and carrying a large broom—approached. As he did so she saw that in his other hand he carried a linen bag that might once have been blue. His eyes, she saw as he came closer, were undeniably blue.

"Miss Seeton?" The man in dungarees grinned down at her. "I'm Ray Raybould," he added, little realising that he had no need to introduce himself. Or did he realise? Did he know how very good-looking—unforgettably good-looking—he was?

Perhaps he did. His grin, as he saw Miss Seeton's expression, smoothed itself to a smile of (it really could not be denied) undoubted charm. "The girls," he said, "have told me all about you, so I know you lodge with Ma Beamish. And I thought—as I spotted you by chance—that it would save time if I gave these to you, rather than to one of the others. That is, it'll save time later—so they won't risk missing the bus if I don't happen to be where they expect to find me."

He held out the once-blue linen bag, and it clanked as Miss Seeton took it. "Nuts and bolts," she said, nodding. "Rivets, and screws, and—and washers . . ."

"I can trust you to pass 'em on to Tilly?" He made the question as close to an instruction as good manners would permit. Meekly Miss Seeton told him that he could.

"Thought so," he replied with another smile. Having handed over his burden, Raymond Raybould seemed to have no great desire to rush back to work. He leaned on his broom and smiled again. "How are you settling in, Miss Seeton?" he enquired, his blue eyes twinkling.

Miss Seeton thanked him and said that she thought, all things considered, she had been fortunate to have found such good friends at her lodgings. Without the great kindness of Beryl and Ruby she could not have made as much sense of her appointed task as she believed, with their help, she had managed to do. "But of course," she concluded, "they are both very nice girls."

"They are indeed," he said promptly, and chuckled. "You think they've got some prior claim, do you?" he went on once he had stopped smiling. "Nothing of the sort, I assure you. Footloose and fancy-free, that's yours truly!"

He pushed himself upright from the broom and swept her a deep, almost mocking, bow.

Miss Seeton frowned. Whether or not he was the conscientious objector Beryl and Ruby suspected him to be, there was something . . . uncomfortable about Mr. Raybould. Something . . . not genuine: some impression of falsehood, of pretence, of acting a part. As he bowed with the broom in his hand, a sudden vision of a knight in armour with his spear or bannered lance at his side, had flashed into her mind. She blinked—it was gone—but the memory, the impression, was not gone. Raymond Raybould was not what he seemed, and her fingers itched to set that vision down on paper before it should fade entirely. Major Haynes, after all, had asked her to inform him of anything out of the ordinary . . .

"You look puzzled, Miss Seeton, and a little flushed." Raymond's tone was sympathetic. "You're hot and tired, of course. It must be quite a new experience for you, working in industry."

Miss Seeton agreed that her particular experience of work had been very different.

"An artist, they tell me," he prompted.

"A teacher of art," Miss Seeton politely corrected him. At first, thinking of Major Haynes and his insistence on security, she had hoped nobody would know, but that hope (she now realised) had been naive. Even a glimpse of her, sketching busily nearby, must have been enough for everyone to work out that she was either a professional artist, or an amateur so talented the government was happy to employ her. Her innate honesty could not allow any misapprehension to persist. Her talent, she knew, was not so great: she was competent, no more; and while there were indeed professional artists who (in her opinion) were very little more than competent, they yet contrived to earn a living from their art, which she had never done—and could not expect to do so for the duration. One could hardly regard the rate of government pay as overgenerous. The major had explained that she would be classed as a Civil Service Shorthand-Typist, adding with one of his smiles that he feared wrangling over her geographic status looked likely to continue for some time. She was based in the Tower, in London, and London rates of pay were higher: but she might be asked to work at any time anywhere in the country, and provincial rates were lower. Seventy-five shillings a week in London, seventy-two shillings out of town—either way, Miss Seeton now reflected, she must not expect to make her fortune.

But of course there was a war on . . .

"I thought," said Raymond Raybould, "that teaching was a reserved occupation—nurturing the impressionable minds of younger generations, and so forth. You strike me as the conscientious type." He glanced at the factory floor plan in Miss Seeton's hand. It was folded, and she held it close to her side. "So what on earth made you come to work in a place like this?"

Miss Seeton thought of Major Haynes, and of that coat-of-arms-headed paper she had signed in the Tower. She drew herself up and gazed into the piercing blue eyes of the man in dungarees. "One might as well," she told him, "ask the reason for *your* presence here, Mr. Raybould, when other men of your—of our—generation are already in uniform."

Raymond let out a yelp of laughter. "Touché!" he cried, and threw the broom into the air, catching it without looking as it fell back. "Suppose I were to tell you that I was a pacifist?"

Slowly Miss Seeton shook her head. "Those with strong views on such matters prefer medical to industrial work, or so I have been told."

"Good grief, I'm no doctor!"

"Neither am I," returned Miss Seeton promptly. "But a basic training in first aid does no harm to anyone—on the contrary, may well do a great deal of good, as I know from my teaching experience. If, however, you are uneasy with the idea of blood, which (again from my own experience) I will concede may be the case with the most unexpected persons, your physical strength could be applied to the national cause in a far more suitable way than sweeping a factory floor.

Whether or not," she added with a shake of the blue linen bag, "the sweepings are useful."

"I can't drive," said Raymond, "if it's ambulance work you're thinking of."

"The fire service," countered Miss Seeton, "would be only too glad to have you volunteer, I imagine."

"Suppose," said Raymond, "that I told you I wanted to do something *now*? The blitzkrieg could start at any minute, we all know that—and firefighters will be needed as well as ambulance drivers—but it hasn't happened yet. And—well, this is at least *something*, Miss Seeton."

Miss Seeton remembered Beryl and Ruby, who didn't want to trim hats when there was a war on, and who thought parachutes were defeatist. A smile began to curve her lips.

"It is indeed," she replied, and shook the bag again.

Raymond returned the smile with interest. "It might," he ventured to tease, "be something just a little more . . . productive than your sketches, Miss Seeton—toward the war effort, I mean."

Before she could reply, he hurried on: "What does Mr. Coleman think about having you here? He's a holy terror for efficiency, I can vouch for that—and, with all due respect to your good self . . ."

"Mr. Coleman?" For a moment Miss Seeton was puzzled. "Oh, yes, the manager. I have no idea what he thinks, Mr. Raybould, about me or—or anything else." She wondered if in this she spoke the truth: she recalled Mrs. Morris having said something about the Spanish Civil War—but what? She decided the subject should be abandoned. "Our paths," she informed Raymond steadily, "have not yet crossed, and indeed I see no reason why they should." Then she recalled how Mrs. Morris had emphasised the conscientious nature of the works manager, and felt her cheeks grow warm. "It would," she concluded, "be an impertinence on my part, Mr. Raybould, when there must be far more important matters to occupy him."

Raymond laughed again. "Meaning I should be getting on with my work and let you get on with yours? You're right, Miss Seeton, I should. So I will. You won't leave the bag behind when you run for the bus, will you? There's quite a lot to be sorted this evening. On a day as hot as this, no disrespect, but everyone's sweating. And slippery hands drop things very easily, don't they?"

With another smile, and a skillful toss of his broom high in the air and back into an unseeing hand, he bowed to Miss Seeton, turned on his heel, and without looking round headed off down the corridor, whistling as he went.

The knight who this time flashed upon Miss Seeton's inward eye had the visor of his helmet firmly closed. Though she had been talking to him for almost five minutes, she felt she knew even less about Raymond Raybould than she had before they met.

She wondered whether Major Haynes should know . . .

Chapter 19

Miss Seeton's thoughtful silence on the homeward journey went unnoticed by her friends. Beryl and Ruby having mutually decided that she had found her factory feet and could cope on her own, they waved and smiled to her as she walked through the gates, but as they had left her to make her own way from the administration block, in the same spirit they left her to find somewhere to sit on the bus and themselves joined in the laughter and chatter and gossip that passed the older woman by.

Miss Seeton continued to be thoughtful after delivering the blue bag of sweepings into Tilly's expert hands and accepting in exchange a cup of tea. She listened and smiled, but she kept quiet as Beryl and Ruby waxed eloquent about the heat, their aching backs, their weary eyes, and their plan to spend the evening after supper trying out the new hairstyle one of the other girls had shown them in one of the few picture magazines that had not yet ceased publication because of the paper shortage, though of course it was much smaller than it used to be, and they supposed it would get smaller still before it got back to its original size, after the war.

Miss Seeton pondered her sketchbook and its govern-ment-funded fellows in her bedroom, and the promises of Major Haynes that more would be available as she might request them. She remembered how the major had looked as she signed the Official Secrets Act . . . but she was far from London, and the Tower, and the assurance of the major's presence. Raymond Raybould had unsettled her. His remarks, followed as they had been by the grim expression of Mrs. Morris as the floor plan was locked away, made her feel . . .

The trouble was that she didn't know how she felt, only that she felt . . . uneasy. *Was* she wasting her time, as Mrs. Morris had implied? Mrs. Morris had not wanted an assistant—had made this fact very clear—and was just as clearly relieved that the assistant was able to occupy her time well away from the Welfare Office, leaving her superior to her own devices.

Her own, more worthwhile, devices?

At the factory next morning, Miss Seeton did not wait for Mrs. Morris to raise her head from the paperwork on her desk. On the previous day she had waited before interrupting the welfare officer's train of thought to ask for the floor plan to be unlocked, but on this occasion she went at once to stand beside the visitors' chair and coughed.

Mrs. Morris shuffled together a few sheets of paper and sighed loudly. She did not look up. Miss Seeton cleared her throat. Mrs. Morris sighed again.

"Mrs. Morris," said Miss Seeton. She did not wait for her superior to respond. "I know that you regard my appointment as both a—an impertinence, and unnecessary. But does Mr. Coleman feel as you do?"

Susan Morris jerked upright on her chair. Her sallow cheeks turned pink, and her eyes glittered.

"He is," Miss Seeton pressed quickly on, "the overall authority here, is he not? Would you feel more able to—to tolerate my presence if his—his official sanction were granted? And," she added as Mrs. Morris opened her mouth, "should he refuse to grant it, then it would be for him to—to advise the ministry that my services were not required. Would it not?"

For a moment the two women stared at each other: Miss Seeton standing, her sketching gear in her hand; Mrs. Morris flushed and still, seated openmouthed behind the desk, her knuckles white as they gripped the pencil with which she had been writing.

At last Mrs. Morris collected her startled wits. "Very well," was all she said as she pushed back her chair and rose to her feet. "Very well, Seeton."

Miss Seeton let out the breath she hadn't realised she had been holding. While she had never thought of herself as either scheming or manipulative—a gentlewoman does not take advantage of the weakness of others—surely the adage that all was fair in love and war must apply at this time even more than usual? Mrs. Morris, it was clear, did not suspect that her warm regard for the works manager was no secret from her assistant—an assistant who by training was an acute observer. Was not another adage that the looker-on saw most of the game?

The game of love. Miss Seeton hid a quiet smile as a brief vision of herself as Cupid flickered into her mind . . . Cupid armed with a bow and arrow that suddenly changed from the rose-pink toys of a Valentine card into sharp, deadly steel as vicious as any bayonet.

Miss Seeton sighed. Love—*and war* . . .

"We've no time to waste moaning," Mrs. Morris snapped as she marched past Miss Seeton on her way to the door. "Mr. Coleman could be anywhere on the premises. He might even," she added as Miss Seeton, with a blush, hurried after her into the corridor, "be asleep—in his office." And now it was the turn of Mrs. Morris to blush. "In which case," she warned, "I have no intention of disturbing him."

"Naturally I would not expect it." Miss Seeton was a little nettled that Mrs. Morris should think her either so tactless or so unobservant. With the factory working round the clock, many men had, in the national interest, refused to go home for days on end. Mothers, wives, and sisters brought in an occasional change of clothes and supplied blankets, wrapped in which their menfolk would sleep on the floor, if necessary, taking advantage of whatever private corner they could find. Her sketches had depicted several of the weary bundles that lay deaf to the industrial hubbub all around them . . .

"And the wives don't really mind," Beryl and Ruby had told her that first evening as she put her eager questions. "They know there's no risk of, well, goings-on because Mr. Coleman is ever so strict."

"*Very* prim and proper," added Beryl, and Ruby giggled her agreement. "He refuses point-blank to let any of us girls sleep over—says it might encourage the men to take liberties—but the rate they're all working, if there's a man in the place with the energy to take any sort of liberty, I'd like to meet him!"

"So would I," said Ruby with another giggle, and Miss Seeton had smiled for their sense of fun. Cheerful minds made willing hands, and willing hands worked harder . . .

"Wait there while I knock."

Miss Seeton jumped as the voice of Mrs. Morris uttered its brisk command. Perhaps (she acknowledged) she should have kept her thoughts from wandering—although what else she could more profitably have done while hurrying after her superior she did not know—but had there really been any need for the older woman to address her as if she were a recalcitrant pupil being escorted to the headmistress?

Then she smiled as she stood meekly where instructed. Of course: Mrs. Morris, already acquainted with Mr. Coleman, would be anxious to spare either the manager or the newcomer any embarrassment, even if she felt it herself. While in these urgent days the snatching of forty winks at one's desk must be no disgrace, the "prim and proper" man who grudgingly allowed his female staff to work, but firmly refused to let them sleep, in his factory overnight would greatly dislike being surprised in his whiskers, with his collar and tie undone. He did not know that such sights were familiar to Emily Seeton from her time at college, when friends of a bohemian turn of mind might elect on the spur of the moment to stay several days in one another's attics, causing much annoyance to those of their landladies who provided full bed and board.

Miss Seeton sighed. In these days of rationing, nobody now could approve such careless, carefree habits . . .

"Come on, Seeton!" Once more a brisk command from Mrs. Morris woke the younger woman from her daydream. She saw her superior beckoning from an open door, and went across to be introduced to the man who would decide her fate.

Mr. Coleman was tall, thin, pale, and more than slightly stooped. Miss Seeton had to blink several times before she could convince herself that he did not wear spectacles: the frown lines on his forehead were deep, as if he spent his every waking hour squinting myopically into the distance.

She reminded herself that here was a widower who had not only lost his son, but who held a position of great responsibility—a responsibility so great that it could be called the ultimate burden. It would not be fanciful to say that the fate of the nation, perhaps the fate of the whole free world, might depend on Mr. Coleman and his fellow managers at other aircraft factories. No wonder, then, that he should wear a permanent frown . . .

"Miss Seeton," said Mr. Coleman, smothering a yawn. Mrs. Morris had been right about his sleeping habits: Miss Seeton noted a crumpled collar, a spike of thinning hair no amount of smoothing could return to wakeful neatness, and a growth of fine, grey stubble on his hollow cheeks and jaw.

"I must apologise again," broke in Mrs. Morris above Miss Seeton's attempt to return the manager's greeting, "for the interruption, Mr. Coleman, when everyone knows how busy you are." The look she shot at Miss Seeton, and the indignation of her pink cheeks, were very eloquent. "That is," she went on, "everyone *ought* to know—ought to appreciate all the hard work and effort—"

"Yes," said Mr. Coleman, interrupting in his turn.

"Yes," echoed the hot-cheeked Mrs. Morris with another indignant look at Miss Seeton. "I'm sorry, but when Seeton here insisted—insisted—that she wanted to have you . . . approve her post officially, I—"

"Approve someone sent by the ministry?" Mr. Coleman's hand strayed to his tie, still loose from his interrupted slumbers. "The ministry assigned her to this factory, Mrs. Morris, and that is good enough for me." Tidying the knot on his tie, he began a slow, dismissive progress towards the door, encouraging his visitors to move before him. "It is not," he said, "my place to question ministry decisions, Mrs. Morris."

"I—well, yes, perhaps, but—"

On the threshold Mr. Coleman held up a white-palmed hand, and Mrs. Morris fell silent. "If," he said, "Miss Seeton's appointment is found to be an error, the ministry will sort it out in its own good time. My time—*our* time—is far too valuable to waste in what we all know would be futile argument. I would have expected you, at least, to understand this."

"Yes," replied Mrs. Morris after an unhappy little pause during which Miss Seeton wished she hadn't started this, and was first to edge her way out of the office. If her main object had been to reassure her superior that there was nothing to be done about the ministry-appointed assistant, this object might have been achieved—but the hidden hope of playing Cupid seemed to have gone badly wrong.

Miss Seeton sighed.

"I told you not to moan!" Mrs. Morris vented the tumult of her feelings on a victim she supposed would not answer back. "For goodness' sake, Seeton, don't—"

This time it was not Mr. Coleman who interrupted her; nor was it Miss Seeton.

It was the sound of running footsteps.

Miss Seeton did not recognise the girl at once, with her hair in a turban and her trim little form swathed in oil-stained overalls; but then she knew red-haired Muriel, the mimic, who came pelting into sight along the corridor and uttered a cry of relief when she saw the trio of adults standing by the manager's office.

"Oh, thank goodness—Mr. Coleman! Mrs. Morris! In the Machine Shop—we've got to call the doctor—get the first aid—there's been an accident!"

Miss Seeton saw the manager's look of surprise and heard the shocked exclamation of Mrs. Morris.

"The drive belt on number-seven lathe," panted Muriel as Mr. Coleman shook himself out of his trance and, without a word, hurried back inside his office. The redhead's voice was trembling now. "Betty was just—oh, it's awful—her p-poor face, her hands—the b-blood—and I think it's b-broken her arm—she was working flat out and it—the belt—it snapped—it just snapped . . ."

But here Muriel burst into tears. Mrs. Morris looked in the direction taken by Mr. Coleman, and glared at Miss See-ton. "You stay here and deal with this," she instructed with a nod for the sobbing Muriel. "We can't have such behaviour upsetting everyone else, or production will suffer. Tell Mr. Coleman I've gone to the Machine Shop with the first-aid kit—from my office."

Miss Seeton noticed that even at such a time the older woman couldn't help the proprietorial emphasis of the last word but one. And she sighed for the wartime shortages that had made possession of a basic first-aid kit so rare a circumstance. It puzzled her that the Machine Shop's own kit had not been called into use, but perhaps the other workers were as distressed and confused as this child here . . .

She shook Muriel by the shoulders, ignoring her tears. "Come now," exhorted the former teacher, "you must pull yourself together. If you want me to come to help your friend—what was her name? Beryl?"

"B-betty," Muriel corrected her after a moment or two with a sniff and a shudder.

"Betty," echoed Miss Seeton, moving aside to allow Mr. Coleman to stride past with a purposeful frown on his face in (she assumed) the direction of the Machine Shop. "And your name is . . .?"

"Muriel," said Muriel, sniffing and shuddering again.

"Then, Muriel, if you want me to come to help poor Betty, you must stop crying and show me the way," Miss Seeton told her firmly. "Besides," she added as Muriel blanched at this casual mention of her injured friend, "Mrs. Morris was right about not allowing production levels to fall. Should you really have left your own machine to run for help? I'm sure you meant it for the best, but the sooner we take you back, the better."

"The—the doctor?" faltered Muriel.

"Mr. Coleman has telephoned," said Miss Seeton, who had no reason to suppose he had not. "Dr. Huxter won't take any longer than necessary, I'm sure, but we mustn't waste time. Which way is the Machine Shop? We will go there at once." Allowances might, in peacetime, be made for shock; in time of war there could be no allowance made. The factory was meant to be working round the clock, and Muriel's absence from her own lathe—understandable though some might consider it—could be regarded by others as unforgivable.

And perhaps, by others still, as treachery.

Chapter 20

Miss Seeton shook young Muriel once more by the shoulders, and the girl braced herself to meet the other's grave eyes. "The Machine Shop?" prompted Miss Seeton, and Muriel nodded meekly, wiping her face with a corner of the turban that had somehow come unwound.

Then Miss Seeton remembered that to reach the Machine Shop involved going out of doors. She hesitated. Muriel, in her hurry, had been prepared to take the risk—but ought not an assistant to set as good an example as a regular welfare officer? Mrs. Morris would, by now, be well on her way to the Machine Shop with not only the first-aid kit, but no doubt also the steel helmet she had collected from the office. Perhaps there would be time—

She felt Muriel's urgent tug at her arm, and realised that on this particular occasion there was no time. As they hurried along the corridor she tried to ease her conscience by silently promising that Emily Dorothea Seeton would, in future, carry her tin hat and gas mask with her everywhere, no matter how inconvenient they might be for someone already burdened with sketchbook, pencils, and a handbag . . .

They arrived in the Machine Shop to find the foreman, his hands on his hips, bellowing at a group of anxious girls kneeling, standing, and otherwise hovering around a crumpled shape lying on the floor—a shape to which Mrs. Morris, on her knees, appeared to minister while Mr. Coleman stood in the background, looking faintly sick, and the heavy thumping roar of abandoned lathes and drills rumbled through the air.

"Get back to work, all of you!" bawled the foreman above the general hubbub. "There's nothing you lot can do for her somebody else can't do better—and it won't help the poor kid to have you crowding her—and if I don't see you back on your machines inside half a minute, I'll have all your pay packets docked if it's the last bloody thing I ever do! Don't you know there's a war on?"

A few of the girls glanced at Mr. Coleman, who could do nothing but stand and look, his face pale and his expression troubled. Miss Seeton soon realised that Betty must have passed out from pain and shock: the injured girl neither moved nor uttered a sound as Mrs. Morris mopped and soothed her, taking no notice of the pool of sticky blood in which she knelt. The pool was spreading. Miss Seeton could not suppress a shiver at the thought of what torments the child would suffer if—when—she recovered consciousness.

By Miss Seeton's side Muriel let out one shrill gasp at the sight of her stricken friend, but as Miss Seeton pulled herself together and frowned, so did Muriel try to follow her example, taking a deep breath and then, with a nod to the foreman, being one of the first to lead a return to the lathes and drills. Within a minute the only people still close to Betty were Mrs. Morris, Mr. Coleman, and Miss Seeton, the latter having been recognised by the foreman as someone who would not panic in a crisis—someone to whom it would be safe to entrust those items he had managed to take from the shop's medical box before the shrieks of Betty's neighbours brought every girl within earshot rushing to her aid and, in the rush, crowding him out.

Mrs. Morris had felt no compunction about elbowing those who stood in her path firmly out of it. Mr. Coleman, less sure of himself, had welcomed Miss Seeton as moral support, and only at her approach with additional bandages and cotton wool had he ventured any closer to the casualty.

"I daren't touch her head, but this really needs a splint," said Mrs. Morris, accepting without question both the presence of her assistant and the roll of bandage offered by Miss Seeton when the older woman tested Betty's arm. "Strap it to the side—isn't that the way to do it?"

"In the absence of a doctor, I believe so," Miss Seeton agreed. "But let us hope Dr. Huxter arrives soon—we can hardly leave her here for very long, but to risk moving her without expert advice . . ."

"What do you say, Mr. Coleman?" Mrs. Morris gave the manager a chance to wield his authority. "Should we strap her ready to be lifted on a stretcher, or just try to stop the bleeding?"

Mr. Coleman opened his mouth, closed it, and shook his head. "I'm sorry," he said at last, and they had to strain to hear him. "I couldn't—above so much noise, I didn't quite catch . . ."

"We can't just leave her like this!" Mrs. Morris almost shouted the words at him as she gestured to the helpless, motionless figure on the floor. "How long did the doctor say he would be?"

Above the racket of the machines it was difficult to make out the manager's reply, and Mrs. Morris was about to ask again when the foreman, who had been tramping up and down the lines of drills and lathes watching the girls at work, waved a thankful hand and roared a greeting.

"Hey, Doc—over here!"

The large figure of Dr. Huxter, nimble in pinstripes, advanced briskly between the piles of metal sheets and plates that stood in rows on the floor between the different machines. Not a girl raised her head as he passed by: they were desperately trying to catch up on the valuable minutes they had lost immediately after Betty's accident.

"Well, what happened?" enquired the doctor as he opened his black bag. "The message said a drive belt broke—is that right?"

"Slashed her across the front and threw her backwards," the foreman told him as Mrs. Morris and Miss Seeton rose to their feet and moved quickly aside. "Poor kid cracked her head on number-six lathe and knocked herself right out—she didn't stand a chance. Whipped her to shreds, if I'm not mistaken . . ."

"You aren't," muttered the doctor, though only Miss Seeton was near enough to hear him, and perhaps only her quick eye saw that the syringe he was busy preparing bore a label identifying the contents as morphia.

He looked up. "You haven't moved her?" he demanded as he rolled up Betty's sleeve.

"No bloody fear!" exclaimed the foreman, and then flushed for the unhappy choice of words. "Leave you to it,"

201

he said, and returned promptly to his supervisory tramping up and down.

Miss Seeton shut her eyes as the needle went into the blue-white flesh of Betty's arm, but reproached herself for her weakness and opened them in time for the doctor, glancing up, to notice her and smile. It was a fleeting smile, but encouraging; and Miss Seeton managed a shaky smile in return as she asked if there was any way either she or Mrs. Morris could be of assistance.

"Not you," said Dr. Huxter. "Too small." He looked from Mrs. Morris to Mr. Coleman. "But if you other two could get a stretcher . . ."

It seemed an eternity before the ambulance drove off towards the hospital, with Dr. Huxter following in his car. In an emergency, Miss Seeton noted, his driving seemed less erratic than at other times. He was, she decided, one of those people who thrived on a challenge . . .

Mr. Coleman watched them through the gates, sighed, and then asked Miss Seeton to take Mrs. Morris back to the Welfare Office to make her a cup of strong, sweet tea and never mind the ration.

"Th-thank you," said Mrs. Morris, who had only allowed the shock to affect her once Betty was out of sight. "B-but my—my hands . . ."

"We'll go to the cloakroom first," Miss Seeton reassured her, and ventured a comforting pat on the shoulder as the bloody fingers writhed together.

It was not until Miss Seeton was drinking her own, half-strength cup of tea—sugared, though lightly, as it would be foolish to deny she was a little shaken by recent events—it was not until then that she could reflect on how factory security was not quite as . . . well, as secure as she had been led to believe. Jemima Wilkes had been adamant that no unauthorised person was allowed to wander around as he pleased: yet Dr. Huxter had appeared in the Machine Shop without (as far as she had noticed) an escort.

Miss Seeton wondered whether the presence of herself, Mr. Coleman, and Mrs. Morris counted as an escort on the way out of the shop, and supposed that it must.

But—what about the escort on the way in?

Miss Seeton wondered whether Lord Beaverbrook's private army was less dedicated to its appointed task than his lordship believed . . .

The atmosphere on that afternoon's homeward bus was subdued. Muriel was not the only traveller who had witnessed Betty's accident, and even those who worked elsewhere on the premises knew every grisly detail, as well as a few more, by the time they had clocked out, changed their clothes, and walked to the factory gate.

Miss Seeton was quite as subdued as any. She was, she had to admit, exhausted. Mrs. Morris had continued in a state of mild shock for most of the morning, having after a few feeble attempts to assert herself left the younger woman to answer the telephone, to take messages, and even to make a few decisions on her own. The office had been busy, very busy—and so had Miss Seeton. Mrs. Morris (resolved her now harried assistant) could be indulged until what was nominally the midday break, although none of the workers ever took it; after which hour, Miss Seeton would administer a dose of the common sense that used to stand her in good stead with hysterical schoolgirls—not that Mrs. Morris was hysterical—and urge her superior to forget her own, mild affliction in the interests of the general morale.

Yet she would not have been human had she not been glad of the chance to prove herself to the older woman. While the dreadful circumstances of that chance must be deplored, they might, in the end, be somehow turned to good. Nobody, not even the normally efficient Mrs. Morris, could expect to solve alone the many problems of a workers' Welfare Office for a factory this size. Suppose (mused Miss Seeton as she made neat, quick notes on a scrap of paper) Mrs. Morris were to fall ill? Or (and here Miss Seeton had to control both her memory and her imagination) have an accident? Until now, the utter busyness of the office had not been clear to one who had most of the time been banished with her sketchbook well beyond interference range. Now, however, that Miss Seeton understood better what Mrs. Morris had to do, her conscience would not permit her to leave the older woman to cope with the work on her own.

When in the end it dawned on Mrs. Morris that Miss Seeton was coping more than adequately on her behalf, the welfare officer rallied. She could not bring herself to thank her assistant for the effort she had made, but she did not throw her out as she had done the day before. The sketchbook and pencils stayed in their corner as Miss Seeton continued, with discretion, to lift some of the administrative weight from the shoulders of Susan Morris.

By clocking-off time Miss Seeton's brain was dulled by the unaccustomed work. Sick notes, budgets, billeting problems, and ration books were very different from the sketches, paintings, and collages of her teaching days. As Miss Seeton said her goodbyes and headed for the bus, she regarded her superior with renewed respect. To have held down this job for so many months without help showed remarkable strength of will—a strength Miss Seeton doubted that she herself possessed.

But there was a war on: and crisis will often bring out the best in people, as it seemed to have done with Dr. Huxter and his driving. Hidden depths . . .

Miss Seeton smothered a yawn. Her eyelids drooped. In the muted, stifling heat of the bus, she could very easily find herself asleep . . .

"We're here, Emily!" Beryl and Ruby were shaking her awake, the shaking on Ruby's part in concert with the faint rhythmic jangles of a blue linen bag. "Come on!"

Miss Seeton snapped out of her daydream, gathered up her belongings, and followed the sisters from the bus. She was glad it was only a short walk to the house; she was glad of the cup of tea Tilly Beamish soon brewed in exchange for an account of Betty's accident the other girls were happy to provide. Miss Seeton expressed her regrets, gave nothing away, and, after a light supper, had an early night.

"You look as if you didn't sleep too well, dear," was the welcome from Tilly next morning. "Bad dreams?" It was clear she hoped the answer would be yes, so that she could dwell again on the details of what had happened to Betty, how much worse it might have been, and what could yet be to come. *Troubles never come singly*, Mrs. Beamish had warned her lodgers the previous night. *Mark my words, it won't be long before the bombs are back . . .*

"I slept very well, thank you," countered Miss Seeton a little stiffly, and again promised her troublesome conscience that she would behave better in the future. She had not slept well: her dreams had been bad. Red, furious, violent visions had repeatedly woken her as Betty's broken body crumpled time after time to the floor of the Machine Shop, her skull smashed by the flailing canvas whiplash of the broken drive belt against the unrelenting metal of the neighbouring lathe, the blood streaming from her lacerated face and hands and skull in a slow, sticky stain.

The fourth time the nightmares woke her, Miss Seeton was wrapped in a tangle of heated sheets, with her heart thumping and the back of her neck as sticky with perspiration as the back of Betty's head had been sticky with blood. Miss Seeton untangled herself, slipped out of bed, and once her eyes had grown used to the darkness, padded on bare feet across cool linoleum to the open window, where she stood breathing deeply for some minutes, gazing at the peaceful valley, listening for the drone of approaching enemy aircraft, and wondering if tonight would be the night when the silence was broken, not by desynchronised engines and ack-ack fire, but by church bells ringing the invasion alarm—the night when England fought, perhaps, her final battle.

" 'Blood, toil, tears and sweat,' " quoted Miss Seeton in a regretful murmur. When it came to the point—nobody now could realistically think the point would *not* come, even if that realism was never voiced aloud—when it came to the point would she, daughter of a soldier, be able to kill in cold—or even in hot—blood?

Blood . . .

Death . . .

"I slept very well, thank you," said Miss Seeton, hoping her blushes did not show. She was thankful indeed when Beryl and Ruby arrived with their new hairstyles and changed the subject.

The workbound bus was still a touch subdued as it rattled its way to the factory, although red-haired Muriel seemed to have taken to heart the example set by Miss Seeton the previous day and soon began imitating Lord Haw-Haw with almost as much enthusiasm as on other occasions. While telephones were few in private homes, there was a box on the village green, from which a torchlit call to the hospital just before bed had reassured Betty's best friend that the girl was thought to be out of danger, even if she would bear the scars and feel the pain for many days to come.

The news had cheered the other girls, but they giggled rather than laughed at Muriel's clowning, and a few voices questioned the reliability of the hospital statement on the grounds that if Betty had in fact died, nobody would admit it for fear of lowering morale.

"Accidents can happen, we all know that," someone with greater faith in Authority retorted.

"Well, who's to say it was an accident?" someone else re-joined with scorn.

Everyone hushed her before the dread word *sabotage* could reach the ears of the driver. Miss Seeton wondered whether she, as assistant welfare officer, should say or do something to distract them, but feared her own authority was not so great and, having hesitated, was lost.

Young Muriel had seen her hesitate and, guessing at part of the dilemma faced by her newfound ally, threw herself with yet more enthusiasm into her Lord Haw-Haw act. "The women and girls of Britain"—she sneered—"are so fearful of being injured by splinters from Jairman bombs that they now insist their milliners should fashion the season's new hats out of very thin tin plate, which will be covered with silk, velvet, or other draping material."

Ruby and Betty, former apprentice milliners, joined in the uneasy screams of mirth as Miss Seeton threw the child—not only a wonderful mimic, but blessed with an excellent, if perhaps in this instance unfortunate, memory—a grateful smile, and made a mental note to commend her to her superior as worth watching.

"Where is the *Ark Royal*?" hooted Muriel, realising that Betty's accident was preying on her mind. With imaginary binoculars she peered at an invisible ship on a horizon that, through the antiblast mesh on the windows of the bus, was equally invisible. "Ship ahoy! Full speed ahead!"

A squeal from the brakes of the bus was echoed by a shriek from young Muriel, who was jerked off her feet and sat down in a hurry. The driver cursed. Those seated nearest the front tried to see what had surprised him.

"There you are!" cried the scornful one after a moment. "I *told* you it wasn't an accident!"

Everyone jumped to her feet and headed for the door to see what had prompted this remark. Miss Seeton, more level-headed, stood on tiptoe and applied one eye to the small unmeshed diamond that was the bus company's sole concession to the idea that passengers might wish to know where they were without having to bother the driver.

The scornful one, decided Miss Seeton with a sinking heart, must be right. If Betty's accident had indeed been an accident . . .

Why were so many police cars parked in the factory yard?

Chapter 21

Miss Seeton, the first to be checked through the gates, had to blink and blink again as the face of "Day" George scowled down at her with dark fire in his eyes, an angry twist to his mouth, and—good gracious—no nose.

But then she blinked and realised with some relief that George's resentment must be directed against, not herself, but (or so she suspected) the police. His nose was out of joint, poor man, although what investigations he could have expected to carry out concerning young Betty's accident she had no idea. The gate, after all, must be guarded. There was a war on. Miss Seeton directed a quick, sympathetic smile towards the now normal-featured George, and hurried on her way to the administration block. An assistant welfare officer should set an example. In their confused eagerness to learn what was going on, the morning shift had crowded out of the bus to pester the waiting night shift about what had happened. Miss Seeton privately lamented the curiosity that would make the girls late clocking on . . . but had to concede that, if anyone were to tell her what there was to know, she could not help but be interested.

A sudden swift patter of feet sounded behind her, accompanied by a rhythmic jangle. "Emily!" cried a voice Miss Seeton knew must be Ruby's. "Oh, Emily—Miss Seeton!"

Miss Seeton turned to wait for Ruby to reach her, and saw that Beryl was in close pursuit of her sister. Both girls were pale and seemed breathless with more than the exertion of the chase; their grey eyes looked almost black and were huge in the white, strained faces.

"Oh, Emily," Ruby said with a gasp as she skidded to a halt beside Miss Seeton and brandished the jangling linen bag wildly in the air. "Oh, it—it's awful!"

As she burst into tears her sister arrived. "Don't," begged Beryl, thumping Ruby on the shoulder. "Don't, Ruby, or you'll make me, too . . ."

Schoolteacher Seeton took automatic command. "Now then, Ruby, crying never helped anyone," she told the sobbing girl with stern kindness. "And the same goes for you, my dear," she added as Beryl gulped once or twice and sniffed. "Take a deep breath, both of you, and tell me—no, Ruby, *you* tell me—what has happened to poor Betty."

"B-Betty? Oh!" Ruby uttered a little cry and hurled the linen bag to the ground. "Oh, no . . ."

Despite herself, Miss Seeton gulped. There was a quiver in her voice as she forced the question: "Is she . . . worse?"

"She—she . . . isn't," Beryl managed to bring out as her sister sobbed all the more. "Isn't . . . d-dead, I mean, but—oh, Emily, but *he* is!"

"He? Who?" enquired Miss Seeton. "And . . . dead?"

"M-m-murdered, they say." Not unnaturally, Beryl stumbled over the word. "Oh, Emily, he was—they say he was—was h-hit over the h-head . . ."

"They say," echoed Miss Seeton, who after years in the staffroom knew how rumours could start. "Who, exactly?"

Beryl answered the question she supposed Miss Seeton was putting. "R-Ray Raybould," she said, and began to cry in earnest.

"Another accident," said Miss Seeton bravely after a horrified pause. "Th-these things happen, girls, especially with everyone so tired, and people will exaggerate . . ."

She didn't sound convincing, even to herself. Had the death of the cleaner—had whatever, in fact, had happened, to whomsoever—been a routine industrial accident, there would surely be no need for the police to be on the factory premises: the cars in the front yard proved that this line of reasoning would not go far. The officers of the law had invaded Lord Beaverbrook's territory, disturbing his private army in the persons of Day George and the Local Defence Volunteers (or rather the Home Guard) for an incident far more serious than a broken arm, a scarred face, or a cracked skull. Betty, the hospital had said, would pull through. Miss Seeton suspected that the same could not be said for Raymond Raybould . . .

But there was a war on, and work to be done. Against the aerial "fury and might" of the Nazis, the Spitfires, as Mr. Churchill had warned, could expect to be launched—and in parts of the country were indeed being launched—at any moment. Those involved, in any capacity, in the manufacture of the lifesaving planes must not be allowed to shirk their obligations, no matter how dramatic the excuse.

"I'll come to help you clock in," said Miss Seeton with a final pat on each shoulder as the girls continued to sob. She bent to retrieve the blue linen bag, and as it jangled in her hand she wondered who would collect the sweepings for Tilly Beamish and her housewife friends to sort now that Raymond Raybould was dead.

If he was dead. Rumour, gossip, exaggeration . . .

"I will come with you," said Miss Seeton, and began to urge the girls back down the path in the direction of the clocking-on machine. While they were queueing she would try to find someone whose reactions were a little less . . . emotional—understandable though emotion might be, in the circumstances—if Raymond Raybould, that was to say, was really dead. And, if he *was* dead—and if his death had been no accident, but deliberate—then she felt sure that this news should be imparted as soon as possible to Major Haynes.

She had, however, no wish to telephone him with mere alarmist rumours. For almost the first time in her life Emily Dorothea Seeton was conscious of a fear of looking foolish. In the national interest she was, of course, prepared for far worse: but if a few moments' conversation could establish the true facts, she would prefer to converse and establish before hurrying to the telephone and calling the Tower of London.

Phone this number (the major had said) *and someone will be in touch. If there's anything in the nature of an emergency, you're to phone* this *number and give the password . . .*

Miss Seeton's heart was fluttering as she slipped into the Welfare Office and found it empty. She uttered a thankful sigh: it would not have suited Emily Seeton at all to have Mrs. Morris commenting with scorn (as she was sure to do) on her young assistant's state of nervousness. The death of Raymond Raybould was indeed being regarded by the police as murder, and Miss Seeton had to tell Major Haynes.

Her heart fluttered still more as she reached for the telephone handset. Had she memorized the numbers correctly? Suppose she were to muddle which was which and quote the secret password to the wrong person? Suppose—?

"Number, please," said the operator's voice in her ear. Miss Seeton licked her dry lips, crossed mental fingers, and did her best to sound confident as she repeated the emergency number.

"I'm sorry, caller, I can't hear you." Miss Seeton's best, it seemed, had not been good enough. She tried again.

"Thank you," said the operator, her voice muffled by the thump of Miss Seeton's heart. "Trying to put you through."

There followed a series of clicks, whistles, and whirrs, above which a completely unknown voice (male) launched into a one-sided argument with someone he addressed as Cutie-Pie. Miss Seeton's cheeks grew warm, and her hand tightened on the receiver. This was an emergency—and the lines were crossed! Should she break the connection and try again?

But then there came the rhythmic burr of the dialling tone, which trilled barely once before someone at the other end was asking who she was and what she wanted.

Miss Seeton's cheeks flamed. She had braced herself for this, but it sounded so—so very melodramatic . . .

"What," she enquired warily of the mouthpiece, "goes up a chimney down, but—but can't go down a chimney up?"

"What was that?" Once again, it seemed, her delivery left something to be desired. "Who is this?"

Heavens! She had forgotten to identify herself—Major Haynes would not be pleased . . .

"My name," enunciated Miss Seeton with care, "is Emily Seeton. I am calling from—from the Spitfire factory to ask what goes up a chimney down, but can't—oh!"

In her shock she dropped the handset back in its cradle, breaking the connection. A sudden hand had grabbed her by the shoulder and, trying to pull her round, shook her off balance, so that she stumbled and nearly fell against—

"Mrs. Morris!" said Miss Seeton, aghast. "Please—let me explain—it isn't—that is, I wasn't—"

"Be quiet!" the older, taller woman spat as she shook her again, not gently. "I *knew* I was right about you!" *Shake*. "I *said* sending you here was a mistake!" *Shake*. "You—you wretched little traitor!" *Shake*. "You spy!" *Shake*. "You—you murderer!"

The repeated shakes and accusations had left Miss Seeton too startled to do anything but try to remain standing. Her face, already pink with embarrassment from the telephone call, now turned a fiery, indignant red. To Mrs. Morris this blush was final proof of the traitor's guilt, and she shook her victim once more with great vigour, released and threw her so that she stumbled again, seized her arm, twisted it round behind her, and marched her to the open door of the office and out into the corridor.

"Not one word from you, my girl!" Mrs. Morris gave her prisoner's arm a swift upward jerk. Miss Seeton winced, but uttered only a brief cry as she stumbled on in the direction she was being forced. "If you open your mouth to a soul," the older woman threatened in a low snarl, "I'll tell them just what you were doing when I caught you, and how you were trying to send a message in some filthy code to the Huns—and then I'll let you go." She jerked Miss Seeton's arm again. "I don't think," said Mrs. Morris grimly, "you'll get very far, no matter how fast you can run. The sentries are armed, re-member, with orders to shoot to kill . . .

"Ah, George." They had reached the cubicle in which the one-armed man sat all day on watch, and Mrs. Morris spoke in her normal voice. "I want you to fetch one of the police-men from outside. Tell him it's an emergency, and don't take no for an answer—and bring him here *at once*."

George looked from Mrs. Morris, bright-eyed and stern, to Miss Seeton, pink-cheeked and flustered. "I didn't rightly ought to leave the door," he said at last. "I'm supposed to be on guard, aren't I?"

"We will remain here until you return," Mrs. Morris told him. "You—and a policeman," she added with another tweak of Miss Seeton's arm.

Despite herself, Miss Seeton gasped. Old George looked more closely at the two women and slowly nodded. "But if you let anyone in that's not authorised," he reminded them as he edged out of the cubicle, "I won't answer for the conse-quences. You keep 'em out unless they've got a pass!"

It was an uneasy few minutes before George reappeared. Miss Seeton ventured—once—to speak, but she did not try again. Her right arm and shoulder were warm and simmer-ing from the tweaks and jerks applied by Mrs. Morris every time her captive displeased her: and of course the welfare of-ficer had never been pleased at the idea of an assistant. There was, Miss Seeton reflected with sad philosophy, more behind this—understandable—mistake than mere hatred of mur-der, spies, and treachery . . .

She sighed—and then yelped. Mrs. Morris hissed at her to be silent, and she obeyed. It seemed the wisest thing, in the circumstances, to do.

The magnificent specimen of police sergeantry who appeared at Old George's side was greeted by Mrs. Morris with a conspiratorial glance and a swift murmur that George must be back in his cubicle before she could reveal the reason for her summons.

"He said it was urgent," said Sergeant Hammersley, whose muscular development was admired by Miss Seeton the artist but contemplated with apprehension by Miss Seeton the suspect traitor, who began to wonder if she would ever be able to hold a pencil or paintbrush without pain . . .

Once George was inside his cubicle, Mrs. Morris ordered him to close the hatch. This, reluctantly, he did, and she turned to address the burly sergeant.

"This—this creature," spat Mrs. Morris, giving Miss Seeton a final shake, "is a spy! I caught her using the telephone in my office to send a coded message," she hurried on as the sergeant tried to express his surprise. "You must arrest her immediately—and not just for spying. I'm sure she knows far more about the murder than we suspect—and if you look inside her sketchbook you'll see how—how helpful it would be to the enemy—you must arrest her and lock her up before she can do any more harm—and keep her locked up until she can be dealt with!"

Just because Sergeant Hammersley was a large, well-built man did not mean that he was a pattern of bucolic stupidity. He snapped to attention at the word *spy* and listened keenly to the rest of the hurried explanation while keeping a close watch on Miss Seeton's reactions.

"So, what have you got to say for yourself?" he demanded as Mrs. Morris drew to a breathless halt. Miss Seeton, whose arm had endured one final vicious tweak, shook her head with tears in her eyes, and said nothing. "She says," prompted Hammersley, "you're a spy, sending messages in code . . ."

For the first time a note of uncertainty crept into the sergeant's voice. This young woman in her quiet tweeds and, well, peculiar hat didn't look like his idea of a spy; she looked English through and through. But then, that might be the Germans' cleverness—a sort of double bluff—and as to whether or not she'd looked guilty when the Morris woman was telling her story, it had been hard to tell, with her being shaken all the time and her arm twisted round and Morris not letting her go in case (he supposed) she made a bolt for it, which—with the police on the premises, not to mention the LDV perimeter patrol—didn't seem likely, unless she was one of the fanatical sort that would prefer a quick death and glory to being locked away in prison . . .

"Messages in code," reiterated Sergeant Hammersley, and produced his notebook. This action prompted him to ask what Mrs. Morris had meant about the sketchbook, and she told him. Her story made him frown—and the unhappy figure of Miss Seeton made him think.

"We'd better take you and your sketches into protective custody, miss," he said at last. "There's a war on, remember, and bloody murder been done, and if you're safely out of the way, then everyone else can get on with what they're supposed to be doing, and if it turns out later we've made a mistake, then—"

"I told you," broke in Mrs. Morris, "I heard her! If she wasn't giving them some sort of coded message . . ."

"That's enough!" Sergeant Hammersley leaped to the rescue as Mrs. Morris vented upon the unfortunate Miss Seeton her frustration at having her word doubted. "Now, that's quite enough, madam, thank you." Sergeant Hammersley loosened the white-knuckled grip of Mrs. Morris and allowed Miss Seeton's arm to relax into his own, more gentle custody. "She won't be giving me any trouble—will you, miss?"

"Indeed, no," the prisoner managed to gasp while flexing her cramped muscles, trying to betray no further weakness. Was she not, after all, a soldier's daughter?

"I'll take you along to the station," the sergeant continued as Mrs. Morris prepared to argue, caught his eye, and subsided. "If you'll fetch the sketchbook, madam, I'll take it along as well, and I'll come back later for your official statement— if it's necessary," he found himself adding. The young woman really did look a most unlikely spy—but he knew he couldn't afford to risk judging by appearances.

Because if he got it wrong, the way things were he could just be putting out the welcome mat for the Germans . . .

Chapter 22

They had (Miss Seeton reflected) been stern, of course, even hostile—but it was a polite hostility, and if the politeness had been somewhat forced, that was only to be expected, as they supposed her to be a spy; and despite popular belief (to which she did not subscribe) that spies were treated roughly, they had not been . . . violent. Mrs. Morris (mused Miss Seeton, flexing her aching shoulder and arm) had treated her with more violence than the police.

They had been brisk and efficient, taking her to a quiet room at the rear of the station to ask her questions, noting her careful answers, and saying—but not threatening—that she should make "a proper statement" later, when they were in less of a hurry. She would (they said) understand their hurry, because there was a war on—and murder on top of that. She had assured them she understood very well, and they had smiled grim smiles and said it was lucky for her that she did.

They told her they would give her time to think things over, and took her to a cell with modest facilities and a door with a stout lock. Miss Seeton heard the key turn behind her and sat down to await rescue.

She wished they had not insisted on keeping her sketch-book: it was, after all, not hers. It was the property of His Majesty's Government, at least insofar as a government department had paid for it, even if she might be considered responsible for it in the short term. But she could see why they had done so—the police, that was to say—and it had seemed wiser not to make too much fuss and, by fussing, to draw attention to herself any more than circumstances had already contrived. The identity card describing her as a civilian war artist did not, in her opinion, look either impressive or credible, at least when the situation was as grave as . . .

"Murder," Miss Seeton whispered in the silence of her cell. "Poor Mr. Raybould. And yet . . . why should anyone wish to murder one of the cleaners?"

The factory complex was large, its staff legion—and increasing daily, as Mrs. Morris had told her, with the enormous growth in output. Miss Seeton knew that for every cleaner she had seen (and sketched) at work, there were a dozen others out of sight, all of them always at work. The loss of one life was regrettable—more than regrettable—but the loss of one worker was . . . incomprehensible. There were more workers to replace him, and more to come . . .

Miss Seeton rubbed her upper arm and frowned. Raymond Raybould had been murdered, then, because of who he was *as himself*, not because of who he was in the working sense. Anyone could sweep a floor. It required, as far as she knew, no special training. One took one's broom, applied it to the floor, and pushed. When the pile being pushed seemed likely to spill, one collected it by means of a dustpan—the industrial size had made her chuckle the first time she saw it—and tipped the contents through a sieve into a sack. Any metal pieces caught by the sieve were dropped into other, smaller sacks or linen bags to be sorted at home by village housewives . . .

Miss Seeton wondered whether anyone had thought to tell Mrs. Beamish to expect her home late because she was in custody, suspected of being a spy. She sighed.

She sat up. *Spies*. Microfilm! Perhaps one of those precious metal sweepings had been, not an ordinary nut or bolt or screw or rivet, but something hollowed out, with a secret message hidden inside . . .

"This is too melodramatic," Miss Seeton scolded herself with a blush. Whatever would Major Haynes think of such fanciful notions?

Major Haynes. (Giles?) Miss Seeton shook herself and blushed more deeply. How fortunate that her dear mother had always emphasised the importance to a gentlewoman of self-control. It had been . . . unsettling to be accused by Mrs. Morris and arrested by the police, but the major had warned his protégée that she must on no account reveal to anyone, or even hint at, her connection with Military Intelligence Section G (Gabriel?) for fear of endangering national security. Despite the looming presence of an extremely large and irritable uniformed inspector of police, she had remembered that warning and refused to tell him any more than—what was the popular phrase?

"Name, rank, and number," she murmured, recalling the inspector's black looks as she had remained steadfastly silent about the cryptic words Mrs. Morris had overheard. "She was in a hurry," Miss Seeton had volunteered at last, and only once. "She might—she might have misheard . . ."

This was hardly a downright lie, but it made her uneasy; and as (not being a quick thinker) she could offer no less sinister interpretation for whatever words she might in fact have said, she said nothing, and had ended up in the cells— waiting for rescue. They looked after their own, the major had emphasised. She would not be forgotten.

She smiled. She was confident that sooner or later this little—entirely understandable—misunderstanding would be cleared up. Her telephone call to the secret number had been answered; she had given the password, and . . .

"Oh, dear." Miss Seeton sighed. How much of what she had tried to say in fact been heard at the other end?

But there was no sense in worrying. She must wait and see—must wait and keep silent about what she knew, just as the major had told her.

She looked around the little room in which she was a prisoner. "Such melodrama," she scolded herself again, and resolved to turn her thoughts in another direction.

Why should anyone wish to—to murder Raymond Raybould? What might he have done to . . . offend anyone so deeply that only his death could . . . atone?

He had implied that he was a conscientious objector. Beryl and Ruby had said the same. His views were no great secret—and he seemed neither embarrassed nor ashamed of them. Perhaps he should have been. In the opinion of many, conchies (unless for avowedly religious reasons) were the lowest of the low. Might someone who had watched a loved one go to war, never to return, have taken exception to the cleaner's declared philosophy and—and carried that exception beyond all reasonable bounds?

"And yet," Miss Seeton reminded herself sadly, "we are fighting this war for the sake of freedom. If one truly has strong moral views about—about killing . . ."

Then she remembered that it might not be long—it might be at any moment—that she, with the rest of the nation, would be called upon to make the ultimate decision whether to stifle those moral views or to uphold them.

If the church bells rang . . .

They did not ring that night. Miss Seeton slept a troubled sleep and woke, stiff and weary, next morning to the sound of a thump on the door of her cell and the jingle of keys in the lock.

"Are you decent, Miss Seeton?" It was Sergeant Hammersley who made the enquiry, to which the prisoner, stifling a yawn as she sat up, replied that she was.

"We're to apologise to you, Miss Seeton." Hammersley popped his head round the door to see her trying to pat her hair left-handed into shape, grinned a shamefaced grin, and allowed the rest of himself to appear. "We've had a message—don't know who, not allowed to ask—that you're on the side of the angels, and we really didn't ought to've brought you in yesterday even if it did look a bit . . ."

"Suspicious," Miss Seeton concluded kindly as he turned red and coughed himself to a halt. "That's quite all right, Mr. Hammersley. In an emergency one should always take every precaution, which you—which the police—did. I assure you that I blame nobody for what was a—an entirely understandable error—and indeed, it is I who should apologise—for the inconvenience to which you have been put. I trust that—that your investigation of poor Mr. Raybould's death has not been too much hindered by . . ."

Now it was Miss Seeton's turn to cough. For a moment she and the sergeant regarded each other in sympathetic silence. They broke simultaneously into smiles of relief; Sergeant Hammersley went so far as to chuckle.

Miss Seeton rose to her feet, trying not to wince as the movement revived the ache in her arm and shoulder. "If you can tell me where exactly I am," she said, "and how I may find my way home—that is, to my lodgings—I will waste no more of your valuable time. Is there a suitable bus?"

"Bus?" Sergeant Hammersley looked worried. "Oh, but the inspector said as you were to have a car—except you'll have to wait, with them all being at the factory, for one to come back, if you don't mind. There's a cup of tea while you're waiting," he offered as Miss Seeton shook her head.

"Thank you, but no," she said firmly. "There is a war on, Mr. Hammersley, and the very idea of—of wasting petrol is as abhorrent to me as that of wasting people's time. The bus will suit me very well, if you can show me the stop and tell me when I may expect the next to arrive."

Miss Seeton regretted her firmness when the bus did not arrive until ninety minutes after the advertised hour. She had begun to suspect Sergeant Hammersley's optimistic forecast when, after twenty-five minutes, she remained the only person waiting in the wooden shelter. After half an hour's still-solitary wait she toyed briefly with the thought of walking home, but with every signpost in the country removed, the milestones defaced or buried, and everyone under government advice to give directions to nobody, it seemed safer

224

to wait rather than risk losing herself and causing more trouble than she already had. *If anyone stops to ask me the way, I have to tell them that I can't say* had been the couplet she herself had rehearsed with pupils of all ages. Before the previous day's little misadventure she might have hoped her appearance would convince the most sceptical that she was no Nazi parachutist, but now she would take no chances. She would, instead, take the bus . . .

She was nodding in a corner of the shelter when the bus pulled up, and as she stretched herself awake her shoulder twinged again. She almost dropped her handbag, clutched at her sketchbook, missed, dropped her gas mask, and dropped her bag as well. While she fumbled about on the ground to retrieve them she blushed, and apologised profusely to the driver when she finally climbed on board.

"You ought to have it in a sling," said the young woman conductor as she took Miss Seeton's money, punched her ticket, and heard her apologise again. "Might be a sprain, or anything—you don't want to take any chances. There's a good doctor in your village, I've heard. He'll see you all right, ducks!"

With a pat on Miss Seeton's other shoulder the bus conductress moved back to resume the conversation she and a plump woman with a wicker basket had been enjoying on the topic of hens and how to raise them.

Miss Seeton, bumped from side to side on the ill-sprung seat, took her mind off her aching shoulder by remembering dear Cousin Flora's chickens in the garden of her cottage in Kent. Poor Cousin Flora: poor Kent. Poor England—whose south and eastern coasts had been evacuated for a distance of twenty miles inland, to make troop movements easier in case the worst should happen. Even the flocks of sheep on Romney Marsh had been sent far away, so that they would not provide food for the invaders . . .

Miss Seeton shook herself and gazed out of the window as the bus rattled along. Over the tops of hedges she could see the fields of ripening grain . . . fields across which the villagers had erected makeshift anti-invasion devices—huge blocks of concrete, rusting cars, farm carts, fallen trees. Tanks, she knew the theory went, would find it difficult to manoeuvre, aeroplanes to land . . .

Miss Seeton shook herself again as the bus rattled into the village. She would have rung the bell, but the conductress had remembered: she grinned and waved at Miss Seeton's smile of thanks, then returned to her fowl talk again.

Miss Seeton glanced up and down the winding street as the bus drove away, but there was nobody about. "Elevenses, of course," she murmured with a sigh for the days of peace when there had been more than one type of biscuit on the plate and several varieties of cake. She shook her head, sighed again, pulled herself together, and headed briskly for home. A quick wash and brushup, perhaps a cup of tea, and she would be able to face the rest of the day undaunted.

She rapped the knocker using her left arm, but Tilly Beamish did not answer the front door. Miss Seeton wondered if she should go to the back, and then remembered the girls of the night shift. A lesser woman would have cursed her own stupidity: Miss Seeton, blushing, muttered a heartfelt "Drat!" and resolved that Tilly should be asked to pass on her apologies for having woken the sleepers, and her offer to—say—sew on a few buttons or sketch a quick likeness if ever their paths should cross. Once, that was to say, her arm and shoulder were easy once more . . .

But for now, she could hardly camp on the step until Mrs. Beamish came home: for all she knew, her landlady had posted her lodger missing and was forming a search party. It was a pity that in all the confusion she had forgotten to ask Sergeant Hammersley whether anyone had thought to tell—

The door opened. A young woman with long, dark hair and a Rubenesque figure wrapped in a patterned robe materialised in front of Miss Seeton, stifling a yawn.

"I do beg your pardon," Miss Seeton began, but the girl waved at her to come in; so she did.

"You must be Emily," said La Rubens, taking a second look at Miss Seeton's hat. The ribbon trim seemed a little sorry for itself. "Yes, I've all heard about you from Ma Beamish—aaaah . . ."

As she yawned again Miss Seeton again tried to apologise, but La Rubens dismissed the attempt with another wave that this time involved her whole body. "I'm Maisie," she introduced herself, smiling. "I'm an aero-detail fitter—and you're some kind of artist, aren't you?"

Miss Seeton agreed that she was, although as she did so she emphasised her current role as assistant welfare officer, even if secretly she doubted whether Mrs. Morris would allow her to continue in that role, given the embarrassment there was likely to be on both sides. The sketching (she explained aloud) was hardly a suitable full-time occupation, at a time of national emergency.

"Like me," replied Maisie with a knowing giggle, while Miss Seeton felt a glow of modest pride at the success of her evasive conversational tactics. She wondered if Major Haynes would approve . . .

"I used to be on the stage," Maisie went on as with a blush Miss Seeton came to her senses and politely asked in what way her new friend found the likeness. "Not that you could call it acting, exactly." Maisie eyed Miss Seeton up and down, then grinned. "More exotic dancing, if you know what I mean." She winked and struck a sudden pose, her arms up-flung, her hips and torso curved, her majestic bosom displayed to full advantage as she teetered on high-heeled slippers. "Marguerite, Flower of the East, that was me, even if it's East Grinstead we're talking about, not the East Indies."

"Oh," said Miss Seeton, who suddenly remembered what Mrs. Beamish had said on her first evening. Country people were, of course, probably less accustomed to persons of a bohemian nature than one who lived and had attended art college in London, and who visited the theatre from time to time.

"I was glad to get out of it, I can tell you." Maisie, formerly Marguerite, struck another pose, even more flamboyant and provocative than the last, and then relaxed. "Far too much like hard work. It wasn't so bad when I was doing life classes around the colleges, because all I had to do was keep still, and none of them tried to get me into bed—well, not the students, anyway. A few of the tutors could be a problem, but . . ."

She shrugged. "Well, the dancing paid better, but you can have enough of feathers and fans and wisps of chiffon, can't you?" Miss Seeton supposed that you could. "So when they asked for girls to help the war effort, I thought why not? Here's my chance to do something useful for once."

Miss Seeton ventured to mention ENSA, but Maisie shrieked with laughter. Then she clapped a hand to her mouth and pulled Miss Seeton through to the kitchen. "Betty—she's still asleep," she said, pointing upwards.

"Betty?" Miss Seeton blinked, then rallied. It was not so uncommon a Christian name. For a moment, though . . .

"They say she's still serious but comfortable," Maisie said, guessing what had startled her. "As if anyone can be comfortable with a cracked skull and a broken arm, never mind her poor face! But at least she's better off than that cleaner—what was his name? We had police all over the show last night, though if there's as many today, I'll be surprised—and what did *you* know about it for them to keep you talking for so long?"

The question startled Miss Seeton a second time, and once more she blinked before, rallying, murmuring some story of a mistake, and not wanting to disturb everyone by coming home late at night . . .

"You should have heard Ma Beamish," said Maisie with a chuckle for Miss Seeton's cry of dismay. "We got the full performance when we came home this morning—how you'd been taken for a spy, and she couldn't believe it, and if it was true it was disgraceful to impose on a poor widow woman in her own home—if I'd been a critic I'd have given her top marks, I really would—but don't take on, duck." All the amusement vanished as she saw Miss Seeton crumple down upon a kitchen chair with a look of horror on her face. "She was just letting off steam, that's all. You aren't a bit like any spy I've seen in the films, and if you really were, why would they let you out? You ought to be in the Tower of London, by rights."

Miss Seeton's look of horror turned to a rosy blush, but fortunately Maisie jumped to the wrong conclusion. "You'll be all right," she promised her flustered new acquaintance. "Tilly's bark's far worse than her bite, you'll see."

Miss Seeton winced; her blush faded. Maisie's careless phrase, intended to reassure, had achieved the opposite end by reminding her of her first day at the factory, and Old George's words about Mrs. Morris.

Mrs. Morris . . .

"I must get on," she said, and climbed shakily to her feet. She would be late for work, but to work she would go, walking every yard of the way, if she must. She would wait for no bus, ask nobody for a lift. She must be there as soon as humanly possible if she was not to betray the memory of her soldier father.

This was *her* war, and she had been given a job to do; and she would do it, no matter what people thought, or how they behaved towards her.

Major Haynes would expect no less of Emily Dorothea Seeton.

Chapter 23

Maisie, though yawning, offered to make Miss Seeton a cup of tea while the other slipped upstairs to powder her nose and tidy her hair. Miss Seeton thanked her, but refused on the grounds that as soon as she was comfortable again, she would be on her way, walking to the factory where she really ought to have been since eight o'clock that morning.

"I know, I know," said Maisie with a grin. "There's a war on, and you want to do your bit. Good for you—but if you're sure, I'd better get back to bed . . ."

Miss Seeton said she was sure, and Maisie followed her up the narrow stairs, her slippers slapping in rhythm as she climbed. Miss Seeton thought of castanets and found herself humming an air from *Carmen* as she hurried through her toilette.

"*L'amour est* tum tum *de* something . . ."

Miss Seeton blushed. *L'amour*, indeed! At a time like this! But they said that all was fair in—

"I must hurry," she told herself sternly; and she did.

It took less than ten minutes for Miss Seeton to refresh herself; within a quarter of an hour of her encounter with Maisie-formerly-Marguerite she was stepping out smartly along the village street, her hat at a businesslike angle, her handbag—sketchbook inside, gas mask attached—over her left arm. She estimated that a steady pace of four miles an hour should bring her to the factory gates well before the midday break that so few people wasted time in eating, and with the sun bright (but not yet high) in a cloudless sky, it was a beautiful day for a country walk. Had it not been for the war, she could have enjoyed the excursion unreservedly.

After twenty minutes she paused by a stile to watch one of the newly completed Spitfires undergoing a test flight almost overhead, soaring from the factory airfield, rolling, diving, looping, swooping, and climbing in the pilot's allocated quadrant of the sky. It was, as ever, a breathtaking performance by a skilled expert, and Miss Seeton did indeed hold her breath as the usual burst of flame from the exhaust roared into the air and the plane returned to the ground. As another Spitfire rose to repeat the exercise, she sighed, shook her head, and walked on.

It was a busy morning for test flights. The sound of Merlin engines was all around, drowning out the song of summer birds and Miss Seeton's renewed attempts at *Carmen*. "*Qui n'a jamais, jamais* tum tum something . . ."

She awoke from her trance to hear the squawk of a motor horn behind her. Above the sound of the Spitfires and her own tuneless warbling she had not heard the car's approach, and turned in some surprise to see who was hinting that she might be taking up too much of the road for safety.

"Dr. Huxter!" She recognised at once the plump-faced, smiling figure leaning from the window of a car, which, seen for the first time close up in daylight, she realised had rather more chipped, scratched, and damaged paint than perhaps a good driver should allow. One had (she reminded herself) to make allowances for the blackout, of course . . .

"Hello, there!" Samuel Huxter inched the car a little nearer, and Miss Seeton, ever courteous, had to fight an instinctive urge to take several steps backwards. "I must say I'm delighted," said the doctor, "to see that they didn't cart you off to the Tower last night. But it was touch and go, I heard!"

"A simple misunderstanding," Miss Seeton told him with a smile. "Entirely understandable, of course, but everything is now settled to the satisfaction of both the police and—and myself, and I am going back to work."

"Hop in," he invited, hopping out to open the passenger door, cursing as the car began a slow forward trundle, and hopping (with an effort) back in again to haul on the brake.

"I'm always doing that," he told Miss Seeton cheerily as she tried to think of an excuse, and failed. "A pity they can't invent a two-driver car, don't you think? A copilot would be a blessing to a bloke like me, eh?"

As Miss Seeton climbed inside she consoled herself with the thought that a passenger seated next to the driver might in the short term be as good a blessing as any pilot—and, in any case, it wasn't very far to the factory.

It would just *feel* like a long way . . .

Dr. Huxter crunched up noisily through the gears and made bright conversation as he drove along, telling Miss Seeton that the news of broken-armed Betty and her concussion was more hopeful than the previous day's reports, and the girl was expected to recover, apart from her face, though it had been a nasty accident and no mistake.

233

"Mind you," he added, "there are those who say that it *wasn't* a mistake—that there have been altogether too many mistakes in recent weeks—but that's just scaremongering, if you ask me. Don't you think?"

Miss Seeton, having shut her eyes as a length of hedge came unnervingly close to her face, gulped twice and said that as she hadn't yet been in the village a week she was hardly competent to judge, but that anything smacking of alarm and despondency was to be deplored as unpatriotic.

"That's all very well," returned the doctor, "but we've got to face facts, Miss Seeton. For every one of *us* there are hundreds of *them*, what with the poor devils who've been overrun and are forced to put everything they've got towards the Nazi war effort as well as the blighters themselves. Don't you, in your heart of hearts, think it's hopeless?"

"I do not," said Miss Seeton with resolution. She was so annoyed that she opened her eyes and grabbed hurriedly at the door handle as the hedge made another approach. "And if you will pardon my saying so, Doctor, a man in your position should perhaps think twice about making such remarks where persons less . . . capable than—than others of making up their own minds might hear you."

Dr. Huxter whistled a few bars of "Rule, Britannia" and drove on without speaking. His whistle was as melodious as the song of Miss Seeton. It was a melancholy, silent pair that arrived at the factory gates.

Once more the doctor squeezed the rubber bulb, and the squawking hoot brought Day George leaping from his sentry box with a rifle in his hand.

"Halt!" he cried, bracing himself to pull the trigger. "Who goes there? Don't you move an inch!"

234

Dr. Huxter poked his head out of the window. "You know very well who I am," he told the military figure in front of him. "Miss Seeton, too. You also," he added with an emphasis his passenger did not understand, "know very well why we're here—so let us in, there's a good chap."

George's eyes narrowed as he stumped up to the car and peered through the windscreen, before moving round to peer through the nearside window. He recognised Miss Seeton and jumped back.

"Let *her* in? Over my dead body!" he cried, waving the rifle in a way that even to Miss Seeton's inexpert eye did not seem safe. "We don't want *her* sort here—taken away by the police, she was, only yesterday afternoon!"

"Perhaps," said Dr. Huxter, "you should ask the police what they think about her this morning. If they agree—if they confirm—that she isn't a risk to security, will that change your mind?"

George brandished his rifle again. "Ah," he said slowly. "Yes, the police . . . But I can't leave my post, Doctor, you know that, whether it's to ask permission or no."

"The police?" Miss Seeton had been so startled by the accusations of Day George that the doctor's words had only just registered. "Are they here again? Oh, dear—what—what else has happened?"

"Ah," said George, in quite a different tone, narrowing his eyes into slits of suspicion as he aimed his rifle with more spirit than skill. "And what were you expecting to have happened, my girl, hey? Only bloody murder again, that's what!"

"What?" cried Miss Seeton, distinctly shaken. She had realised even as soon as she uttered her earlier words that the presence of the police should come as no surprise, as they would be continuing to investigate the death of Raymond Raybould. She had been prepared to laugh at her folly for having thought the worst; but now . . .

"As if you didn't know," scoffed George, stepping a few paces nearer. "With the doctor giving you a lift and all, trying to pretend he didn't tell you, you—you damnable fifth columnist!"

Miss Seeton turned to look at Dr. Huxter, who managed a rueful smile. "I'm afraid so," he said. "I wasn't driving this way for pleasure, you know, or even on a routine call. One of the Beaver's Army was found with his head smashed in a couple of hours ago, but I was at hospital, and the message only just reached me."

"Oh," said Miss Seeton. "Oh . . ." It was not that she thought herself unduly squeamish—indeed, she was grateful to the doctor for having broken the news without feeling the need to wrap her in cotton wool, although she wondered that he had not mentioned it on the journey—but it was nonetheless a shock to learn that within the space of twenty-four hours two violent deaths had occurred in this out-of-the-way place, as well as an accident that, the more she considered it, might not have been an accident after all.

She had to telephone the major. Quickly.

"I assure you," she said with a smile to George, "that I am nothing so despicable as a fifth columnist, or a spy, or—or anything but a patriotic Englishwoman. And as such my place is inside those gates, at work, not—not wasting time out here. Doctor, don't you agree?"

"Well," said Dr. Huxter. Miss Seeton followed his gaze to the business end of George's rifle and understood why he had temporised.

"I assure you," she reiterated, and then came to a halt as she realised that she did not know George's name, which made making a direct appeal somewhat awkward. In the circumstances, one could hardly feel the *tu* form of address entirely suitable. "I assure you," she said for the third time, "that—that my intentions are—are as honourable as yours, and—"

"Quiet!" George's bellow was urgent, not angry. With his free hand he shaded his eyes and squinted upwards into the distance. "Listen!"

Dr. Huxter stuck his head right out of the window and turned in the same direction. "Theirs," he said grimly after a few tense moments. "More than one, by the sound of it. Let us in, man—you can't expect a woman to stay outside during an air raid!"

George was about to speak when the siren began to wail. He shouted something Miss Seeton could not quite catch as the barrage balloons were winched into the sky and the ack-ack guns started blazing, and ran to open the gates, first darting into the wooden hut for his steel helmet, which he clapped on his head even as he gestured with his rifle for the doctor to make haste.

Dr. Huxter needed no second bidding. The gates were open the merest crack, and his foot was on the accelerator, urging the car through the widening gap with a scream of tortured metalwork that set Miss Seeton's teeth on edge. The whine of the balloon winches and the pounding snarl of the ack-ack guns—so few of them—was joined by the clatter of falling shrapnel, and Huxter cursed as he pulled the car against a breezeblock wall.

"This'll be the last of my paint," he told Miss Seeton as he switched off the engine. "And I think we'll have to run for it . . ."

They were outside the car, staring together into the heavens. Miss Seeton's eye was keener than the doctor's. "I think so, too," she said. "I see five aircraft and I don't believe they're ours."

"Nor does anyone else," he returned, seizing her by the hand and cursing as he tangled with her gas mask and bag. "We run for it, same as the rest of 'em—there's a shelter over there and a slit trench a bit closer. Which do you prefer?"

Miss Seeton glanced at the mass of people now erupting from the various factory buildings, all of whom seemed to be heading for the shelter. "The trench," she said, "if it's closer—I don't know—"

"I do," he told her. "It is," and he began to run. For so large a man he moved speedily, and Miss Seeton's shorter legs had to work hard to keep up with his stride. Every time she slackened her pace or faltered, he tugged on her hand, which made the bag and gas mask bump and tangle. But Miss Seeton ignored them: she ran and ran.

Others ran, too, as the droning *thud-thud-thud* of enemy engines drew ever nearer. Out on the airfield they were abandoning the tractors used to disperse the Spitfires on the ground and were plunging into trenches, or taking cover by the few trees left standing when the ministry acquired the land. The siren wailed, the ack-ack blazed, the shrapnel clattered, and Emily Seeton ran, hand in hand with Samuel Huxter, running for their lives.

But not fast enough. One of the aircraft peeled away from its fellows to swoop overhead in a long, vicious curve.

"He's making a dummy run!" cried the doctor, panting.

There came a swift, sharp series of bangs, and Miss Seeton saw dust spurting up in a moving line a few yards ahead of her. Huxter cursed once, glanced up, and ran on.

"Missed," he wheezed, still running. "Machine gun . . ."

Even at such a moment Miss Seeton found time to be shocked at the very idea of being machine-gunned on English soil. They had no right—

There came a roar behind her, and a thump, and a shower of earth through which she felt herself flying . . .

And Miss Seeton knew no more.

Chapter 24

Her head was throbbing with sharp, vicious needle-darts. It felt strangely . . . heavy, like the rest of her small person, and hot. Or possibly cold. Miss Seeton wondered if she might, for the first time in her life, be suffering from a migraine. If she was, she hoped it would be the last.

Cautiously she opened her eyes.

She closed them again at once. The glaring white light all around her turned the needles into daggers, and she felt more than a little sick.

She moved her head on the pillow and tried to stifle a moan as the daggers turned into corkscrews and sickness bubbled its acid way up into her throat. She gulped and began to shiver—and gulped a second time—and groaned.

"Easy, now," said a woman's voice that rang with a curious echo. A cool hand rested for a moment on her cheek and then slipped round under the back of her head. "It'll make you feel even worse if you're sick, but if you really can't keep it back, don't worry. There's something here to catch it . . ."

The nurse—that voice, those words, could belong only to a nurse—produced a kidney-shaped white enamel bowl into which Miss Seeton, as corkscrew points scored painful lines across her brain, vomited with impressive accuracy and thoroughness. With her eyes blurred by tears and exhaustion, she fell—or rather, was gently laid back—on the pillow, and as her head filled with a slow, rushing roar Miss Seeton drifted out of the all-white echoing world into velvety, pain-sparkled darkness.

The next time she opened her eyes the pain was almost gone, replaced by a dull, general ache. The light still glared but held fewer daggers, and the world, ever white, was less blurred. The rushing roar, like the pain, was almost gone. She moved her head on the pillow and caught her breath as . . . nothing happened.

She sighed, relaxed, and warily tried to move—to test—the rest of herself. Hands: bandaged, but at least the fingers worked well, if a little stiffly, though the palms—*ouch*—were sore. Arms, shoulders—more stiffness there . . . feet, toes, legs—

"Oh," gasped Miss Seeton, wincing. "My legs . . ."

The violent spasm on top of the general ache made her eyes water. As she blinked and sniffed away the tears she realised that one of the white blurs that had seemed to fill her troubled vision was the hump of bedclothes—hospital bedclothes—on a frame over the lower part of her body.

"My legs . . . must be . . . broken," whispered Miss Seeton.

But she knew that the only way to face up to a problem was not to ignore it in the hope that it would vanish of its own accord: problems never did that.

"My legs," said Miss Seeton out loud in a voice that barely shook, "are broken."

"No, they aren't," said another voice, even louder, and if it shook, Miss Seeton did not notice. "Don't you worry," the voice went on. "You'll be all right, duck. I've heard them say so more than once these past couple of days." The voice took on a slightly apologetic note. "Well, it's not that I'm given to eavesdropping, I wouldn't want anyone to think that, but when they're right beside the bed talking you can't help hearing them, with the curtains so thin and all. Can you?"

"I—I suppose," Miss Seeton conceded, "you c-can't." She turned her head, without the daggers and corkscrews, to look in the direction of the voice. Beyond the immediate focus of her blankets and a wooden locker at the side of the bed, everything began to blur again. "I c-can't see you." Miss Seeton faltered. "My eyes . . ."

"Concussion," said the voice. "They said that, too." The voice coughed. "And you'll be over the worst in another day or so, and off home to free the bed for some other poor basket, no offence meant. My name's Ivy, by the way," the voice continued as Miss Seeton began blinking and sniffing again, and shivered with (she supposed) shock.

Or relief. Ivy had spoken with conviction: there seemed no reason to doubt her optimistic forecast. Miss Seeton would soon be safe at home . . .

"Home? No . . ." Miss Seeton's memory lurched, lunged, and dragged the name out of the depths. "Mrs. Beamish . . ."

"Not me," said Ivy. "Not guilty! And you can't blame anyone but them bloody Germans for you being in here with your head in a turban and your poor brains scrambled like eggs, not to mention your knees—blown clean off your feet you were, I heard, and not the only one."

Miss Seeton's memory lurched again. "The . . . doctor?" she brought out, once more feeling his grip tighten on her hand as they ran beneath—ran in fear of their lives away from—the swooping Nazi plane towards the shelter of the slit trench she did not believe they had reached . . .

Or had they? Memory's faulty display showed Day George brandishing his rifle at the sky as the face of Mr. Coleman bent over her, blurred and twisted, anxious, out of focus, while Samuel Huxter's voice issued instructions . . .

"The doctor?" Miss Seeton asked again, more loudly.

"He'll be along in an hour or so," Ivy told her. "When they brought you in you were right out of it, believe me, and sick as a dog when you finally came round, so they'll be pleased as Punch when you start talking to them sensible like the way you are now, and not just on account of wanting the bed."

"Oh," said Miss Seeton, somehow too tired to make the effort to explain. She closed her eyes again and slept.

The aftermath of her experience left Miss Seeton too weak to argue when the nurses replied to her questions about Dr. Huxter that she was not to worry about anything except getting well soon. Shock (they insisted) took different people different ways. To be within an inch of your life from a machine gun and then being blown off your feet by a bomb, bashing your knees and almost cracking your skull, would be enough to give anyone a shock. She was to lie quiet and rest, and soon, if she was good, the hospital doctors would discharge her into the care of her landlady.

Although the raid on the factory had been heavy, because normal round-the-clock service was resumed within a matter of hours, none of the girls was able to visit Miss

Seeton to cheer her weary days with their giggles and gossip. They did not, however, forget their new friend, sending messages and picture papers when Tilly Beamish struggled into town, just once, to see her, bringing in lieu of garden flowers (the Dig for Victory campaign had had its effect) a bunch of hedgerow blossoms for her lodger's enjoyment. Miss Seeton thanked her, smelled them, sneezed, and had a relapse.

"We're sending you home today," the consultant informed her when he did his rounds on what she understood to be the fifth day since the bombing. "Nurse will come by later to remove your bandages and give you sticking plaster and—and so forth, instead. Then, if you take things easy most of the time, and do your physio exactly as we showed you, you should be good as new within the week—and, yes, back at work," he added, answering the question he thought he saw in her eyes.

"Thank you," said Miss Seeton. "But talking of nurses—and doctors—"

This neat thematic link to her most pressing question was ignored by the doctor as he continued his professional harangue. "But I have to warn you," he said gravely, "that those knees could give you trouble in later years no matter how thorough the physiotherapy."

"Doctor," said Miss Seeton with a faint smile, "if you can guarantee that I will live to see my later years, and to see them in freedom, you might be surprised at the thoroughness with which I shall apply myself to my physiotherapy."

For the first time he looked at her as a person, and not as a case history propped up on pillows with a temperature chart hanging on the end of the bed. "Yes," he said slowly. "Ah, yes, if we could only see into the future . . ."

But this was neither the place nor the time. The consultant became brisk and professional once more. "We'll leave it to your good sense, Miss Seeton," he said with a nod, and moved on to talk with Ivy.

Tilly Beamish had accepted Miss Seeton (and the weekly rent that came with her) as a lodger under the impression that she was a small but essential cog in the mighty ministry wheel. She had accepted with even more enthusiasm, because it was more exciting, her supposed identity as a spy. The message from the police, alerting her to the young woman's imminent release on the highest authority, had left Mrs. Beamish quite bewildered, but after milking the situation for all it was worth in the village tea-shop, she had resolved to make the best of things by spoiling Miss Seeton as the heroine of the hour.

Heroines do not sneeze themselves into unconsciousness at the first sniff of kingcups, charlock, and herb robert. After alerting the nurses, Tilly had hurried away, telling Ivy to be sure to tell Miss Seeton they were looking forward to having her home again. Her room (she promised) would be ready and waiting, and the only flowers in it would be the wax wreath from Beamish's funeral, which it had always seemed a crying shame to tidy away, and now she would get it out again as something for Miss Seeton to look at while she was resting in bed, her being an artist as she was.

"That is a kind thought," said Miss Seeton when Ivy had broken the macabre news; she supposed that it was, even as she recalled Dr. Huxter's warning the first night that if she didn't keep her suitcase locked, Tilly Beamish would know all there was to know about her, and more. "But I doubt if I'll feel like sketching for a little while yet. My eyes don't blur the way they did, but they grow tired so very easily . . ."

"Well, you do look tired," was Tilly's greeting as Miss Seeton yawned her way down from the bus in which she had dozed most of the way home. The conductress had shaken her awake as they rumbled into the village, and Miss Seeton's eyes had blurred not from weariness but from relief as she saw Mrs. Beamish waiting for her at the stop.

Tilly kept up a flow of chatter as they made their way along the street to the cottage, after which journey Miss Seeton felt uncertain of her legs, and sat breathing heavily for a while before forcing herself to climb the stairs. Tilly had told her she could go straight to bed, and this now seemed the most sensible thing she could do, despite the ache in her knees at every upward step.

She was recovering her breath in bed, with a woollen shawl crocheted in happier days by her mother around her shoulders, when she heard a brisk rapping at the front door. One of the neighbours, no doubt, dropping by for a chat, which Mrs. Beamish was sure to enjoy. A man? Delivering a parcel, perhaps, although why Mrs. Beamish should sound so indignant about it—but a gentlewoman does not snoop. And she was really very tired after her exertions. Miss Seeton let her weary gaze drift across to the wax-flower wreath under its glass dome set by Tilly in proud splendour on the chest of drawers, and closed her eyes.

She opened them again as the castanet clatter of feet up the stairs was followed by another brisk rapping, this time on her bedroom door, accompanied by an enquiry from Mrs. Beamish—who sounded most annoyed—as to whether or not she was decent. Miss Seeton blinked, adjusted her shawl, and after a puzzled moment or two intimated that she was.

The door opened.

"Thank you, Mrs. Beamish," said a voice that had the invalid sitting up on her pillows. "I'll do my best not to tire her, I promise . . ."

And in walked Major Haynes.

He was dressed in tweeds, and his neatly furled umbrella was brown. He smiled at Miss Seeton before turning back to close the door, very firmly, in Tilly's face, and paused to listen for retreating footsteps.

There were none.

He grinned as he approached the bed. "Mrs. Beamish, it seems, means to defend your honour to the death," he said as Miss Seeton smiled shyly up at him. "Let me know when you want to scream, and I'll open the door so that she doesn't miss it."

Miss Seeton's smile became a twinkle of mischief. "That would be most considerate of you," she replied, "and I thank you. But—such a surprise to see you . . ."

"I'd have been here earlier, if I could—as soon as we learned of your little contretemps with the police—but at least we managed to sort it out for you in the end." The major glanced at the chair on which Miss Seeton had made a neat pile of her discarded clothing, raised his eyebrows in a silent query, and received Miss Seeton's nod. He laid his umbrella on the bed, swept the clothes up in his arms, looked for somewhere to put them, and reeled back in horror as he saw the wax wreath.

"Good God!" He dropped the clothes beside the umbrella, shuffled through them, found Miss Seeton's petticoat, shook it out, and draped it over the glass dome with a muttered "Rest in peace" while Miss Seeton tried to stifle her giggles.

"They told me," he said, settling himself on the chair, "that you were convalescent. The quality of your convalescing is open to serious doubt, with a monstrosity like that leering at you in such a way that would put ideas into the head of someone with less sense than you, Miss Seeton."

Miss Seeton accepted the compliment with another twinkle and a discreet murmur that the wreath was one of her landlady's most prized possessions, brought out of retirement, as one might say, for her to use as—as artistic inspiration, when she was feeling well enough again.

"Yes," said Major Haynes, becoming serious. "They told me you'd fallen on your hands and knees as well as bumping your head. The damage won't be lasting, they said. I sincerely hope that's true—and not just because of your work for us."

Miss Seeton blushed, and lowered her gaze. "I fear," she said, "that there has been little opportunity, in the circumstances . . ." She stopped. She looked. She shook her head and looked again.

"I wondered if you'd spot it," said the major. "It's my own idea—had it made specially. A bicoloured, reversible umbrella!"

Miss Seeton lifted her head to smile. "I *thought*," she said, "it was the same, but the other was black, and—well, it seems slightly bulkier than a normal umbrella, now that I see it close to—although this would be caused by the extra seams in the fabric, no doubt."

Major Haynes regarded her thoughtfully. "You don't miss a trick, do you, young Emily? I beg your pardon," he added as Miss Seeton turned pink. He was a little red himself as he went on: "It's a brolly with a secret, this one. I told you I had it made specially—I'll show you."

He jumped to his feet, seized the umbrella, twisted the handle . . . and stabbed into the air with a swordstick. Miss Seeton's eyes widened. The major laughed and stabbed once more, with some force, in the direction of the petticoated wax wreath dome. Miss Seeton giggled. The major caught the petticoat's lace trim with the tip of his sword, tossed, twirled, and began a deft juggle of white satin above Miss Seeton's head, the fabric swirling and billowing like some exotic canopy tethered by a shining metal cord. His movements were swift, graceful, and energetic. Miss Seeton was reminded of a toreador caping a bull, or a flamenco dancer with his cloak awhirl as he leaped. There was, she decided as she admired the performance, no inch of Major Haynes that was not pure muscle, tuned to perfection. She had always enjoyed watching an expert at work . . .

Or at play. With a sudden "Olé,!" of triumph, the major gave his wrist a sudden flick. The petticoat flew across the room to drape itself in its former elegant folds over the dome. Breathing only a little harder than usual, he slipped the sword into its umbrella sheath and sat down.

Miss Seeton's hands were still too sore for clapping, but she contrived to mime vigorous applause, nodding and smiling as she did so. The major rose to take a modest bow before sitting down again.

"To business," he said with a sympathetic glance for her bandages. "I know you haven't had much time, and your . . . stay in hospital can't have helped, but there's always a chance that you might have come up with something. Miss Seeton—where is your sketchbook?"

Chapter 25

"She looks jolly," was the major's observation as he turned a page to reveal a sketch of Jemima Wilkes in flying kit, perched on the wing of a Spitfire and waving her helmet in the air while the breeze ruffled her curls.

He had made very few comments as he leafed through the sketchbook while Miss Seeton's heart sank at his silence—a silence broken only by the discontented feet of Mrs. Beamish clumping, after a very meaningful barrage of coughs, down the stairs. Miss Seeton sighed. She—or rather, her work—had clearly disappointed him. Yet . . . competent, surely, even if uninspired: and had he not assured her, back at the Tower when she signed all those forms, that Section G would be pleased with whatever she did? Drew, that was to say. She had tried then to explain—talent, not genius—he had said it did not matter . . .

"We could certainly use a few of these for a leaflet or two," said the major as he flipped the sketchbook shut and stared down at the cover. He heard another sigh from Miss Seeton and looked up. "Make a change from sandbags, eh?"

This time she was not cheered by the little joke they had grown to share. She sighed yet again, and her voice was troubled as she embarked on an apology for having, well, wasted his—and the government's—time, and money, and—

"Hold on!" broke in the major. "What's all this? Who said anything about a waste of time?"

"The—the journey here," said Miss Seeton, her cheeks beginning to glow. "And—and everything," she finished helplessly. Her hands, had they not been sore, would have writhed into knots on the coverlet, but her fingers were able to dance a most unhappy dance, and they did.

Major Haynes muttered something and reached across to take her hands in his, holding them until they stilled, saying nothing as he held them. When at last he released her he was smiling.

"Too conscientious, my girl, that's what you are," he told her. "You've been worrying about this all along, at a guess." Mutely Miss Seeton nodded. The major nodded back. "Away from home for pretty much the first time—fretting about what might be going on back in London—trying to make sense of assembly lines and machinery when you've never seen anything like it in your life before . . . It's no surprise that you're worried. It's only natural." He grinned. "And I'll apply a metaphor from nature and call you a fish out of water, doing her best to try to keep afloat. Sound right?"

"About right, yes," said Miss Seeton, smiling now with relief that he understood so well.

"At another guess . . ." Haynes began, and stopped. When Section G had first discussed employing Emily Seeton, they had agreed that, though the experiment might well fail, it was worth a try. Had she known what they really wanted of her, she would have worried even more during her time at the factory—time that would then indeed have been wasted.

And if he told her the truth now, conscientious as he knew her to be, the same would happen. She was sure to worry herself out of any possible use to Section G. She would become self-conscious, straining with dutiful patriotism to relax as she had been relaxed when she drew those earlier, almost psychic sketches . . . with the result that anything she drew would reflect that strain, and the experiment—his experiment—would without doubt have failed.

One is not accepted into the intelligence service without intelligence. Major Haynes had plenty, and was a quick thinker. "At another guess," he said, "you need . . . well, forgive the impertinence, but speaking as a friend rather than a—a colleague . . ." He patted her hand again and coughed. "As a friend," he hurried on, "may I suggest that you need to put your worries in their proper perspective? Look them full in the face. Get them down on paper and—and yourself safely back in the water once you've seen they aren't so dreadful, after all."

The ingenuity of the logic pleased him, but it had been hard work. If he hadn't been holding Miss Seeton's hand, he would have mopped his brow.

Miss Seeton hesitated, then nodded. "You are right, I fear," she said. "I have *not* been facing up to my worries in the way I should have done—and of course it is exactly like riding a horse—not that I ever have, except for seaside donkeys as a child, which is hardly the same thing—or rather, falling off it."

For a second time Major Haynes had to think quickly. "By analogy with jumping straight back on the minute you've checked there are no bones broken," he said. "Exactly."

Miss Seeton was smiling. "Dear me," she said. "Fish and horses: it reminds me of our discussion that first day, you know, about the outing with the children to the zoo, and the girl in the kiosk who looked like little Miss Brown, and Sandy Powell—and the goldfish, of course."

Major Haynes pounced at once on this invaluable cue (*was* the girl a mind reader?) and said, "Talking of *sandy*, and thinking of those blessed bags of ours, how about a sketch or two now you seem to be more in the mood?" He turned Miss Seeton's hand over and inspected the palm. "My poor dear—you *did* come down with a bump, didn't you?"

"I exercise my fingers daily," said Miss Seeton, which was hardly a direct answer but somehow reassured him. "Such a charming girl—though very busy, of course, with so many people injured far worse than I—but she told me to play an imaginary piano whenever I could, and said what a pity it was that I cannot knit."

"The seaboot stocking—I remember." Haynes released her hand and chuckled. "You could try jotting down a few impressions of the unfortunate man who had to wear it, just to get you started . . ."

Miss Seeton found that somehow or other she was holding a pencil in one hand and the sketchbook in the other. "Go on," urged the major. "Let your subconscious rip. Show me what's been bothering you. The bogeyman is never so scary once you've seen he's not under the bed." As he spoke he lifted the frilled valance and peered. "Nobody home," he said. "And nothing to worry about. So—show me!"

For a time Miss Seeton did not move, except to close her eyes. While she concentrated, Major Haynes was also motionless, watching her face and, when they gave a sudden twitch, her fingers.

Miss Seeton opened the sketchbook to a blank page, and stared. There was a pucker between her brows as she broke the silence with a gusty sigh and set furiously to work with the pencil—swift, flowing, hazy lines, scribbled shadows and hatchings that looked, from where Haynes craned his head to see, like a dark jumble of shapes without form or reason.

The pencil flew back and forth across the paper; Major Haynes watched. And waited. And hoped . . .

Miss Seeton wilted, lying back on the pillows and letting the pencil slip from her grasp. "I've done my best," she said as the major reached out to take the sketchbook from her. "Do you . . . do you think it will work?"

Haynes did not answer. It was now his turn to concentrate. He saw . . . a man—but not the sailor who had been his suggestion. This was a man in typical Spanish costume—heeled shoes, flowing cape, flat hat beneath which his features were out of focus—juggling with bandaged hands half a dozen small black balls to each of which, on closer inspection, short lengths of string were attached. Beside him, affecting a remarkable pose in her draperies and metal breastplates, was a veiled, exotic dancer with mystery in every curve of her body. In the background overhead a group of aircraft marked with crosses swooped and soared, while a billowing parachute carried earthwards to safety an indistinct human figure that might have been male or female.

The short lengths of string . . . were fuses. The small black balls were . . . bombs, in traditional style. The aircraft marked with crosses were . . .

"Not the Luftwaffe, surely?" The major traced one of the crosses with his forefinger. "These . . ." He studied the

Spanish man's bandages. "The Red Cross?" he asked Miss Seeton, who nodded, though she looked rather more puzzled than pleased at his quick understanding.

"I'm sure I can't think why," she said, "apart from the dreadful accident to poor Betty, when Mrs. Morris and I tried to help with our sadly limited first aid and Mr. Coleman—the works manager, you know—was so disturbed, until the doctor came." She hesitated. "Which in a man, I suppose," she went on, "one may concede, particularly as it was his responsibility, even though in these days we are all asked to do what we can and one would have hoped . . . only perhaps he can't. There are many people who dislike the sight of blood. Or so I imagine he must regard it, for he is very conscientious, and the head of any organisation has to accept ultimate responsibility for what happens under his—his jurisdiction, does he not?"

"He does," said Haynes after a moment or two. He stared again at the picture. *The* exotic dancer—Mata Hari? That a spy should be foremost in Miss Seeton's mind should come as no surprise, but . . . the bomb-juggling Spaniard? "Why Spain, my dear?"

Miss Seeton began to explain the sound of castanets each time anyone went up or down the stairs, and the capelike effect of her swirling petticoat, and—this with a delicate cough—her admiration of the major's splendid physique. By the time she finished, it was hard to say who was the more embarrassed of the two in the quiet little bedroom.

"I see," said Major Haynes. "Yes, and I thank you for the compliment. Er—his face is blurred, but . . . were you thinking of Mr. Coleman when you drew this?"

Miss Seeton hesitated. "It was when the bomb dropped, I think, as we were running to the trench, for I have a memory of his gazing down at me while the doctor was . . ." She sat up. "Dr. Huxter! I had entirely forgotten him! Major Haynes, please tell me—was he hurt? Is he safe?"

"Emily Seeton, you are a shocking flirt," said the major with a grin. Then he became serious. "Didn't anyone tell you? Have you only just remembered? The concussion . . ."

Miss Seeton was shaking her head. "I believe I recall asking the nurses once or twice, but nobody would say anything, and after a time I fear that I let the matter slip from my mind. The concussion, no doubt, as you say."

"Delayed shock," agreed the major absently as he studied the sketch again. "As for your friend Huxter—is he the chap coming down with the brolly?"

Miss Seeton turned pink and said that she didn't think so, and if the major knew anything about him, she would like to hear it. "He might," she explained, "have saved my life, with his superior knowledge of the factory grounds and where we could take shelter in the emergency. I hope that nothing has . . . When he didn't come to see me, I wondered . . ."

"A flirt," said the major, "but a grateful flirt. Yes, by all accounts, Huxter did indeed get you to shelter just in time— picked you up and carried you after you fell, so I'm told. That man knows his way around, all right . . ."

As he broke off, Miss Seeton found that she was—not angry, but irritated, at her continuing ignorance. "But is the doctor *all right*, Major Haynes?" she demanded, turning even more pink in her indignation.

"What?" Haynes looked up from the sketchbook. "Oh, of course. My apologies. There was a second round of bombing after the lot that caught you—a direct hit on the Machine

Shop—and while Huxter went over to see what could be done, part of the wall collapsed on top of him."

The colour drained from Miss Seeton's cheeks, and her eyes were dark with horror. "Oh," was all she said. "Oh, dear . . ." And her hands, despite the pain, writhed together on the blanket.

"They won't have told you because . . . some of the girls were killed," said Major Haynes, once more taking her hands in his. "A lively piece with red hair was one—but Huxter came out of it alive," he added as Miss Seeton's small frame shook with a suppressed sob at the news that she would never again hear merry young Muriel—she was sure he meant Muriel—poking fun at Lord Haw-Haw. *Famine stalks side by side with Winston Churchill today. England will become a land of skeletons by the wayside.* Anything less skeletonlike than the dogged figure of Winston Churchill was hard even for Miss Seeton to imagine—but now she would no longer have to try. Miss Seeton gulped and sniffed.

"I'm sorry," said the major. "But—you asked." Miss Seeton, with another sniff, nodded. "And," Haynes went on, "didn't we agree that it's better to face up to the facts, no matter how unpalatable?"

Miss Seeton, in a trembling voice, confirmed this.

"Huxter's in another hospital with a crushed pelvis," said the major. Intelligence learned most things, sooner or later. "He's a regular jigsaw puzzle of pins and wires and plaster, but he'll live, though it's doubtful if he'll walk properly again." He did not add *if ever*, but Miss Seeton, for all her distress, was no fool. He did not need to add it. The tears spilled down her cheeks, and she wrenched her hands from those of Major Haynes to hide her face from his sympathetic sight.

Awkwardly he patted her on the shoulder. "I'm sorry," he said. "I'll leave you now—you'll want to be left alone for a while." He cleared his throat. "I—I've brought you another sketchbook and some more pencils. I'll leave them on the dressing table and . . ."

He picked up the original sketchbook and, with a final glance at the Spaniard, closed it. "I must be off," he said. He picked up his swordstick umbrella, slipped the sketchbook in his pocket, and patted Miss Seeton once more on the shoulder before, without a backward glance, walking quietly from the room.

"I've had to tell her what happened after she was knocked out," he told Tilly Beamish, who met him at the bottom of the stairs to bar his escape until he should confess to such sins as might have been committed during his time in her lodger's bedroom. "She's pretty upset, but—"

"Of course she is," retorted Tilly with scorn. "Father and son the Huxters have doctored this part of the world, good men both of them, and to bomb and cripple the likes of him—if I could only get my hands on that Hitler . . ."

As she paused for breath the major seized his chance. "She's upset," he said again, "but a good cry will do her a world of good—I suspect she's been bottling it up for some time. It would be a kindness if you could take her a cup of tea in, say, half an hour, and sit with her awhile if she wants to chat." He directed the full force of his charming smile at Mrs. Beamish, who found herself smiling back.

"I might," he told her, reaching automatically for the pocket that contained the sketchbook, "be seeing Dr. Huxter later on. If I do, I'll send him your regards, shall I?"

Dr. Huxter—who knew his way and seemed to move freely around a factory that was high security . . .

Chapter 26

When war had been declared on Germany in September of the previous year, more expensive branded petrol was immediately replaced by blended "pool" at a cost of one shilling and sixpence per gallon. Petrol was rationed from the twenty-second of the month, and while every car owner could obtain his basic coupons by presenting the car's logbook at his post office, the amount of petrol thus permitted did not take him far. Supplementary coupons could be issued for such domestic or business purposes that were deemed essential, though drivers' views on what might or might not be essential seldom agreed with those of the authorities to whom they had to apply. Only if one was engaged upon work of national importance could a car's use be considered patriotically permissible, given the growing efficiency of the U-boat blockade.

By the late summer of 1940, even to visit the convalescent Emily Dorothea Seeton, civilian war artist seconded to MI5 Section G and injured in its service, Major Haynes had not been granted the use of a car. He had followed in Miss Seeton's wake and come by train from London, although at his destination he had been met by a police car with a uniformed driver who was bursting to know who the stranger—and what his business, so obviously secret—might be.

"Why, they told us she wasn't a wrong 'un," he had said as the car drew up outside Tilly Beamish's house. "Phoned from London to say to let her go. Was that you? Changed your mind? Or is she really one of yours?"

Major Haynes looked with new interest at this young man who, without being told, had deduced so much so quickly. He countered these questions with questions of his own. "Do you enjoy being a policeman? Have you ever thought about a more . . . challenging job?"

"Ah," said his chauffeur. "Well, now." He turned to focus on the major a gaze that was both contemplative and shrewd. "More of a challenge than being a village bobby? Well, and maybe I have, at that." Then he grinned as he jerked his head in the direction of Tilly's front gate. "Don't you go rushing into things, mind. Think it over. I'll still be here when you get back."

When Major Haynes emerged from Mrs. Beamish's house and made his way down the path, he saw the young policeman slumped in the driver's seat, dozing in the warmth of the July sun. Something about the nonchalance of the posture made Haynes open the front gate very quietly and shut it with even greater care. He walked almost on tiptoe to the passenger door, but was forestalled when, without appearing to notice him, the young policeman reached out a long arm to click the handle down. The door drifted open, and Haynes climbed in.

"Watched for you in the glass," came the greeting as the major settled himself on his seat. "Easy enough to tilt the wing mirror—and easy enough for folks to think I'm asleep on the job, isn't it?"

"It is," said Haynes, impressed. "Yes, indeed. Tell me, are you local to these parts?"

The young policeman chuckled. "Ah, we ain't all of us in the country the idiots you city types like to think, even if what education's come our way's been a bit basic. But a bloke with common sense picks things up—and goes on learning—right the way down the line. Doesn't he?"

"He does," Haynes agreed with approval. "Then you must know the Huxter family pretty well."

"Oh, it's not him," was the prompt and confident reply. "Whoever your lot's after, it's no more the doctor than that welfare girl of yours lodging along of Mother Beamish—not that I'd care to be so sure about the rest of 'em up at the factory, mind. Naming no names, but if you was to ask . . ."

Haynes looked at him. In silence, he looked back. Haynes nodded. "I'm asking," he said slowly, "whether Mr. Coleman is quite as . . . competent as the manager responsible for the production of aeroplanes vital to this country's survival ought to be—a manager who, until the war came, was happily running one of the largest motorcar factories in the country. A factory that was a byword for efficient productivity . . ."

"Ah," said the young policeman.

That was all he said, and as soon as he had spoken, he started the car and drove off. He did not need to ask where the major wished to go, and Haynes saw no need to tell him.

When they arrived at the factory gates, there was some argument with Day George, whose temper had not been improved by the recent bombing incident, and who was determined to let nobody in without authorisation. He still felt guilty for having weakened under the persuasion of Dr. Huxter and Miss Seeton: had they not been running for shelter when the Nazi plane made its first attack, they might not have been injured. Day George and his numerous siblings had been brought into the world by Samuel Huxter's father; George did not care for the idea that it might be partly his fault that the son had only by inches missed a premature reunion with his deceased parent.

"Well, look here, if you don't believe *him*," said the young policeman at last, with a jerk of his thumb towards Major Haynes, "or them papers he's shown you—you know who I am right enough, don't you?"

George conceded that he did, adding hastily as he sighted along his rifle that the place could be full of fifth columnists for all he'd been told to the contrary, and it was his job to stop them.

"Then I'll be a hostage." The young policeman turned to wink at Haynes, and turned back before the other had time to speak. "For the major's good behaviour, see? Just let me pull the car off the road, and you can keep me in sight the whole time he's inside. What about that for an offer?"

Quite how it happened George never knew, but within a minute the police car and its young driver were the only witnesses to the presence of Major Haynes on the factory premises. The major had nodded his thanks to the young man whose noble sacrifice (his curiosity by now must be almost unbearable) had made access possible, and slipped past the sentry hut before George worked out what was going on.

Military intelligence had obtained a floor plan from the Ministry of Aircraft Production, but Haynes knew that the manager, working with the rest of the factory around the clock, might be anywhere on the site at any time. It would be a matter of hunting him down and luring him into a quiet corner for a serious talk. The admin, block might be a good starting point for his tour: he was curious to meet, if he could, the woman whose suspicions of Miss Seeton had landed the young artist in police custody.

One-armed George popped his head through the hatch and glared at Major Haynes. The major, recognising a martial gleam in the older man's eye, uttered a few cryptic phrases that had the Great War veteran grinning with pleased reminiscence, and waving the newcomer past with only a cursory look at his papers. "Third door on the left, sir," he said. "And don't bother to knock."

There was, however, no Mrs. Morris to be found in the Welfare Office. Haynes took advantage of her absence to check one or two of those filing-cabinet drawers with the most promising labels. He was delighted to discover that all, without exception, were locked.

"Easy to pick, of course," he reflected as he jingled the short lengths of hooked wire kept always in his jacket pocket. "Most people couldn't, though, so Morris scores on security. That's a point in her favour . . . unless it's a double bluff." Such ploys were not unknown in his line of business.

And the business of . . . what other person, or persons, in the Spitfire factory?

He tried the manager's office next. He did not knock on the door. He opened it and saw a male figure draped across a blotter on the desk. At the sound of the opening latch the figure shot upright, its thin frame quivering in alarm.

264

"Wh-ho are you?" demanded Mr. Coleman, his eyes bright. "What do you mean by b-bursting in here?"

Once more Major Haynes produced the identity papers over which Day George had cast so suspicious, and Old George so casual, an eye. "I would hardly call it *bursting*," he said quietly as he laid them on the yawning manager's desk. "But I apologise for having startled you. From the look and the sound of you, you need all the sleep you can get."

Mr. Coleman swallowed the rest of his yawn, and shuddered. "Your people must know more about that than I do, Major Haynes—if that is your name." The major bowed, but said nothing. "I've no doubt you are kept informed by B-Beaverbrook's minions as to the exact number of hours each and any of us manages to snatch from working." Mr. Coleman took a deep breath, blinked, pushed the papers back across the desk, and waved towards a chair piled with papers that, to the major's keen eye, looked like blueprints. "Please sit down," he invited.

Major Haynes hesitated. Mr. Coleman began to look uneasy rather than drowsy. The major swept the pile of blueprints up in his arms and dropped them on the floor. He took the chair, carried it to the door, closed the door, tipped the chair on its back legs and its back under the door handle, and walked back to Mr. Coleman . . . his prisoner.

"Why," asked Major Haynes softly, "did you do it?"

The factory manager gaped at him. "What?"

Major Haynes did not reply.

"Did I do what?" persisted the factory manager. "What—what in heaven's name do you mean?"

Sadly Major Haynes shook his head. "A man with a clear conscience," he said, "would have asked me what the devil I meant by jamming his office door with a chair and locking him in. You merely ask what in heaven's name I mean. You can't be *that* sleepy. The game's up, Coleman." He added in a sympathetic tone: "And it's hardly been either a game or heavenly for you—has it? Though I've no doubt your conscience is clear, in your own morally contorted fashion."

The works manager gaped at him again. Major Haynes nodded. "An innocent man would by now either be telling me I've gone raving mad," he said, "or shouting for help. You, on the other hand, have done no more than twitter. On the whole I don't care for the philosophy that silence is proof of guilt, but in this particular case I'm willing to make an exception."

Mr. Coleman's eyes darted from the door, blocked by the chair, to the window—which, despite the heat, was closed against the factory sounds from outside. He had, after all, been trying to sleep when Major Haynes arrived. He looked at the metal paperweight gleaming on his desk, but there would have been little point in trying to throw it to break the glass. He would not have been able to climb through even the largest panes, which in any case were so heavily taped with brown paper against blast they would probably not have broken.

"Better give in gracefully," advised Major Haynes, who had watched the other man closely, reading his mind in his expression. "There's no escape. We'll probably see you hanged for a murderer, but we might, and I stress the *might*, not use our option to have you shot as a traitor. We know about you, you see."

"Do you?" Coleman, whose shoulders had sagged, pulled himself together. "Then I wonder that I was ever appointed to this job . . . if you knew *all* about me. Perhaps you knew less than you ought."

"Or thought," amended the major neatly. "There's something in that line of reasoning, I agree, but we know rather more now—and what we know is enough to know the charges will stick. Don't think I'm bluffing," he added as the manager's face registered scornful disbelief. "We have a witness statement that you are the one behind the sabotage—for which we concede there might have been some sympathy for you—as well as the one who killed two people within a space of twenty-four hours last week, for which we can feel no sympathy at all."

His hand had strayed to the sketchbook in his pocket as he spoke of a witness statement, but his eyes never left those of the works manager—who, now that the accusation had been made, seemed almost relieved.

"Sympathy?" he cried, his mouth twisting sideways in a rictus of ironic mirth. "Sympathy? My son—my *only* son—killed fighting—flying—in Spain—my wife dead of a broken heart within the year—everything I've worked and cared for in my life, lost—wasted—senselessly—and you talk to me of sympathy?" He reached for the paperweight and gripped it in a white-knuckled fist. "You can always take one with you," he quoted grimly, his thin body tensed as if to spring.

"And that one won't be me," said the major. "Untrained killers need luck, and surprise, on their side. You have neither just now . . . But last week was a different story."

"Last week," echoed the manager. Once more his shoulders sagged. He let the paperweight thump from his opened fist on to the desk. "Luck . . ."

"Bad luck, the worst possible, for them," said Haynes. "But good luck for *you* in the furtherance of what we'll call your campaign. For you, the killing of a couple of people who learned too much counted for nothing against the greater number of deaths—pointless deaths, in your view, of young fighting men in their prime—you were hoping to prevent by your sabotage. You tried all along not to do any serious damage, didn't you? That's why it took a while to register that there really was something sinister about the number of mishaps that were occurring on this site—although never to a finished plane, when a test pilot might have been killed."

Haynes sighed. "Perhaps that very fact should have been a pointer, but we missed it. The pilots were safe. They never had to use their parachutes on your account . . ." Even at such a time he had to smile. Mr. Coleman, his eyes clouded with misery, did not notice. "You spared them," Haynes hurried on, "and it wasn't just because you knew them as individuals, colleagues, with names and families of their own . . . You could, I'm sure, have squared your conscience as you squared it when you killed the other two—but they were young, as your son was young, and like him they had lives to live, a future to look forward to. You could see no reason why even one young man should lose his life, his future, in support of this war . . . any war."

The major's voice was low as he ended: "I told you that we knew about you—that we had some sympathy—but we make no allowances when national security is at stake. You were believed to be setting patriotism above your personal philosophy in your work here—and that belief of ours was mistaken. We do not often make such mistakes." Once more the major's hand strayed to the sketchbook in his pocket.

"Fortunately this mistake was retrieved before things went too far in the wrong direction."

"The wrong direction?" In his white face the eyes of the manager suddenly blazed. "War is *wrong*! Fighting is *wrong*! The waste of *a single life* is wrong, never mind the thousands—millions—who will die in the very near future thanks to the stubborn blindness of the politicians!"

Haynes regarded him sadly. "In the very near future," he echoed. "Yes. Let me tell you, Mr. Coleman, that by your actions you may, you *may*, have saved the lives of a handful of airmen for a brief period—but believe me, it has been only a delay. And I know that you *do* believe me. The time is fast approaching when every man, woman, and child in this island will have to face up to the realisation that it is fight, or go under. Kill, or be killed. I regret as much as anyone that this is not an ideal world—but it is not. In an ideal world, I agree, pacifism would hold sway above all else. In an ideal world, there would be no room for Hitler. But Hitler, Coleman, has found plenty of room for himself and is making more—by invasion, by conquest, by terror—every minute of every day."

He paused. Mr. Coleman said nothing. The major picked up the paperweight. It was a brass shell case. He sighed for the irony.

"Kill, or be killed," he repeated. "You have two deaths on your conscience. The Home Guard and the cleaner—were *they* going to kill *you*? An elderly man, and a conscientious objector? I think not."

"They . . . knew too much," said the manager, unable to resist the stern challenge in the major's eyes.

"They found out too much," Haynes amended. "No doubt it was by accident, as there have been so many other *accidents* at this factory over the past few months—but you couldn't make their deaths look like accidents, could you? There was no time. They might reveal what they had found out to someone with the authority to stop you. You killed them as soon as you knew that they knew, and it was impossible to avoid having the police called in."

"The police learned nothing," said Coleman quickly. "If— if there was, as you say, a witness to . . . what happened, why was I not . . . questioned—arrested—earlier?"

"This," the major told him, "was a very special witness. Very special indeed." And his hand strayed once more to the pocket that held Miss Seeton's *very special* sketchbook.

Chapter 27

"He relied on the Chesterton effect," Haynes explained to his colleagues back at the Tower. "In the same way that the postman in the celebrated short story was invisible, so was Coleman. As works manager he could go anywhere on the premises at any hour, day or night, and nobody would be in the least surprised to see him."

"Except that they *didn't* see him," said Chandler. "Not to notice him, that is. Thank you, Haynes. We take the point."

"Not too sharply, though," said Aylwin. "He'd obviously been seen—noticed—on two occasions at least, or he would never have killed those chaps. Odd sort of behaviour, for a pacifist."

"For the greater good," said Chandler. "That was his justification, of course. Did he tell you what exactly it was they noticed?"

The major shook his head. "He babbled on at me for a while about war, and waste, and government skulduggery and so forth—not that it was all entirely babble, of course, if it could only be applied in an ideal world. Or applied rather earlier in the proceedings than where we are now."

"This house," muttered Captain Grange through his beard, "will under no circumstances ever fight for its King and country. Ha!"

"Don't let's get started on the Oxford Union," begged Chandler as Cox, the cynical, uttered a loud snort. "It was seven years ago and a different world." And with this plea he successfully squashed any attempt to argue (as many did) that the notorious university debate of 1933 had done much to encourage Hitler in his grandiose national land-expansion schemes. Hindsight suggested the vote might not have been carried with such enthusiasm had the voters possessed foresight . . . but it was, as Chandler said, seven years ago.

"My guess," interposed Haynes before an argument could start about anything else, "is that the Home Guard spotted Coleman fiddling about with some widget he had no business to be touching. The poor old chap's health wouldn't support his working full-time at the factory, but we know he had a certain amount of engineering experience in his background. He would have understood rather better than a casual bloke-on-patrol that what the manager was doing was potentially damaging, and my suspicion is that he challenged him about it and . . ."

"Had his head bashed in for his pains," said Cox darkly. "So much for the rewards of virtue!"

"The same theory holds, presumably, in the case of Raybould," said Chandler.

Everyone sat up.

"Raybould," said Captain Grange. "Ha! If Beaverbrook had only *told* us, things might have been very different."

Aylwin grinned at him. "I thought the Royal Navy view was that everything should be done in duplicate where you can? If not in triplicate?" He reeled back as if a thought had just struck him. "Good heavens! Suppose—"

"Fool," snapped the captain with a scowl. The resultant awkward silence was broken by Haynes.

"The Beaver has his own approach to problems," he said. "I agree it would have been advisable for him to consult us before sending in his own undercover agent, but given the urgency I can see why he wasted no time with red tape and simply got on with the job."

"Got Raybould on the job, you mean," said Aylwin. "Was the man a genuine conchie? I wouldn't put it past the old man to have arranged a—a pool of the blighters, ready to spy out the land in all sorts of dodgy situations."

"Currying favour as patriots," said Cox, "when they're not prepared to fight. Ugh."

Chandler said quickly that the war was being fought for the safeguarding of freedom, including the freedom to hold genuine religious or philosophical beliefs. As it happened, however, Raybould was *not* a conscientious objector. He was an army captain, wounded at Dunkirk and still technically on furlough, whose convalescence had been . . . interrupted by an appeal from Lord Beaverbrook, a family friend.

"He was good for sweeping," he explained, "but not much else. The shrapnel wounds gave the mortuary quite a shock when they looked him over. In theory he was barely able to walk, but when Beaverbrook told him what he suspected was going on he made a tremendous effort and . . ."

He finished with a rueful shrug, and a sigh that was echoed round the table.

"A good man, by all accounts." The naval captain paid tribute to his army junior in a gruff, regretful voice. "If only we'd been told, we might have got someone there sooner as—as backup."

"We sent Miss Seeton," said Chandler.

All heads turned as one towards Major Haynes, who bowed quietly in acknowledgement of the salute.

"Much good she would have been in a scrap," said Cox as Aylwin chuckled.

"She came up with the answer," said Haynes, indicating with a forceful gesture the sketchbook lying on the table around which they sat. "Don't ask me how she knew, but she did. That girl has a—an uncanny gift, there's no getting away from it."

Aylwin eyed him shrewdly. "Thought you said she wasn't pretty?" he said with another chuckle.

"She's not," said Haynes calmly. "No glamour at all. She's quiet, ladylike, has her own way of looking at things . . . and somehow, I don't know how she does it, she makes you look another way at her, too."

"A quaint little body," agreed Chandler. "I can see the attraction to those who appreciate the . . . unusual."

Aylwin snorted. So, in a very different way, did the misogynist Cox. Captain Grange cleared his throat. Chandler glanced at Haynes, who bowed again. In the awkward lighting of the little room, it was difficult to tell if he was blushing or not.

"So," resumed Chandler, "the unusual Miss Seeton drew a peculiar picture, and you took the risk—the grave risk—of accusing Coleman on the strength of this doodle *and nothing else*. You called it a witness statement, but the girl was hardly a witness. She wasn't there. She didn't see either of the murders take place—how could she?"

Haynes shook his head. "I told you, I don't know how she does it—any of it," he said. "But she *was* a witness: she witnessed Coleman's response to the bombing raid and to the accident, a genuine accident, to young Betty. There was honest shock, horror, in his reaction to the kid's injuries—remember, he'd always tried to avoid hurting anyone as far as he could, especially the younger workers with their lives ahead of them. Miss Seeton seems to have . . . latched on to this in some way I—we—can't understand . . . Maybe it was the bump on the head, poor girl, that made her extra sensitive, but we have to accept there was a definite tendency in that direction even before she was blown up. Otherwise," he concluded, "we wouldn't have been so bothered by Steptoe's original report. And we would never have sent her to the factory in the first place."

"We take," reiterated Chandler, "the point."

"Might try using her again," suggested Captain Grange. "Seems to have done well enough here," he added as everyone looked at him in some surprise. "Worth a try," he said once more, and subsided with a fit of coughing.

Chandler returned quickly to the main topic under discussion. "Raybould," he said, "being a cleaner, had as much right to wander the place as Coleman. Whatever he saw that roused his suspicion of Coleman we can't guess—and before anyone suggests it, I don't propose asking Miss Seeton to sketch *her* guesses, thank you. Leave her where she is, at least for the moment."

"When's she coming back?" asked Cox, carefully not looking at the major. "And do we send a personal escort when she does?"

"Miss Seeton," Haynes informed him in level tones, "who has, it seems, quite remarkable powers of recuperation, will

275

shortly be taking over full-time as workers' welfare officer at the factory following the—ah—unexpected collapse of Mrs. Morris after the . . . regrettably fatal accident to Mr. Coleman. She, that is Emily—Seeton," he added just too late to prevent Aylwin's chuckle, "will remain there in the interests of the general morale until a more suitable, permanent replacement can be found." Then he let a grin soften his features. "And they'd better hurry up," he said. "She *means* well, but . . ."

"But," supplied Chandler as his colleague fell silent.

"Says it all, really," said Captain Grange. "About the girl, I mean. No doubts now about her loyalty, patriotism, sense of duty, and so forth. But . . ."

"Quite," said Major Haynes as the naval beard wagged up and down in a paroxysm of speechless confusion.

Cox, who had been scowling in his normal manner at the sketchbook on the table, looked at Haynes. "Coleman's death was," he enquired, "an accident?"

"I made very sure it was," the major told him. "He knew the game was up, and he knew he had a choice. End up going before a court, risking publicity—even MI can't guarantee to catch everything before it gets in the papers—with the subsequent loss of morale—or the alternative of what must, I suppose, be called the Gentlemanly Way Out."

"Offered to lend him your revolver and lock him in the library, did you?" Aylwin was as irrepressible as ever.

"I asked him to take me on a guided tour," said Haynes. "Accidents can happen in the best-regulated factories, particularly when they've been working flat out round the clock for weeks and everyone is always more than half-asleep even when they're theoretically awake . . ."

There was a thoughtful silence, broken at last by Captain Grange. "Good," was all he said, but he echoed the general sentiment, and Haynes once more inclined his head.

"And nobody smelled a rat?" This from Cox.

"Accidents," Haynes reminded him, "happen in the best-regulated circles. The police were glad to have it sorted out without a lot of . . . unpleasantness. My driver—the young chap who's coming to see us next week—told me the locals had wondered all along about the wisdom of putting Coleman in charge of the place, but they assumed he'd been vetted and, as we did in fact suppose, was putting the needs of his country before his private philosophy."

Captain Grange coughed. "Did the decent thing in the end," he said. "In one way you can see his point of view—son killed, futility of war—but . . ." And again the beard signaled its confusion.

"So kind of Hitler to give us one last chance to see it for ourselves," said Aylwin after another short silence. He grinned. "If you'd told me it was April Fools' Day coming round again four months late, I'd have believed you!"

"Bit of a cheek," said Chandler, "littering the countryside with leaflets. *Last Appeal to Reason*, indeed! As if anyone in his right mind would believe a single word of that lunatic's speeches!"

"No doubt the Reichstag swallowed it whole," said Cox. "Now *we're* the aggressors—after what the blighters have done to Czecho and Poland and Denmark and France and—"

"Useful salvage, though," put in Haynes as Cox paused for breath. "Paper pulp is in increasingly short supply, and every little helps. Once it's been mashed and bleached and whatever else they do, what was originally written on the stuff won't hurt . . . any more than it hurts now," he added with a laugh.

The others laughed with him, Chandler quickly reminding them of how those people lucky enough to find one of the Nazi propaganda leaflets dropped over southern England during the night of 1st August had been putting them up for auction, all proceeds going towards the war effort. Britain, with her back to the wall, knowing the situation could explode at any minute, still contrived to keep her sense of humour.

With courage, resolve, and a sense of humour, much can be achieved in a nation's darkest hour . . .

The German assault on London—the capital's first serious daylight raid—began in the late afternoon of Saturday, 7th September, to endure for seven interminable hours and twenty unforgettable minutes. In a sinister formation one and a half miles high and covering eight hundred square miles of sky, the enemy aircraft (almost a thousand—three hundred of them bombers) crossed the Channel and headed inland to their target. So ferocious was the eventual onslaught that invasion code word *Cromwell* was flashed from post to post across the country, and church bells were rung as the whole world throbbed and roared and howled and the sky darkened with wave upon wave of aircraft dropping over three hundred and fifty tons of bombs to such effect that, by Sunday morning, four hundred and forty-eight Londoners were dead, and sixteen hundred seriously injured. Twenty-eight British fighter aircraft were lost in the counterattack, and three more were destroyed on the ground.

Those in the know rejoiced at this change of Nazi strategy from aerial combat between military pilots to wholesale slaughter of innocent civilians and the destruction of their homes. Those in the know were well aware that, though the desperate shortage of fighter aircraft was—thanks to Lord Beaverbrook—less desperate than it once had been, it would take very little for the shortage of pilots—all of them exhausted, some flying with no more than ten hours' combat practice behind them—to render the Battle of Britain lost.

But the Battle of London—the Blitz—had begun. Grim as its beginning had been, with the threat of worse to come—it was to be more than seven weeks before the bombing ceased, and then only for one cloudy night—it had bought for Britain a breathing space. The chiefs of the air staff, the government, and the Intelligence services knew that the price at which it had been bought was high, but that no price, in the circumstances, would—or could—have been too high. Hitler's invasion plan had failed. Britain—with luck, and hope, and prayers—might have a chance.

Far from London Miss Seeton heard the news, and ached to be at home rather than where she was. While Hampstead was not bombed on the seventh, communications were disrupted, and Alice was unable to send a message that she was, for the moment, safe. Her daughter knew where her duty lay: she would not press for her replacement at the factory, but she worried, and her dreams were very troubled.

Release and her replacement came on 10th September, the day after Hampstead's first bombs fell. Miss Seeton, weary and travel-stained, reached home next day to find all the mainline stations closed and another air raid in progress, so that it was not until very late in the evening of the eleventh that she picked her shaky way through the blackout to the welcome little porch, to be greeted with a maternal kiss, a smile, an envelope, and two wrapped packages.

"It's your birthday," Alice reminded her with another smile. "Poor Emily. You had forgotten, had you not?"

"I. . . had," Emily agreed, stifling a yawn. "I'm sorry—but I—I've had rather a lot on my mind recently." She told her mother nothing of what she had been thinking, or doing, and Alice knew better than to ask.

"Mr. Churchill gave such a splendid speech on the wireless," she said. "One cannot say that he minces matters, of course, but it is better to be told the truth and have the chance to face up to one's difficulties, wouldn't you say?" She gave her daughter no time to agree. "He told us," she went on, "that Hitler has transport barges all along the Channel coast, and there are batteries of guns everywhere, and thousands of troops, and we must expect invasion next week because of the weather . . ." She watched as Emily unwrapped the first of her packages. "Your aim," she said quietly as the paper fell away, "will be steadier than mine, but I polished them with great care—it seemed the very least I could do."

"Th-thank you," was Emily's reply as the bullets lay shining in the palm of her hand.

"You can always take one with you," said Alice to her daughter, who was still gazing at the bullets. "Your dear father's regimental sword will suit me best, I think, and is with his revolver on the hall table, which seems the most sensible place for it—unless they land on the roof, in which case I think the noise will wake us and there will be time to run downstairs and shoot them once they have tumbled to the ground—or stab them as they lie there. They are sure to be winded by their fall, which ought to slow them down long enough for us to play our part. Aren't they?"

"Yes, of course," said Emily, after a pause in which she marvelled at how adversity could change—could surprise—people. Her gentle mother's plans to repel Nazi invaders were hardly practical, but they showed a fighting spirit of which Hugo Monk Seeton need not, when his wife and daughter met him again, feel ashamed . . .

"Oh," said Alice, "and something else—a letter for you—now, where did I put it? There was no time to send it on, as you had said you hoped to be back soon."

It was the now familiar brown OHMS envelope, but addressed in an unfamiliar hand. The letter inside invited Miss E. D. Seeton to attend the Tower of London at two-thirty in the afternoon of Friday, 13th September. Miss Seeton smiled as she checked the postmark. Section G must have known well before she did when she would be coming home.

The signature, in blue ink, was both neat and legible. It was not *Haynes* . . . it was *Chandler*.

"Miss Seeton, thank you for coming," was Chandler's greeting at the sentry-box end of the bridge. "I hope you and yours suffered no great inconvenience in this morning's raid?"

Miss Seeton, stifling a sigh, assured him that while she—and her mother—had been unaffected by the four hours of bombing, she was sorry to have heard from a policeman that Buckingham Palace had been hit.

"More than once," Chandler told her. "Of course, things could have been worse, when you remember the blighters were here for eight hours last night as well. There's been quite a little party, all over town—the House of Lords had an incendiary, and they dropped another in Downing Street—though if they were hoping to get Churchill, they didn't."

"I'm very relieved to hear it," said Miss Seeton.

There was a pause. "Yes," he replied at last. "Look, Miss Seeton . . . let's go up to my office, shall we?"

He offered no more small-talk as he led his visitor through the hidden passageways and across the courtyards of the Tower. "First," he said, "I want to tell you that we're more grateful than we can say for your efforts at the factory. You deserve a medal. We'll have to see what can be done—though, of course, we can't promise."

"Good gracious, of course not," said Miss Seeton, shocked at the very idea. A few quick sketches, a short spell of office administration, a handful of silly girls who needed (and received) a swift lesson in common sense could be taken—had been taken—by an art teacher in her stride. Even that foolish misunderstanding with Mrs. Morris had been sorted out with remarkably little inconvenience to anyone save herself, who was a soldier's daughter, while the bump on the head and the damage to her knees could have happened to anyone in an air raid. They certainly did not merit any form of official decoration, which is what Mr. Chandler seemed to be saying.

"Of course not," said Miss Seeton, gazing high overhead to where swirling white vapour trails showed the presence of those who truly deserved a medal. *All our hearts*, Mr. Churchill had said, *go out to the fighter pilots*. With most of that sentiment, Miss Seeton would not disagree.

"I'm sorry," she said as she realised that Chandler had been speaking to her, and she had heard nothing. "I do beg your pardon, but I was . . . distracted."

"You've had a time and a half of it," he said with some sympathy. "Look—don't let's go indoors just yet. Fresh air is such a blessing, and while the sunshine lasts . . ."

Miss Seeton glanced at him. For some reason, he seemed to be uneasy. She did not care to think what that reason might be, and embarked upon an anecdote from her time at the factory, when one of the pilots reported a maniac kettledrummer inside his engine whenever he dived. He was accused of hallucinating, insisted it was either a kettledrummer or a midget with a machine gun, and was mollified only when it was found that the petrol tank's self-seal covering had split. At high speeds it flapped between the tank and the armour plating with a vibration so very staccato that anyone could have been forgiven for thinking the plane might shake to pieces in midair.

"You seem to have picked up the jargon quite nicely, Miss Seeton." Chandler smiled, though the smile appeared forced. "So you enjoyed your assignment?"

"A teacher," Miss Seeton replied, "should try to keep an open mind and make the most of each new experience. In that respect, I may say I found it interesting—if not necessarily enjoyable—but in time of war one must do what one can, without complaint, for one's country. As I believe I did."

"You did, yes." Chandler hesitated. "For one's country . . . Look, Miss Seeton, it's about Jerry."

Miss Seeton's gaze rose automatically to the swirling vapour trails of battle.

"No," said Chandler, "I'm sorry, I meant Gerry. Haynes. Gerald Haynes . . ."

"Gerald," echoed Miss Seeton. Here was one piece of the puzzle solved.

She suspected she did not want to know any more of it.

But she was a soldier's daughter . . .

"Major Haynes," she said. "My departmental superior, as one may call him."

"That's the chap," said Chandler. He took a deep breath and began to gabble. "Look, Miss Seeton, soldiering's a bloody, begging your pardon, business, and Gerry had to go down to Dover on . . . business I'm afraid I can't tell you, and they got it pretty badly the day he was down there with bombs, and shells from the coastal guns—and nearly fifty people injured—and . . . and seven people killed."

"I see," said Miss Seeton quietly.

"Yes," said Chandler.

Miss Seeton found that gazing so intently into the sky had dazzled her. She looked away, pulled a handkerchief from her pocket, and wiped her eyes.

"It was quick," said Chandler at last. "He . . . couldn't have known a thing about it. He . . . hadn't wanted to go, you know, but when you're in the forces, orders is orders, and the job was . . . necessary, believe me, and he managed to finish it before . . . He'd been hoping you'd be back in time for . . . It was your birthday, you see."

"I see," said Miss Seeton again. "The date was . . . in the files, no doubt."

Chandler nodded. He did not speak. Neither, for a long time, did Miss Seeton.

"I think," said Chandler at last, "he would have wanted— have liked—you to . . . Come with me," he concluded with a brisk shake of his shoulders. In silence, Miss Seeton followed him; from kindness, he did not look round.

"After you," he said as he unlocked and opened the door of his office. Miss Seeton walked in and waited.

"Here." He strode across to the hat stand, and from one of the hooks lifted down . . .

"The major's swordstick umbrella!" cried Miss Seeton.

Chandler thrust it at her. "Go on, take it. He said he gave you a demonstration—very proud of his skill, was our Gerry. He had it made specially, did he tell you? That's why it was his password—that daft riddle."

Miss Seeton, accepting into her startled hands the bi-coloured brolly, stared at it for a moment. Then a gentle smile crossed her face. "What," she whispered, "goes up a chimney down, but can't go down a chimney up? Of course!"

She was oblivious to the salutes of the sentries as she made her way slowly from the Tower. In the office Chandler had thumped her on the shoulder in a comradely gesture before escorting her to the sentry box on the bridge, where he said he knew he had no need to remind her that she had signed the Official Secrets Act, and that because she had done such a splendid job for them she should not be surprised if they were to call on her again. The country (he ended) owed more to her than perhaps she realised.

Miss Seeton tried to reply that the country owed her nothing, but her voice was as mute as her heart was full. She clutched the umbrella as if it were a talisman, and, when Chandler thumped her shoulder again, she could only nod and walk away.

At the far end of the bridge she stopped. She did not look up at the sky, but down at the umbrella in her hands. *The job was necessary. He managed to finish it.* For this, at least, she could be glad. He had died for his country: her country. Mr. Churchill's words came back to her . . .

"Never in the field of human conflict was so much owed, by so many, to so few."

Glossary

The following expressions were well understood in wartime Britain, but may be unfamiliar to American readers seventy years later:

Ack-ack, anti-aircraft

Almoner, old-fashioned term for (medical) social worker

ARP, Air Raid Precautions (later, Civil Defence organisation)

Barrage balloon, large balloon tethered by wire ropes, causing enemy aircraft to fly higher above the target and to drop their bombs with less accuracy

ENSA, Entertainments National Service Association (entertainers to the armed forces)

LDV, Local Defence Volunteers; civilian force of non-enlisted men, later renamed the Home Guard (and, thirty years on, nicknamed Dad's Army for the benefit of a highly successful television series)

Maginot Line, the French fortifications that had been expected to prevent invasion by the Germans but didn't (the Germans wisely went round the end of the Line rather than attacking it)

pillbox, a small concrete fort, generally half-buried in the ground

WVS, Women's Voluntary Service; the "Ladies in Green" who were (and, with an additional "Royal" in their name, still are) committed providers of tea, sympathy, and even more essential unpaid social services

Preview

It's practically a Royal Marriage! The highly eligible son of Miss Seeton's old friends Sir George and Lady Colveden has wed the daughter of a French count.

Miss Seeton lends her talents to the village scheme to create a quilted 'Bayeux Tapestry' for Nigel and his bride. But her intuitive sketches reveal a startlingly different perspective—involving buried Nazi secrets, and links to a murdered diplomat and a South American dictator . . .

Serene amidst every kind of skulduggery, this eccentric English spinster steps in where Scotland Yard stumbles, armed with nothing more than her sketchpad and umbrella!

The new Miss Seeton mystery

COMING SOON!

About the Miss Seeton series

Retired art teacher Miss Seeton steps in where Scotland Yard
stumbles. Armed with only her sketch pad and umbrella, she
is every inch an eccentric English spinster and at every turn
the most lovable and unlikely master of detection.

Further titles in the series —

Picture Miss Seeton
A night at the opera strikes a chord of danger
when Miss Seeton witnesses a murder . . . and paints
a portrait of the killer.

Miss Seeton Draws the Line
Miss Seeton is enlisted by Scotland Yard when her
paintings of a little girl turn the young subject into a
model for murder.

Witch Miss Seeton
Double, double, toil and trouble sweep through
the village when Miss Seeton goes undercover . . .
to investigate a local witches' coven!

Miss Seeton Sings
Miss Seeton boards the wrong plane and lands
amidst a gang of European counterfeiters. One
false note, and her new destination
is deadly indeed.

Odds on Miss Seeton
Miss Seeton in diamonds and furs at the roulette table? It's all a clever disguise for the high-rolling spinster . . . but the game of money and murder is all too real.

Miss Seeton, By Appointment
Miss Seeton is off to Buckingham Palace on a secret mission—but to foil a jewel heist, she must risk losing the Queen's head . . . and her own neck!

Advantage, Miss Seeton
Miss Seeton's summer outing to a tennis match serves up more than expected when Britain's up-and-coming female tennis star is hounded by mysterious death threats.

Miss Seeton at the Helm
Miss Seeton takes a whirlwind cruise to the Mediterranean—bound for disaster. A murder on board leads the seafaring sleuth into some very stormy waters.

Miss Seeton Cracks the Case
It's highway robbery for the innocent passengers of a motor coach tour. When Miss Seeton sketches the roadside bandits, she becomes a moving target herself.

Miss Seeton Paints the Town
The Best Kept Village Competition inspires Miss Seeton's most unusual artwork—a burning cottage—and clears the smoke of suspicion in a series of local fires.

Hands Up, Miss Seeton
The gentle Miss Seeton? A thief? A preposterous notion—
until she's accused of helping a pickpocket . . . and stumbles
into a nest of crime.

Miss Seeton by Moonlight
Scotland Yard borrows one of Miss Seeton's paintings
to bait an art thief . . . when suddenly *a second* thief strikes.

Miss Seeton Rocks the Cradle
It takes all of Miss Seeton's best instincts—maternal and
otherwise—to solve a crime that's hardly child's play.

Miss Seeton Goes to Bat
Miss Seeton's in on the action when a cricket game leads to
mayhem in the village of Plummergen . . . and gives her a shot
at smashing Britain's most baffling burglary ring.

Miss Seeton Plants Suspicion
Miss Seeton was tending her garden when a local youth was
arrested for murder. Now she has to find out who's really at
the root of the crime.

Starring Miss Seeton
Miss Seeton's playing a backstage role in the village's
annual Christmas pageant. But the real drama is behind the
scenes . . . when the next act turns out to be murder!

Miss Seeton Undercover
The village is abuzz, as a TV crew searches for a rare apple, the Plummergen Peculier—while police hunt a murderous thief . . . and with Miss Seeton at the centre of it all.

Miss Seeton Rules
Royalty comes to Plummergen, and the villagers are plotting a grand impression. But when Princess Georgina goes missing, Miss Seeton herself has questions to answer.

Sold to Miss Seeton
Miss Seeton accidentally buys a mysterious antique box at auction . . . and finds herself crossing paths with some very dangerous characters!

Sweet Miss Seeton
Miss Seeton is stalked by a confectionary sculptor, just as a spate of suspicious deaths among the village's elderly residents calls for her attention.

Bonjour, Miss Seeton
After a trip to explore the French countryside, a case of murder awaits Miss Seeton back in the village . . . and a shocking revelation.

Miss Seeton's Finest Hour
War-time England, and a young Miss Emily Seeton's suspicious sketches call her loyalty into question—until she is recruited to uncover a case of sabotage.

About Heron Carvic and Hamilton Crane

The Miss Seeton series was created by Heron Carvic; and continued after his death first by Peter Martin writing as Hampton Charles, and later by Sarah J. Mason under the pseudonym Hamilton Crane.

Heron Carvic was an actor and writer, most recognisable today for his voice portrayal of the character Gandalf in the first BBC Radio broadcast version of *The Hobbit*, and appearances in several television productions, including early series of *The Avengers* and *Dr Who*.

Born Geoffrey Richard William Harris in 1913, he held several early jobs including as an interior designer and florist, before developing a successful dramatic career and his public persona of Heron Carvic. He only started writing the Miss Seeton novels in the 1960s, after using her in a short story. Heron Carvic died in a car accident in Kent in 1980.

Hamilton Crane is the pseudonym used by Sarah J. Mason when writing 13 sequels and one prequel to the Miss Seeton series. She has also written detective fiction under her own name, but should not be confused with the Sarah Mason (no middle initial) who writes a rather different kind of book. After half a century in Hertfordshire (if we ignore four years in Scotland and one in New Zealand), Sarah J. Mason now lives in Somerset—within easy reach of the beautiful city of Wells, and just far enough from Glastonbury to avoid the annual traffic jams.